TROOP 18

Visit us at www.boldstrokesbooks.com

By the Author

Trigger

Pathogen

Troop 18

TROOP 18

by
Jessica L. Webb

2017

TROOP 18

ISBN 13: 978-1-62639-934-1

This Trade Paperback Original Is Published By
Bold Strokes Books, Inc.
P.O. Box 249
Valley Falls, NY 12185

First Edition: March 2017

CREDITS
EDITOR: JERRY L. WHEELER
PRODUCTION DESIGN: SUSAN RAMUNDO
COVER DESIGN BY MELODY POND

Acknowledgments

A big thank you to my readers for loving Kate and Andy as much as I do. It's a huge gift to know that people have connected with these characters and keep coming back to find out more about their story.

Thank you to everyone at Bold Strokes Books for helping Kate and Andy find a home.

As always, special thanks to my editor, Jerry. Your insight makes me a better writer.

Dedication

For my wife, Jen. Your gift to the world is living a life full of confidence. I am happy I get to witness it every day. I am learning.

CHAPTER ONE

A ndy walked into the diner, the bell on the door jangling its unacceptably cheery welcome. She shrugged off the momentary dip in conversation as a half dozen diners looked up to see who had joined them at this late hour. Andy sensed mostly curiosity. A few people shifted in their seats in an unnecessary effort to show their good behaviour and lack of guilt. Andy normally found that response amusing, but right now she didn't care. Right now she just needed somewhere to sit and something to eat.

Andy walked to the back corner near the windows, one hand resting deliberately on the belt at her hips. She sat down, placing her RCMP hat on the opposite seat. It didn't matter, she was eating alone. Again. Andy pulled the menu out from behind the ketchup, sugar, and vinegar and fought the urge to put her head in her hands, to feel the pressure of the pads of her thumbs pressing on her eyes. Instead she scanned the menu quickly.

She knew they were out of Vancouver because they didn't have artisanal bread, a gluten free section, or an organic stamp of approval. Just sandwiches, burgers and fries, two fifty extra for a side salad. Andy slid the menu back and looked out at the headlights of cars coming down off the highway, most of them too fast on this bend, so close to Vancouver, so close to home. She'd parked her car so the drivers could spot the reflective letters of her cruiser. She didn't have jurisdiction to pull over a speeder, but she hoped it would pull their foot off the accelerator, even just until they were off the mountain.

"Hey there, what can I get for you?"

Andy had heard the waitress approach, but she'd kept her eyes turned until the last possible moment. The waitress was in her early twenties with short, spikey, unnaturally black hair, and a smile she was working to the best of her late night diner waitress ability. Andy felt the girl's slick look of approval. The waitress cocked one hip in Andy's direction, her eyes widening with interest, the curled corners of her black eyeliner making her look especially young. Andy wanted to sigh, stand up, and walk out. She wasn't sure she had the patience for this.

"Club sandwich on whole wheat and a coffee, thanks," Andy said, her tone polite and completely unengaged.

"Sure thing," the waitress said, still trying. She wrote down the order, pushed the notepad into the back pocket of her too tight jeans and headed to the rear of the diner. If Kate were here, Andy would have bet her money the waitress was right now sauntering back to the kitchen, showing off her inked back, a suggestively placed tramp stamp showing just above the waist of her jeans.

Kate.

Against her will, Andy's shoulders slumped slightly. No one would notice, but the momentary lapse of control made Andy feel weak. She deliberately squared her shoulders again, clenched her jaw, and watched the headlights on the highway descend the gradual slope of the mountain.

Seven weeks. Forty-six days since Kate had walked out of the hotel room in Hidden Valley where they had just solved their second case together. Kate had asked for time, and Andy had given it willingly because she had seen Kate struggling— the nightmares, the uncertainty, how she avoided certain topics. How she continually pushed herself for everyone else, including putting her life in danger. But she never paused to think about how it impacted herself. Kate never thought about Kate.

Andy did. All the time. She'd never stopped, really. From the moment she'd walked into Kate's ER almost seven months ago,

Kate had taken up residence in Andy's thoughts and in her heart. She'd moved in so easily, so unconsciously Andy had almost been unaware of how quickly she had fallen for Kate Morrison.

Andy wished she could smile and feel comforted by the memories of their first few weeks together. How Andy's heart had hammered in her chest every time Kate came anywhere near her, how she'd seen the same reaction in Kate's wide, brown eyes, and how hard it had been to resist touching her. Andy wished she could close her eyes, sink into the thought...

The waitress intruded on Andy's thoughts. "Here you go. Club sandwich on whole wheat and a coffee." Andy berated herself for not hearing the waitress approach. She hadn't had time to bring herself back together. "Sugar's on the table, and I'll bring you some cream. Though I've decided you aren't exactly the cream type," the waitress said, flirting shamelessly now.

Andy's anger kicked her in the stomach, but she tightened her muscles against it. Control. "This is fine, thanks." Polite, aloof, not a hint of a smile.

The waitress hung around a few seconds too long, waiting for Andy to look up. She didn't, dismissing her with absolute silence and hoping to God she would get the message. Andy's patience was thin these days. Her anger was consistently too close to the surface, triggered too quickly by too trivial things.

It wasn't hard to figure out why. Andy knew she could give Kate all the time and space in the world if only she could be sure Kate would come back to her in the end, forgiving Andy for all the things she had done to push her away. Andy's certainty slipped a little more with each day that passed. She had initially thought it would be a few weeks, a month at the most. And here she was, December first, staring down the holidays, and Andy had been sure she would have heard from Kate by now. Something. Anything.

Andy bit into her sandwich, not tasting it. Fourteen hours into a ten hour shift, and her body was hungry, empty. She was out on the edges of Vancouver closing up a domestic assault call which had turned into a drug bust that rippled over into the outer boundaries of Vancouver. Andy had been on the first call and was waiting around for the initial evidence gathering at the crime scene so it could be officially handed over to the Greater Vancouver Drug Enforcement Section. She should have given the job to a less senior officer. In fact, the look on the constable's face as she told him she'd stay up here and wait was nothing less than incredulous. Andy didn't care. She had her reasons for not wanting to go home.

The last bite of sandwich sat on the plate, surrounded by a pile of pale fries Andy had no intention of eating. She picked up the coffee, staring blankly out the window, counting cars and wondering how long she could sit here with herself.

Her cell phone rang. Andy immediately clenched her stomach muscles again, preparing to not see Kate's number on the screen. It was her boss, Staff Sergeant James Finns.

"Wyles," she said into the phone. She pushed back her plate, hoping the waitress would come to clear it while she was on the phone so she had an excuse not to engage.

"Where are you, Sgt. Wyles?" Finns sounded angry, which was uncharacteristic. Her supervisor was usually even-keeled, no matter what Andy threw at him.

"Half an hour north-west of Abbotsford, waiting to hand over the investigation to the DE guys," Andy told him.

"And may I ask why Constable Jones is enjoying a night off while you're working overtime? Again?"

Shit. This wasn't good. "Thought I'd be nice," Andy said.

"*Nice* would be if you could put in a regular work week so I don't have to keep submitting reports to explain your time extensions."

Andy didn't say anything, waiting for the directive she could sense coming.

"Constable Jones is on his way back. You're off the case, you're off shift. I don't want to see you until Monday morning, Wyles. Got it?"

"Sir…" Andy wanted to reason with him. The thought of two days off was awful.

"Don't argue, it won't get you anywhere. You haven't had a weekend off in almost three months." Andy heard him take a breath. His voice had lost the edge of anger by the time he spoke. "I don't know what's going on with you, Andy, but take these two days and come back for a new assignment on Monday."

Andy hated that he could see through her, that he was changing her schedule based on her personal life, not on the merits of her work. Andy wanted to shift against that feeling of weakness again. She sat perfectly still. Just one more try.

"Let me wrap this up, Staff Sgt. Finns. It's just a few hours—"

He cut her off again. "No, you're off shift. Make me repeat it again, and I'll write you up."

Andy was shocked. Her supervisor had never spoken to her like this, but she'd never given him a reason to before.

"You have two choices. Take the weekend off and meet me in my office at eight o'clock Monday morning or keep pushing and meet the staff psychologist at eight o'clock Monday morning."

Not really a choice, then. "See you Monday," Andy said shortly. She couldn't make a graceful exit from this conversation.

"See you Monday." The phone went dead.

Andy hit the disconnect button and spun the phone in her hands a few times, a habit she hadn't gotten around to breaking yet. Then she stood and walked directly to the cash register near the front door, deciding not to wait for her cheque. The owner himself came out to serve her, smiling ingratiatingly, shifting uncomfortably. Andy paid in cash while the man fidgeted, his cheap white button-up shirt stained and frayed at the edges. Andy looked around out of habit more than interest until she saw the liquor license in its plastic frame behind the till. Expired six months ago. The owner handed Andy her change. She wanted to explain to him exactly how little she cared about his expired liquor license, how it barely registered on her radar. How so little mattered because Kate had been gone for forty-six days.

Weak.

Leaving a tip at the register, Andy pushed her hat back on her head and left, the bells jangling her exit. As she walked to the car, she unconsciously scanned the parking lot, probing the night beyond the pools of light surrounding the diner. Nothing moved except the cars down the highway. Andy pulled herself into the cruiser, jammed her keys into the ignition and sat. Where to go? Not home, not back to her apartment. She checked her watch. Already half past midnight. She thought about phoning Jack, knew he'd still be awake trying to hack the universe. But Andy wasn't sure she could handle his unabashed optimism. No matter how much Andy glared at him, she couldn't shake his certainty that Kate would be back. It drove her crazy, but it was also a relief. Andy relied on her partner more than she let on.

The only other person she knew would be awake at this hour was her best friend, Nic. Brilliant, funny, more energy than three people, Nic. Andy pulled out her phone and thumbed her a text. Nic and her partner Erika had a nine-month-old son, Max, Andy's chubby, spirited godson. She didn't want to phone the house and risk waking anyone. Approximately fifteen seconds after she hit send, her cell rang.

"Andy, what's shaking?" Nic said as soon as she heard Andy pick up.

"Nothing, really. Stuck in my cruiser outside Abbotsford, and I needed someone to talk to," Andy said staring out the windshield.

"Oooh, want me to Google Abbotsford gay night life? I'm sure I could find you something," Nic said excitedly and Andy could already hear her tapping at the keys of her laptop.

"No, Nic, I'm not looking for a bar."

"Why not? You're young and hot and you wear a uniform. I'm disappointed in how seldom you put these assets to good use."

"I'm not exactly single," Andy reminded her with a sharp voice, her fingernail digging into the soft plastic of the steering wheel. Nic knew about Kate, and she knew how Andy felt about her. Andy had never introduced them though, having been protective of Kate and their time together.

"You're not exactly not."

"Look, I've already fended off one baby dyke tonight, I'm really not looking for a repeat. I just…" Andy had no idea how to finish the sentence.

"You're just wallowing."

"I don't wallow."

"Yeah, well I said I'd never produce offspring. Love makes us do crazy shit."

"I thought you taught political science, not philosophy," Andy said. Nic was an associate professor at UBC and had been a graduate student and assistant coach for the women's basketball team when Andy was on the team as an undergrad.

"You're a funny girl, Andy. Now, get off the phone, find a radio station that will drive you absolutely mad, preferably something with a gyrating bass, and then drive home."

"That's the last place I want to go, Nic." Andy hated how vulnerable she sounded, but surely it was allowed with her best friend.

"I meant your parents' place. You're less than an hour away, aren't you?"

"Yes."

"Then go! You know your dad will be thrilled to see you, and your mom will love nothing more than to spend a few hours using her x-ray vision on you all the while cooking the most incredible food and spoiling you like the youngest and favouritist child that you are."

Andy cracked a smile. It wasn't a bad idea, really. "Fine, I'll go."

"Good. Say hi to the folks. Come over when you're back in town. We've got a bottle of wine with your name on it."

"Okay—"

"Wait! Hang on." Andy could hear her moving through their loft apartment, opening a cupboard, then muttering quietly under her breath. "A…N…D…okay, wait…there! Now the Bin 50 shiraz has *Andy, Queen of Wallowing* written on it. So you know which one to open when you come over."

"Nic…" Andy said, only half pissed off.

"What? You prefer king? Chancellor?"

"Bye, Nic."

"Be good to yourself."

Andy turned the key in the ignition, checked the traffic both ways and pulled onto the highway, heading towards her parents' house. Nic may be a pain in the ass, but they'd been friends a long time, and she knew her almost better than anybody. Nic had always looked out for Andy without babying her, something Andy detested.

Andy didn't take Nic's advice about the radio, instead turning up the heater and opening her window halfway, creating a natural white noise. This stretch of highway didn't have much scenery—mostly subdivisions and small towns, but a few early Christmas lights shone optimistically into the night. As she often did, Andy remembered Jack driving Kate home from Hidden Valley while she had stayed through the painfully long process of booking their suspect. Andy had quizzed Jack relentlessly after, wanting to know if Kate had said anything on the drive, how she looked, any indication how she was doing. As if Jack could predict the trajectory of Kate's breakdown any better than Andy could. Apparently Kate had done almost nothing the entire two hour drive except cry, not letting Jack talk or comfort her. As Jack had pulled up outside her apartment, Kate had looked stricken, and she'd asked him to drive to her mom's place. Then, she asked Jack to have Andy find her sister's silver ring, the one Kate had accidentally left in an on-call room at Valley General Hospital.

Leaning back in her seat, Andy reached into her pocket and pulled out the ring, warm from her own body heat. Kate had given no other direction. After a few days worrying over this seemingly trivial item, Andy had stuck it in her pocket and carried it around. She'd watched Kate twist this ring around her fingers so many times, usually when she was nervous or thinking. Andy knew what it felt like under her own fingers when she held Kate's hand. The warmth of it, the smoothness, the familiarity. It reminded Kate of her sister, Sarah, and all the things Kate was sure she'd done wrong.

Andy sighed and put the ring back into her pocket. It was a reminder to Andy now, of all the ways she'd screwed up. All the ways she hadn't been able to protect Kate, all the things she'd said and done that had pushed Kate farther away. Andy still couldn't believe how she'd managed to fuck up this one thing that was more important to her than anything else.

She stabbed at the button for the radio, flipping rapidly and angrily through channels until something loud and obnoxious reverberated back at her. Maybe she'd take Nic's advice after all.

Andy ran the near-dark path through the woods around her parents' place, the air damp and cold against her already warm face. She was only half an hour in, her muscles now stretched and loose, her breathing rhythmic and unconscious. Time to push, then. She lengthened her stride until she had to pull in her core muscles to balance it out, her heart working a little harder to keep up. Andy focused on the way the air burned on the way in, keeping her eyes two steps ahead on the path, planning her footfall, judging the slight slope down to her right. When she felt comfortable with that, she pushed again and again until she was hours into this run, the sun shining its muddied light through the branches above her. She only let herself settle in on the last turn toward home and she was hurting by then, her fingertips tingling, the now predictable waves of nausea flipping through her stomach.

She hadn't pushed herself like this since her cadet training at Depot, and that was over a decade ago. Most of the cadets in her troop had been worried about passing the physical exam, but Andy had only been concerned about excelling. Eleven years later, Andy knew she couldn't push her body the way she had back then. But she had been pushing hard for the past month. It was an outlet, a desperate attempt to keep her life moving. It was punishment. Andy hadn't run at all the first few weeks after closing up the viral threat case in Hidden Valley. For the first time in a long time, she felt unsure, unbalanced. Her own apartment seemed unfamiliar, and all her old pre-Kate routines seemed wrong. She'd become sluggish and sick. By the third morning of waking up and puking, Andy knew she needed to do something. So she'd run. She went right back to her morning twenty kilometres without a gentle re-emergence. She pushed until she was forced to lean against a tree and throw up the thin, watery contents of her stomach. At least there was no shame in that.

Andy took a turn on the path, slowing her pace, wanting to finish her run on the far side of the house. She was slightly dizzy and knew she was going to be sick the second she stopped. She'd left the house before her parents were awake, but they were sure to be up by now, taking in whatever BC winter sun they could through the large windows in the dining room that overlooked the yard. Andy wanted to avoid her parents seeing her like this. The sprawling, mismatched house came into view, and Andy came to a stop outside the cleared yard. She walked in a large circle, hands on her hips and head back as she pulled in breath after breath of air. The muscles in her thighs reached their peak of burn as she doubled over and threw up, feeling disgusting but almost instantly better. Andy stood straight again, wiped her mouth on the inside of her shirt, and walked to the back door of her parents' house.

Her mother was at the door, looking her up and down the way only a parent can. Andy was a full foot taller than her mom, but that look had always made her feel small and exposed. Andy stood silently and took it, red-faced and sweating, her body slightly shaky now with exertion and a chill. When she couldn't handle it any more, she bent down and untied her shoes, letting them drop to the floor.

"Your father is hurt you didn't wait for him this morning," her mother finally said, a carefully laid question in the comment. Andy shrugged and wiped her face on her sleeve. "I was up early." It wasn't a lie. She'd barely slept, restlessly moving on the single bed usually used by her nephew until it was morning enough to run. Her answer brought on another long look from her mom, and this time Andy shifted uncomfortably.

"She'll need something to come back to, Andy." Her mother pulled Andy's face down, kissed her cheek, and walked back toward the kitchen.

Maybe this hadn't been a good idea after all. Or maybe Nic knew exactly what she was doing.

Andy followed her mom through the house, but that feeling of being exposed stayed with her, as if her heart was outside her body, uncomfortable and dangerously visible. Suddenly, Andy's shirt seemed too thin. It couldn't possibly offer enough protection. She wanted her softbody armour vest, wanted to pull it over her head and tighten the straps until it sat just right, its layers of bulletproof material all the protection she needed. It was a ridiculous thought. A weak thought. Unworthy of Sgt. Andy Wyles. She took three slow, steadying breaths as she mounted the stairs up to the next level, the sun bright through the dining room windows.

"Look who I found at the back door, Simon," Andy's mother was saying, taking her seat at the table.

"Hi, sweetheart!"

Her dad stood, unfolding his long frame and crossing the kitchen to give Andy a hug. Andy let herself feel a moment of comfort. Nothing had ever felt like a hug from her dad. It was exactly what she needed, but it didn't help that feeling of her heart being outside her chest. He stepped back to take a look at her. He always looked proud, like he couldn't believe how lucky he was to have her as a daughter.

"You training for something, Andy? Looks like you're putting on a lot of muscle," he commented as he sat back down. This was a pretty typical question from her dad, who had also been her running coach. He was the one who had set up her training schedule for Depot.

Andy didn't answer right away, getting a drink of water from the tap first, the only thing her stomach could handle right now. "No, not training." She felt her mom's brown eyes boring into her. Andy ignored it and leaned back against the counter, taking small sips of water.

"I take it you haven't heard from Kate?" Her dad took a bite of toast, a thick smear of honey on top.

Forty-seven days. "No," Andy said quickly, wanting to head off any more questions.

"I'm sorry, sweetheart. I guess she just needs some more time." Andy shook it off. She didn't want her parents to think she'd come here to wallow.

Andy pushed away from the counter. "I'm going to take a shower."

"No, come and eat first," her mom said in the same commanding tone she'd been using on Andy since she showed up at the front door as a two year old holding her biological mother's hand. She'd inherited her adoptive mother's steel core, a gift of environment rather than biology.

Andy considered resisting her mom's directive, but her stomach was now growling its discomfort. So she took her usual seat and pulled a muffin out from under the faded and thin tea towel. Still warm from the oven, the oats and blueberries melted in Andy's mouth. She hadn't enjoyed food in a long time.

Without asking, her mom got up and poured her a coffee, bringing it back to the table with the same interrogative look in her eyes. Andy didn't bother hiding. She knew she was hurting. Nic knew, Jack knew, her parents knew. Probably even Staff Sgt. Finns knew, though she'd avoided the topic of Kate with him as much as possible. Maybe a little outside input wouldn't hurt. Or maybe it was exactly what she needed. Andy's mom handed her the coffee and sat down again, saying nothing.

"Are you here for the weekend?" Andy's dad said.

"I'll head back to the city tomorrow morning."

"Well then, before you take your shower, think you could help me with a few roof repairs? I was going to call someone in to fix the flashing, since your mother won't let me up there on my own," he said, obviously disgruntled.

"I enjoy the benefits of your income, dear," Andy's mother said mildly, picking up the paper and flipping it over.

Andy wanted to smile. The familiar rhythms and conversations of home soothed her. But nothing could quite cover the fact that Kate was still gone, and Andy couldn't be certain that she was coming back.

"Sure, I can help out with that. Have you had the gutters done?"

Two chores turned into three, then four, and the grey day slipped by as Andy and her dad tackled a never-ending list of repairs to the old house. In an old green slicker and a climbing harness, Andy climbed on to the roof. Her father passed her tools and called out instructions. Even when the freezing drizzle slipped the occasional cold drip through an unseen rip in her jacket, Andy enjoyed the sensation of being outside, her hands and thoughts occupied. Andy didn't stop herself from thinking about Kate, but she didn't wallow. She wanted it to make sense, to order her thoughts and events until a logical conclusion could be made. Evidence could be gathered, assumptions broken down, questions asked, pieces fit together. Andy had to discover some line of questioning she hadn't yet pursued, some fault she hadn't yet found in herself that had driven Kate away. She could find a way to make up for it, if only Kate would come back and give her the chance.

No. Not true.

Andy had plenty of evidence to suggest whatever was going on with Kate had begun long before they met. Andy could not take responsibility for Kate never dealing with losing her sister or what she had done to try to save her. And Kate had been dissatisfied with her job at Vancouver East emergency room before Andy had walked in last May. Kate's unwillingness to ever put herself first was an almost ingrained trait. Andy had become all too familiar with Kate's reaction to something that hurt or hit too close to home. Kate's shoulders would lift slightly, as if bracing for impact, and she'd give a small shake of her head. Then she'd relax, or seem like she was. At the very least, she'd force her body into a more neutral position, like she was convincing herself and everyone around her that she was fine. Fine.

Andy wasn't fine, and right now she didn't mind showing it. She dropped the last handful of rotting, half-frozen leaves from the eaves trough into the bucket below. Standing carefully on the slippery, rough shingles, Andy stretched her back and looked up into the winter grey sky, searching uselessly for the afternoon sun behind the clouds. Eventually, a short gust of wind threw more drizzle against the heat of her neck and Andy decided it was time to climb down.

Andy stood under the hot shower for a long time, her whole body turning pink except the four inch long jagged strip above her left hip, a small, muddled mass of scar tissue Andy fingered lightly. The memory it brought had nothing to do with getting shot down at the wharf in Seattle or the first round of stitches, or even of getting blown up or kicked and the second and third set of stitches that followed.

It made her think of the Montana cabin she and Kate had shared together for three days. She remembered Kate not so carefully pulling off Andy's bandage, inspecting her wound, touching the stretched, red edges of skin around the dark stitches, her forehead wrinkling with concentration and worry. Andy remembered whining. She really hated to be babied. Her last girlfriend, Rachel, had driven Andy up the wall by babying her. Kate had let Andy carry on as she cleaned the wound, applied a topical cream, taped a fresh bandage in place, and then finally told Andy that if she referred to her chosen profession as babying one more time, they were going to have an issue. Andy had fallen in love just a little bit more with Kate Morrison then.

Andy smiled as she made her way back downstairs, dressed in faded track pants and a worn hoodie from one of her older brothers. It felt good to smile, and Andy tried to hold onto the tenuous bout of confidence. Of course Kate was coming back. She couldn't possibly come to any other conclusion.

Andy found her parents in the kitchen, her mom rinsing asparagus stalks in the sink, and her dad carefully patting them dry and wrapping each one in a thin strip of prosciutto. A pile of ingredients sat by the stove: olive oil, garlic and a papery white onion, arborio rice, cream, white wine, and a paper bag with what Andy guessed to be mushrooms. Andy could imagine three steaks in the scratched-up glass dish marinating in the fridge right now.

As Andy entered the kitchen, Elaine smiled and gestured to the ingredients. "Would you mind?"

Andy didn't mind something else to keep her head and hands occupied. Not at all. She poured some olive oil into the saucepan, deftly peeled and diced the onion, and added them to the pan when it was hot. Cooking onions was her favourite smell in the world. As she stirred in the rice, she felt a pang in her chest. Her favourite was Kate's skin after a shower. Andy's shoulders dropped again, her confidence from moments ago gone. Forty-seven days and not a word.

"Will it help to talk about it, Andy?" her father said.

Andy concentrated on stirring the rice, watching the grains turn from white to translucent as she poured in the vegetable stock. "Honestly, I don't know."

"Well, I'd like to, if you don't mind," her mom said, snapping off the tough end of an asparagus stalk and dropping it in the compost bucket. Elaine didn't wait for an answer. Andy hadn't really expected her to. "When I met Kate, I thought that I'd never met someone with such extremes of strength and vulnerability."

Her mother had an uncanny ability to see right to the very heart of people.

"She's stronger than I am," Andy murmured, wondering why she'd never said this to Kate.

"I imagine she is, but she has so little self-awareness. Your strength has always been knowing who you are and what you want and not being afraid to show it or seek it out. I have no doubt Kate knows exactly who you are, Andy. But not herself. And that," she said, pointing her paring knife at Andy, "is not your fault."

Andy uncorked the wine and added a couple of splashes, watching the alcohol sizzle and burn off. She stirred methodically, not changing speed, moving the wooden spoon around the bottom of the pan. Good risotto took time and patience and an understanding of the balance of liquids and heat and absorption.

With a guilty twist in her stomach, she remembered practically yelling at Kate while they were on assignment, hurling Kate's lack of self-preservation skills in her face as if Kate was doing it intentionally to piss Andy off. It was her biggest weakness, and Andy had shoved it in her face. It didn't matter that Andy had been so angry because she'd been scared. It made no difference that she'd been unwilling or unable to see the extent of Kate's struggle. She was supposed to love Kate, not accuse her.

Andy's hands shook as she roughly chopped the mushrooms and added them to the saucepan. She flexed her hand irritably, took a long, slow breath, and continued to stir.

"What am I supposed to do?" Andy said into the silence that had fallen. She didn't look up, aware that both her parents were looking at her. It had been a while since she'd asked them for advice.

"Take care of yourself, sweetheart. I think it's all you can do," her father said, wiping his hands on a dishcloth.

"And trust her," Elaine said. "Kate told you what she needs. So trust her."

Andy shifted this idea, simple yet new, trying to decide if she could do it. She lifted a few grains of the now-creamy rice, blew on it lightly then tasted it. The seasoning was perfect, the rice still firm. *Could she do it? Could she be patient and trust Kate?*

Maybe. That was as close as she could get. Maybe.

CHAPTER TWO

Andy woke early on Monday, rolled out of bed and got into her running gear. She could feel cramps low in her abdomen. Perfect. Andy hated running when she had her period. Everything felt off, her joints too loose, her gait awkward. But she hated more the thought it would stop her from running. So she ran. But she didn't push. Just her regular route, no more running until she puked. Getting caught by her mother had been embarrassing enough to snap her out of it.

A run, a shower, breakfast. Pulling on her uniform one piece at a time, Andy felt more and more like herself with each addition. At the front door, she zipped up her storm jacket and settled her hat on her head, its brim low over her eyes. At the last minute, she tucked her black watch cap into her pocket, just in case she was going to be out on the street today. She really had no idea what Finns was going to hand her this morning. As she drove her cruiser through pre-rush hour Vancouver streets, Andy thought about Finns mentioning an assignment, like he already had something in mind. She hoped they could bypass any mention of their last conversation, but knew at the very least she was going to be under some heavy scrutiny. Andy felt up to it today. Finally.

Andy took the stairs up to her cubicle, greeting a few others with a quick good morning or a nod of her head. Andy knew full well she intimidated the shit out of a lot of people. That wasn't her intention, at least, not most of the time. She was who she was, she did her job the way she thought best, she worked hard, she worked as a team. How others perceived her was pretty low on her list of things to worry about. Taking off her jacket, Andy scanned her desk, looking at the picture of her niece and nephew, telling herself she'd have to get a new one soon, with her sister-in-law due to give birth any day. There was a picture of Max, too, his blue eyes almost disappearing as he grinned. Andy still had the picture of herself, Kate, Marie, and Tyler stuck under the metal trim and the picture brought Andy comfort for the first time in a long time. Yes, it had been forty-nine days and yes, for some reason the number fifty caused an inexplicable tremor in her body. But here she was, surviving.

Andy checked her watch. Another ten minutes until her meeting with Finns. She headed to the staff room, hoping someone had started the coffee so she didn't have to. She found a fresh canister, dark and hot. Andy filled her mug, scalding her tongue with her first sip, thinking about how many times she'd stopped in at Kate's ER to bring her a hot coffee, knowing she never made it through one without it getting cold. She missed the way Kate's whole body changed after her first coffee in the morning: transitioning from groggy and adorable to alert and moving, wanting to be three steps ahead, her brain always so many different places at once. Andy suppressed the sigh, took her mug of coffee back to her desk, then went in search of her boss.

Staff Sergeant James Finns had been her supervisor for the last four years and Andy had a great deal of respect for the man. He was expected to announce his retirement any day, but Andy was in no hurry for this to happen. He had high expectations of Andy and kept a close eye on her, but he also let her work the way she needed to and trusted her with assignments normally given to more senior officers. It was easier to respect him than Superintendent Heath who seemed to value ambition, ass-kissing, and status above hard work.

After bringing some much needed positive media to the RCMP last spring with the resolution in Seattle as well as her part in saving Heath's eighteen-year-old granddaughter from a lovesick ex-boyfriend, Andy was in his good books. She had insisted over and over that Kate was the one who had resolved the tense situation, but Heath maintained she had done her part and would be rewarded accordingly. In the past, Heath had made it clear he couldn't stand Andy and she was fairly certain her sexuality had something to do with it. So being on Heath's good side wasn't a bad place to be. She just had no intention of taking him up on his offer.

Andy was surprised to see Finns' door closed, but she checked her watch again. It was just before eight, so she knocked. He called out for her to enter, and she pushed open the wooden door. Her old mentor, Lincoln Henry sat across from Staff Sgt. Finns. He had more greying hair than Andy remembered, but his smile was still bright. He stood as soon as Andy entered, shaking her hand, thumping her on the back, and showing how happy he was to see her. Andy knew full well she owed a lot of her success in her career to Lincoln. They sat down across from Finns.

"You've had a busy year, I hear, Sgt. Wyles," Lincoln said.

"Busy is one word to describe it." She wanted to chat, but she couldn't help but wonder what was going on. "How's Henry?" Andy had brought Lincoln's eldest son, a new member of the RCMP, out to Seattle, wanting someone she trusted who could keep an eye on Kate.

"Henry's posted up in Slave Lake, I think probably freezing his balls off right now. He's working hard and having a good time. You know Henry."

"Tell him I said hi, next time you talk to him," Andy said. She remembered Henry tying a bandage over Kate's bloody, dripping arm. She let the impact hit, spread, and diffuse. Kate was fine. Scarred but fine. Absent forty-nine days, but fine.

"He'd like that," Lincoln was saying. "He thinks you're a god, of course."

"Everyone could use a few of those when they're starting out." Henry was a good kid. Star struck by Andy or not, he'd more than proven himself on his first assignment out of Depot. "What brings you out here?" Andy said, still trying to figure out what was going on. "Last I heard, you and Anna had moved out to Regina so you could take a position out at the training academy."

"Running the show, more like it," Staff Sgt. Finns said. "Say hello to Depot's newest Chief Superintendent Training Officer."

"Really?"

"Yes, really, Sgt. Wyles," Lincoln said dryly. "Think I would joke about a four name position change? And keep it quiet. The official announcement's not until next week."

"Congratulations," Andy said, holding out her hand. Lincoln shook it firmly. "But it still doesn't answer my question."

"Nothing's changed, has it?" he said to Finns. "Still utterly single-minded, I see."

Andy shrugged, still waiting for an answer. If the two of them wanted to sit around and talk about her later, that was fine. She wanted to know what was going on.

Lincoln shifted his weight in his chair. "I need your help with a situation."

"What kind of situation? Where? Here or Depot?"

Lincoln held up a hand. "Let me give you the history. We've got forty-eight troops out at Depot right now. The most senior troop is coming up on their medal ceremony in a week and the most junior troop is so fresh they're still tripping over their own feet in wheel formation every morning. It's one of the middle troops, Troop 18, that's the problem." Lincoln stopped and rubbed his hand up and down his jaw in a gesture that took Andy back a few years. "Now, I'm new to this role, but even the most veteran instructors are telling me they've never seen anything like this troop before. To say they're a tight knit group is a massive understatement. In the four months that this troop of sixteen has been together, they've formed a very tight bond."

"Why such a small troop?" Andy said. Troops were usually made up of thirty-two cadets, though there were always a few who couldn't hack the physical and mental intensity of the RCMP's national training academy. Andy's own troop had started out at a full thirty-two. Twenty-four made it to graduation, a high number.

"It started off as a small troop, just twenty-four cadets. I guess no one willingly comes to Regina in the winter," he said wryly. "We almost didn't run it, but we decided to go ahead. Anyway, two dropped out of their own accord in the first month and three more cadets couldn't maintain the physical requirements of training and were gone within six weeks." Lincoln ticked them off on his thick, rough fingers. "By week fourteen, the troop was really coming together. We weren't sure if it was because they were such a small group to begin with or if they were just a really together troop. Whatever it was, they gelled quickly. But then twenty-four-year-old Justin Thibadeau, a young Acadian kid, had a heart attack during a training exercise. Just dropped to the ground in front of his troop. One minute he was there, and the next he was gone. Coroner said it was some kind of inherited heart condition."

Andy knew what kind of impact a death like that would have on a troop. It would be a shock to the system, a jarring absence, a reminder every morning at roll call that someone was missing.

"How did the troop take it?" Finns said after the silence had stretched.

"Rough. He was a good kid, well-liked. We suspended class, brought in a grief counsellor, gave them some time." Lincoln stopped again, looked between Finns and Andy then shrugged. "Then we figured they had to get back at it, so we threw them back into drills and class and training."

Andy could tell by the way Lincoln now shifted in his seat that he was unsure they'd made the right decision. Andy hated that feeling, the awkwardness of second guessing yourself, of admitting that you were uncertain. "And how did they do? After you threw them back in, how did they adjust?"

"At first? Fine. They pulled together even more so, really leaned on each other. You know how troops are. They're so…"

Lincoln struggled to find the word, his hands talking for him, forming a kind of ball in the air in front of him.

"Insular," Andy said.

"Yes, insular. But Troop 18 took it to a whole other level. They kept to themselves, basically only interacted with each other. It was almost like they couldn't relate to the troops around them or the instructors any more."

As Lincoln paused again, Andy quelled the restlessness inside her. She knew there was more to this. Almost as if Lincoln could read her mind, he looked up and met her gaze. "That makes six cadet absences accounted for," Andy said quietly. "What about the last two?"

"The last two just recently had their Cadet Training Agreement with the RCMP cancelled," Lincoln said.

"What for?"

"They were caught with drugs and alcohol during inspection at their dorm."

Stupid, Andy thought to herself. *Extremely stupid.* There was absolutely no privacy in the dorm rooms with fifty cadets in tight quarters and only a thin partition separating your space from everyone else's. Inspection was strict: leather gloves placed exactly so in the right drawer, every button done up on the uniform hanging in your closet, military corners on your bed. Attention to detail, organization, uniformity, and ability to follow orders precisely were all the hallmarks of Depot. It would take either a great deal of stupidity or an inflated sense of ego to think you could get away with anything out there.

"What kind of drugs?" Andy said, needing this to make more sense.

"Street grade marijuana, less than twenty dollars' worth."

"That's not much. Personal use then, not selling."

"Both passed the drug screen, though," Lincoln said. "As did the rest of the troop. As did all the other troops."

"What else?"

"Two weeks after those two were relieved of their contract, two hypodermic needles were found in a classroom recently vacated by Troop 18. They were clean, nothing on them. No one stepped forward, and punishment got us nowhere. We did a complete strip down search of both dorms, but we only found a few contraband items, mostly food infractions. However, two of the Troop 18 cadets had a large quantity of cash on them."

"Suspicious but not against the rules," Andy said. She was trying very hard to build a case given this perplexing assortment of information. She lined up her questions, then shelved them. "What do you need from me?"

Andy first looked at Lincoln, then followed his gaze to her supervisor. Finns cleared his throat before he spoke.

"As I'm sure you are well aware, Sgt. Wyles, the RCMP has had its fair share of bad press recently. An entire troop being dismissed is not the kind of thing the COs are particularly interested in sharing with the media, particularly so soon after they lost a cadet. But it will be picked up and exploited, and we'll spend the next year trying to defend our practices, traditions, and relevance in today's national police force."

Andy understood. This situation would make the Commissioned Officers very nervous. Still, she waited. Lincoln picked up where Finns had left off.

"I want you in there. I want you to come in and take the lead. No one's been able to crack this group, not their drill instructor, not their classroom instructors, not the variety of counsellors we've brought in, and certainly not me. But something tells me that you can. I think we need to bring in an outsider, someone not responsible for their day to day instruction and inspection, someone they're not answering to."

Andy's instinct gave a kick. She glared at Finns though he only looked back at her impassively, giving her nothing. Andy turned back to her old mentor.

"Why are you requesting me, Lincoln? There must be a couple dozen people who could do this job, and I'm sure none of them are two provinces over."

"I need a unique perspective. I don't want this troop coddled, but I don't want them manhandled either. It helps that you've got a high profile these days. A lot of the cadets and officers already feel like they know you from media reports and, well, you know how the family talks."

Andy let this fact shift her perspective, adding a certain kind of weight to his reasoning. She'd never craved this kind of attention, either from the media or from within, from 'the family,' as Lincoln put it. But Andy also had no intention of shying away from it. At best, if it helped her on an assignment, she'd use it. But something was still bothering her. Andy locked her gaze on Staff Sgt. James Finns.

"Is this an offer or an order?"

"An offer," Finns said. "I can't order you to Regina, but I can support you if you decide to go," he told her, his voice neutral and his hands clasped on the desk in front of him.

Andy scanned his face for signs of deception but found nothing. Still, she was suspicious.

"Is this an offer because you don't believe I'm fit for regular duty, sir?" Andy said, almost able to control the fear that made her voice sound angry. She wasn't sure what she would do if he answered in the affirmative. Just the thought made shame well up in her, and she clamped down on it as she watched her supervisor's face and waited for him to answer.

Lincoln answered, his tone serious. "Once I realized we needed some kind of drastic outside support on this, I immediately thought of bringing you in. *I* did, Sgt. Wyles," he said again, more firmly. "When I called Staff Sgt. Finns a few days ago to run it by him, he told me you were going through something personal, but you were fit to take on any task as always. He also made it clear it would be your choice, that we should respect your assessment of the assignment and your decision to take it on or not."

Andy considered that answer. It added up. She trusted it. There were still too many holes in the story, too many facts she needed to sort through, but the challenge of it tugged at her.

"Give me two hours," she said, looking first at Lincoln, then at Finns.

"I'll do you two better," Lincoln said, grinning. She could tell he already knew she would take this on. "Let me buy you lunch."

Andy managed a smile. It really was good to see him. "Fine, lunch." She nodded her exit to both men, stood and walked to the door, the muscles in her thighs protesting her run from two days ago.

Andy sat at her desk, thumbing through messages on her phone without really absorbing any of the words, half-focused on her desk phone blinking its waiting messages. Normally, the waiting messages and unanswered calls would drive Andy crazy, but she'd kept her phone off and in the car over the weekend, a first for her. It had felt surprisingly good to be cut off, to not be constantly anticipating the next problem or request. Only a handful of people needed to know where she was. Finns had ordered her off-shift, Nic had known where she was, and Jack was used to Andy not answering his call for two days. He would just send a slew of texts until Andy grew tired of reading them and phoned him back. And Kate…well, Kate had asked for time.

Andy shook her head, deciding to ignore the messages. Needing time without interruption, Andy escaped back down the stairs, reaching the street before anyone could intercept her. She headed toward Cambie Street, the closest Starbucks to the RCMP headquarters. Andy vaguely remembered taking this same route with Kate, but she didn't stop to think about it. For once, she was too occupied to berate herself for recent failures. She focused not on the details of the troop's transgressions or guilt, but the fact that Lincoln wanted to bring in an outsider, someone the troop wasn't already familiar with, someone they didn't already answer to. Did Lincoln mean it would help to have someone who didn't know the cadet who had died, who could see them for the troop they were instead of the troop they'd started out as? Still, it sounded like the death of their troop mate had triggered something in the group. Something that required a secret to be kept.

A thought began to form, the smallest germ of an idea. Andy ran with it, dealing with obstacles as they came up, weighing the advantages and disadvantages with as neutral a viewpoint as possible. It would take a lot of work, a lot of planning. And it would take some convincing. She needed to present Lincoln with a solid plan, and she had just a few hours to do it. By the time she was back at her desk, scalding coffee in her hand, Andy had convinced herself this was what needed to happen. But she needed to formalize the plan. Andy put down her coffee and picked up the phone.

❖

"You want me to bring them here?"

Lincoln looked up from the ten-page report Andy had handed him as they sat down at the restaurant for lunch. It was more of a café, with a dozen small tables and a modern-retro counter with stools taking up the long wall. It was busy and loud enough that you felt utterly cut off from everyone else.

"It's north of Kamloops," Andy said. "A day's drive from Regina."

"A long day," Lincoln grunted, flipping through the pages of her report, his sandwich sitting untouched on his plate.

Andy ate her soup, feeling an uncharacteristic bout of nerves. Having spent the last four hours on this, she wanted Lincoln to agree with the plan and let her run with it. It was a long shot, but she knew Lincoln trusted her opinion.

Finally he closed the pages and picked up his sandwich. Andy let him think, waiting with a stillness that belied the turmoil rampant in her body.

"I thought Kurtz had bought into a B&B up there, when did she branch out?"

"Last year. She and Tara bought the acreage north of their property, including a series of rundown cabins from the forties. She's spent the last year and a couple grand retrofitting the cabins—mostly environmental upgrades, solar power, that kind of thing. She's hoping that they can open it for corporate retreats by next spring."

Sergeant Major Rosalie Kurtz, retired, known to all as simply Kurtz, had taken Andy under her wing in her first few years in E-division. Between Lincoln and Kurtz, Andy had been well taken care of. Kurtz had even helped Andy manoeuvre out of a difficult position with Dr. Mona Kellar, a twisted forensic pathologist who had targeted Kate just a few short months ago while they were on assignment up in Hidden Valley.

"Smart move," Lincoln said, making short work of his huge sandwich. "Positioned between Vancouver and Calgary. They'll do well, though I'm not surprised. Kurtz was always ten steps ahead of everyone else."

Andy kept eating, waiting for some hint that Lincoln was taking her plan seriously.

"So you think this place is ready for Troop 18, do you?"

Andy heard the layers of questions, could tell instantly Lincoln was challenging her to present her case. She knew him well enough to know she had about three minutes to convince him.

"There are seven fully operational cabins. That's four cadets to a cabin plus three additional cabins for instructors. Bathrooms in each cabin, hot water available but limited. There's a camp kitchen and a meeting hall that would easily do for a classroom."

"What kind of shape is the place in?"

"Inspection isn't due until March, so Kurtz is offering us only the buildings she is sure would pass today. The others are off limits."

"And what's she going to charge us?" Lincoln flipped to the last page of Andy's report where she'd summarized an approximate cost associated with this venture.

"Nothing." She finished off the last of her soup, put the spoon carefully in the bowl, and pushed it to the side of the table. "Though Kurtz has a long list of repairs, she would be happy to give it to Troop 18 in exchange for use of the property. She thought it would be team building."

"That's not exactly what Troop 18 needs," Lincoln said, putting down the report for the second time. Andy knew she hadn't convinced him yet. Lincoln tapped the report with his finger. "Your plan is missing something. When and how do you address the issues with the troop? How do you intend to get to the bottom of this thing?"

"I don't." Andy spread her hands flat on the table.

"Explain."

Andy didn't shift in her seat or lean forward to add weight to her words. Either he would accept what she had to say next or not.

"You said it yourself. This troop is like nothing Depot has ever seen before, and none of the usual tactics are working. So let me build them up, not break them down. Get them out of the environment that they've figured out. Let's see them regroup and rebuild. I want to see the leaders of this troop come to the forefront while keeping an eye on the followers. My guess is this troop is spending all their time and energy on covering up. Let's give them some room and see what happens."

A long, hard look from Lincoln. She'd presented him with a risk, something he wasn't prepared for. But she'd also presented him with a viable alternative, and he'd already admitted what they were doing right now was not effective.

"Are you giving them enough rope to hang themselves?"

"No, that's not my intention. If this group is as tight as you say they are, I don't think that should be punished out of them. It should be encouraged and moulded, but not punished." Now Andy did lean forward, wanting only Lincoln to hear her next words. "If they do hang themselves, it's because they chose their secret and each other over the RCMP. Which means they were never going to make it, anyway."

Lincoln ran his hand along his jaw. He picked up the file and flipped some pages.

"Tell me about the obstacles," he said, and Andy knew she had him convinced. She couldn't help grinning at him before launching into her summary.

"Location obstacles include no cell phone reception at camp, and if we get unseasonable amounts of rain there could be a road wash-out. As it stands, it's a twenty-minute hike from Kurtz's place up to the camp. Which brings us to my biggest concern, which is staffing. I think four staff on-site should be sufficient, though I'm not sure how many volunteers you're going to find."

Lincoln waved this concern aside. "I've got three instructors who would jump at the chance, and I believe Sergeant Trokof would add a measure of decorum and structure to this adventure."

Andy attempted to keep the disbelief off her face. It clearly didn't work as Lincoln leaned back and laughed. Sergeant Albert Trokof, who inevitably had become Sergeant Jerk-off in the few moments of private conversations between cadets, had been old when Andy was in Depot eleven years ago. Everyone at Depot had exacting, high standards, but Sergeant Trokof was brutal.

"I didn't think that man ever left Depot, let alone Regina," Andy said to Lincoln, who grinned.

"I think he's up for the challenge, and I think the troop needs the same predictability of routines. Besides, he's got a soft spot for this troop."

"And I didn't think that man had a soft spot."

"Just you wait until you meet this crew. There's something very compelling about watching them together."

"Either way, I'll leave staffing up to you as well as the schedule. Sgt. Trokof or one of the other instructors can take the lead, as long as it's not me. I'll take them through their morning run, I'll lead them in training exercises, I'll even help them cook. They'll follow me because I'm a senior officer, not because I'm evaluating them."

Lincoln flipped back and forth through the pages of the report. Andy stopped herself from fidgeting, sensing how close she was. She wanted this badly. While she waited for Lincoln to speak, she evaluated her motives. She wanted to take on this challenge, and she had to admit that getting away from her recently pathetic routines was part of wanting to go. But she wasn't running away. Andy tested the thought and found it acceptable.

"Okay," Lincoln said finally, slapping the report back down on the table. "Okay, I'll give you Troop 18 for three weeks. They need to be back at Depot on Christmas Eve. We're either at the bottom of this thing by then or we're retracting their contracts for Christmas. No pressure."

Andy didn't smile. There was pressure, a lot of it. But suddenly she wanted to twist with excitement, she wanted to be moving, putting this thing into action.

"When do you want them?"

"Two days," Andy said promptly, obviously surprising Lincoln. "Put them on the bus on Wednesday, overnight this side of Edmonton, have them to me by noon on Thursday."

"You can be ready in two days?"

"If I start today." Andy checked her watch. "Right now."

Lincoln gave her a smile Andy recognized, a mixture of confidence and pride. "See, my instincts don't steer me wrong," he said.

Andy raised her eyebrows. "Except the time you ordered clam chowder from that dive in the east end."

Lincoln groaned at the memory and held his stomach. "You had to remind me, didn't you?"

Andy grinned and finally shifted in her seat. She really did want to get going.

"All right, Sgt. Wyles. I'm entrusting Troop 18 to you starting on Thursday at noon. Do you know what you're getting yourself into here?"

"Not at all, sir."

"Well then, I think that's an excellent start."

CHAPTER THREE

A ndy pulled her foot off the accelerator, the Yukon easing into a lower gear, its engine quieting to a dull roar. The town of Clearwater B.C. came into view, small and dismal on this wet, grey day. Gas station signs and overhead wires dominated what could have been a beautiful view of the mountains and the surrounding trees, but Andy barely noticed the scenery as she pulled into town and came to a complete stop at the red light. The gear packed into the back of the Yukon shifted only slightly as she pulled on to the next leg of the highway, less than twenty minutes from her destination.

It was just before noon on Tuesday. Andy had spent the day before ploughing through the intimidatingly long list of supplies they were going to need to feed and shelter twenty-one people for three weeks. Twenty-two, Andy corrected herself. Sixteen cadets, four instructors, Andy, and a Depot medic. The medic was one of the three additions the COs had made to her plan since getting it approved by Lincoln: an on-site medic, a weekly face to face check-in with a senior officer, and weekly drug tests of the cadets, the first one within twenty-four hours of arrival. Andy was still trying to figure out how to get sixteen urine samples from a remote location to a lab.

Andy checked the directions on the print-out Jack had given her, though she was beginning to recognize the area. She'd been here twice before: once a few years ago in the fall to help Kurtz and Tara move in, and then again the summer after to help demo one of the outbuildings. That had been a fun weekend. Eight dykes with hammers and crowbars and four boxes of beer resulted in a huge pile of rotting wood, fungus-covered shingles, and dirty squares of linoleum. Andy was one of the few who had stayed through the hangover the next morning to help haul it all away. She stayed partly because she owed Kurtz and partly because she enjoyed spending time with Kurtz and Tara, though they were both close to twenty years older than Andy.

A green and white sign at the edge of the road announced the turn-off to Clearwater B & B, welcoming travellers, vacationers, and adventurers to a small piece of heaven. Andy turned the Yukon into the drive, gunned the engine up and over the crest of a hill, the grounds of the B & B coming into view. She'd heard Kurtz describe first seeing this piece of land five years ago, how she had instantly fallen in love with it. Even on this grey day, the distant view obscured by drizzled fog, it was incredible.

Low meadows were edged with tall evergreens that became denser and wilder the more you looked. The house itself looked like part of the foggy scenery, with its light grey siding, dark grey roof, and large windows on all sides reflecting back the expanse of grey sky. Andy followed the gravel driveway up to the house, an old Lab coming around the side of the garage, barking dutifully, wagging its tail in slow, excited circles. Andy climbed out of the car and stretched her spine, feeling the tightness in the back of her legs from sitting for so long.

"Andy Wyles, how the hell are you?"

Kurtz walked out on the veranda that wrapped the front of the house, leaning over the rail and looking down at Andy. She was always shorter than Andy thought, somewhere around five-six, though in Andy's memory they were closer to the same height. She had short, steel grey hair, cut neatly around her ears, the curls on top not moving an inch in the slight wind. Her blue eyes were set into an unassuming, lined face that could easily be overlooked. Kurtz usually corrected that as soon as she opened her mouth.

Andy took the steps two at a time, Kurtz giving her a crushing, bruising hug. Andy wasn't sure how she did it, but Kurtz was almost fifty-five and could still probably out muscle half of Troop 18.

"Good to see you, kid," Kurtz said, pounding Andy on the shoulder.

"You too, Kurtz. Thanks again for doing this. It's a huge favour."

Kurtz shrugged. "Hey, I'd rather test out the camp on a bunch of pansy cadets than paying corporates from Calgary. You guys can help me work out the kinks and put in a few days of hard work. We'll call it even."

Andy smiled at the retired officer. Maybe she was actually going to pull this off. She looked down at the Yukon, stuffed with supplies. She still had a lot of work to do in the next forty-eight hours.

"Don't even think about it," Kurtz said, following Andy's gaze. "Tara's got soup and sandwiches waiting inside, so come on in."

Andy pushed off the railing and followed her inside.

Greys, blues, and green dominated the inside of the huge house. Soft and muted, the colours blended together in a comforting, calming palette. Andy smelled chicken soup, and her empty stomach instantly gave a growl of appreciation. She followed Kurtz back to the kitchen where Tara stood ladling soup into large, white bowls. Tara was short and round with a long braid down her back. As the two of them entered, Tara turned and gave Andy a warm smile.

"Hi Andy, grab a seat."

The chicken soup and homemade bread were unbelievably good. Kurtz asked her a million questions about the troop, the history, and the cast of characters about to descend on her unfinished camp. Andy answered as best she could. She had the files on all sixteen cadets but hadn't done much more than scan them. She was hoping to have time to read them tonight.

"And how about your love life?" Kurtz said. "Last I heard, you were madly in love with a redhead."

Andy tried not to choke on her bread, her mouth instantly going dry. She swallowed, fighting successfully for calm. "Still am. But Kate's taking some time." She hoped it was vague enough not to prompt more questions and still clear enough that she didn't want to talk about it.

The silence was uncomfortable. Andy stared at the raised pattern on the tablecloth. She shouldn't have been surprised when Kurtz filled the silence with a question.

"You her first?"

Andy had the sudden desire to lash out, her anger, her defenses rising quickly. But at the very least, Andy had control. "Yes."

"Well, we know damn well not everyone handles it easily."

The anger and self-recrimination hit Andy so hard in the belly that she stood abruptly, making a mockery out of her illusion of control.

"I should get going," Andy said, her voice a monotone. "Thanks for lunch, Tara." Andy left the table, knowing she was being rude. She owed her friends better than this. She was out of the house, down the stairs and almost to the car when Kurtz caught up to her.

"Andy, hang on," Kurtz called and Andy stopped, one hand on the door of the Yukon. She met Kurtz's look with guarded eyes. "Tara wants to know if you're staying here tonight. We've got a group coming in sometime in the next few hours, but there's a room for you."

"I'm not particularly good company, Kurtz," Andy said, the closest she could come to an explanation or an apology for her behaviour.

"You don't need to be. But if you'd rather be on your own, there's the honeymoon cabin, just outside the back meadow. You've only seen it in pictures, I think…"

Kurtz trailed off, and Andy had to guess it was the expression on her face that did it. Kurtz had sent pictures of the cabin they'd built over the demolished building site. It was small, sweet, private, and built entirely of renewable resources and powered with solar energy. It had reminded Andy of their small cabin in the Montana mountains where Andy had truly and completely fallen for Kate. After seeing the pictures, Andy had thought about bringing Kate here, even just for a weekend, dreamed about spending days together in bed. But the thought was too hard, and Andy let the sadness tug at her as she clenched the door of the Yukon, her knuckles going white with strain.

"I should head up to camp, get things set up. I'll need to put in a lot of work before the troop gets here Thursday."

Kurtz held Andy's eyes for a long time before she spoke. "Did you know I couldn't stand you when you first started at E-division?"

Andy looked at her, startled. "No."

"I thought you were such a cocky little shit, giving people the evil eye when they said something you didn't like, not in the least bit afraid to be out of the closet. I heard reports that you even threatened that asshole, Brown, when he wouldn't stop referring to people as faggots."

Andy remembered Brown, a constable two levels above her. He was the worst kind of cop: testosterone-fuelled, inflated ego, stupid. She'd asked him flat out not to use that word again. He'd laughed at her, not only was she a rookie but also a woman. And gay. Too many strikes against her to pay the slightest bit of attention to her request. Andy had finally told him privately to either stop using the word or explain to his buddies how a gay rookie chick had given him a black eye.

"When you showed up," Kurtz said, "I'd been on the force twenty years already, so tightly closeted I couldn't even say the word 'lesbian' in my head when I was in uniform. And it was nothing to you—nothing at all. And that seriously pissed me off. It took me a long time to figure out that you weren't cocky, just completely unapologetic. Barely making a dent in your twenties, new to the uniform, and you could give a flying fuck what people thought of how you lived your life."

Andy considered Kurtz, reading her stern, lined face. "What are you getting at, Kurtz?"

"Maybe you should consider not everyone takes to this as easily as you did."

"I know that," Andy said, annoyed. But guilt also flashed through her, heavy and uncomfortable.

"Do you? Do you have any idea how high you set the bar? How impossible that might be to achieve?"

Andy said nothing, concentrating on unclenching her fingers from the door frame of the Yukon. She needed some time and some space to think through what Kurtz had just said and decide whether it was perspective or judgement. "I should get going," she said finally, not sure what else to say.

"Anything you need, just let us know, okay?"

Andy could barely nod her head in appreciation before she pulled herself into the truck. She slammed the door, jammed the key in the ignition, and backed down the driveway.

By sundown, Andy was exhausted. She parked the Yukon at the end of a small, gravel road, the one Kurtz and Tara were fighting the municipality to be able to pave properly and extend right up to the camp. The walk from the truck to the camp was less than fifteen minutes, but it took her five hours and eight trips down the gravel path to unload all the gear. It was back breaking and mind numbing and Andy loved every second of it. The camp itself was set in a clearing between giant boulders of the Canadian Shield, surrounded by brush and trees. The cabins formed a rough semi-circle, a large rectangle of grass out back forming an old sports field and some cracked, old concrete holding up a rusty, listing basketball hoop. The siding on the cabins was dark-stained shingles, but the windows were bright and modern, and the solar panels on each roof even more so.

Andy stood under the one, humming hydro pole and surveyed her surroundings as darkness crept onto the grounds. If she had any more energy, either physical or mental, she would feel satisfied. This place was perfect: the privacy, the trails up into the mountains, the cabins. Even the kitchen cabin was bigger than Andy had first thought. They might even all be able to squeeze in for mealtimes. She walked there now, feeling cool air on the back of her sweaty neck, hands shoved into the front of her favourite sweatshirt.

Moving boxes around, Andy found a can of some kind of stew, a can opener, and a spoon. She didn't bother lighting the camp stove, and she didn't think about the incredible meal that Tara had likely provided for her guests tonight. Andy sat on the steps of the kitchen cabin and ate out of the can, watching the colour leach out of the surrounding landscape. By the time she had finished dinner and closed up the cabin against bears and racoons, it was dark. Andy walked the short distance to the cabin she'd randomly chosen for the night, her bag slung across a bed. She took an extra armful of wood on her way in, though the woodstove had already warmed the cabin.

Andy had avoided being on her own as much as possible the last few weeks. But somehow out here it was okay, welcome even. Other than the crappy supper and the load of work she had in the next two days, she felt all right. Kurtz and Tara were only a ten minute run down the steep hill, the truck a fifteen minute walk. She made a note to purchase some two-way radios in town. Without a cellphone, they'd need some way to communicate with the main house and the outside world. Andy's own cellphone was already off, the only noise in the cabin now the muted crackle of the fire. Opening her bag, Andy pulled out a handful of troop personnel files and sat at the simple wooden table in the centre of the room.

This was the real work. Trying to understand who these cadets were, what exactly they were hiding, and why. She had few illusions this project was going to be easy. Certainly it wouldn't follow any usual pattern she had for mining information. There would be no interrogation, no carefully placed questions, no set-ups. Andy hoped their carefully constructed pact would begin to break down out here, and they would begin to see the only way out of this was to give up whatever secret they were so vigilantly guarding.

It was well after midnight by the time Andy had read all sixteen cadet profiles. She reminded herself not to make assumptions, given their ages, backgrounds, and levels of education. She needed to keep an open mind. When the cadets arrived, they would give her more information from the way they acted than any report could hope to cover.

Andy pulled at the cord for the light and curled herself under the covers. The only light came from the glow of the woodstove and the edge of orange light cast by the hydro pole through the window. Andy closed her eyes, consciously calmed her breathing, and wondered which memory of Kate would follow her into sleep.

❖

By the time Troop 18 arrived on Thursday, Andy and the camp were both ready. Cabins were arranged, the kitchen was stocked, trails mapped, and the water tested. Andy had picked up groceries, four radios, boxes of matches, pillows, and a basketball when she'd gone into town the day before, the last items on her very long list. She'd avoided the main house, a cowardly act she wasn't particularly proud of, but she'd been enjoying the solitude and didn't want to inflict herself on others until she was sure she could behave.

Andy had dressed carefully that morning, surprised and amused by her nerves. She wasn't a cadet and was no longer subject to Sergeant Trokof's inspections, but she still dressed as if she needed to satisfy those rigid demands. In fact, it was the unmistakable timbre of Sgt. Trokof's harsh, commanding voice that announced the troop's arrival. Andy walked into the centre of the clearing to meet the cadets and named them in her head as they appeared on the gravel road.

Angela Hellman, age twenty-four, three-year university degree, from a small town outside Ottawa. Jacob Frances, fourth generation RCMP cadet, thirty, the oldest member of the troop. Bertrand Petit, twenty-five, a giant at six five, reminding Andy strongly of Jack with his curly hair and long, dark lashes. Tracey Prewitt-Hayes, twenty-six, top of her class so far in everything but fitness, eyes like a hawk. They marched in formation down the path, Trokof's drill sergeant voice bringing up the rear of the troop.

Andy wasn't surprised to see them in the brown uniforms of a more junior troop instead of the blues they should have earned this many weeks into training. She recognized an example of Depot punishment, the giving and taking away of kit items so cadets knew exactly where they stood. Another measure that had failed. As the cadets marched into the centre of the clearing, commanded by the drill sergeant's voice to stand at attention in two neat rows, Andy stood impassively with her shoulders squared and her hands clasped behind her and waited. She was welcoming them, but this wasn't her show.

Sergeant Trokof approached Andy. His blue uniform fit his medium frame with impeccable precision, grey hair short and neat under his cap, high browns gleaming up to his knees, and the same stick he'd carried eleven years ago tucked smartly under one arm. Andy unconsciously sucked in her stomach, lifted her chin a fraction, and reminded herself she was no longer a cadet. She was allowed to look him in the eye.

"Sergeant Wyles," Sergeant Trokof yelled, his usual pitch when in the vicinity of cadets. "It is my absolute dishonour to present you with the most worthless troop at Depot, Troop 18."

He turned to stand beside Andy with one precise movement, stamping his boots into the gravel, both of them now surveying the cadets. Not one of them moved, shifted, or even let their eyes travel around their new surroundings. They were incredibly controlled, very disciplined. But Andy knew from experience being disciplined was easy. It was freedom and choice and space that could trip you up.

"Thank you, Sergeant Trokof. May I address the cadets?"

"Yes, Sergeant," he barked.

Andy surveyed the cadets again, letting the silence stretch, wondering when someone would break rank and look. There, a quick flick of her eyes from Cadet Krista Shandly, age twenty-one from Gander, Newfoundland, the youngest member of the troop. She blushed when she got caught, Andy detecting mainly curiosity but also embarrassment.

"Welcome to Camp Depot," Andy said to the cadets in the same voice she would use with her junior officers back in Vancouver—direct, business-like, but not harsh. "I'm sure you've already guessed by Sergeant Trokof's presence that this isn't going to be a vacation. Whatever else you think this might be, you should know this is the last chance for Troop 18 to prove you're ready to be Mounties."

Again, no one shifted. Andy scanned the serious, blank faces of the cadets in front of her, counting them in her head, wondering where the dead Acadian cadet had stood, where the troop felt his physical absence.

"You will answer Sergeant Wyles with 'Yes, Sergeant,' when she speaks to you," Sergeant Trokof warned.

Silence.

"What do you answer?" he roared.

"Yes, Sergeant!" the cadets yelled back.

Sergeant Trokof turned to Andy and spoke to her under his breath. "They're not cute, they're not bright, but Lord almighty these cadets can follow an order in unison."

Andy was surprised to hear the faintest Newfie accent in his voice. Rumour had it that Sergeant Trokof had hatched from an egg at Depot, a fully-formed RCMP officer, such was his single-minded attention. Andy suppressed a smile.

"I'd like to talk to the right mark," Andy said, referring to the cadet each troop chose early on to be their leader.

"Cadet Prewitt-Hayes, step forward!" the Sergeant yelled, and Andy wasn't the least bit surprised to see the hawk-eyed keener step forward smartly. She had a long face and brown eyes, and her auburn hair was braided neatly under her hat. Prewitt-Hayes seemed very young and very serious.

"Cadet Prewitt-Hayes, you and your troop have one hour to unload your bus and set up in the four cabins behind me," Andy said. "Anything not put away exactly as it should be will be confiscated. Any questions?"

"Yes, Sergeant!" Cadet Prewitt-Hayes focused on a point off to Andy's left. "Permission to ask a question, Sergeant."

"Go ahead, cadet," Andy said mildly.

"Are we bringing the instructors' gear off the bus also or just our own, Sergeant?"

"That will be your second task, cadet. Just worry about your own kit for now. Anything else?"

"Permission to go, Sergeant!"

"Granted."

Cadet Prewitt-Hayes spun on her heels, waved one arm above her head, pointed back down the path to the bus and yelled, "Doubling!" Every member of the troop turned and sprinted.

As the cadets disappeared around the bend, the three instructors and an extremely disgruntled-looking woman in civilian clothes stepped forward. Andy guessed this was the medic, and she didn't look particularly happy to be here.

"Ten bucks they send Foster back for the keys," one of the instructors said. He had a shaved head, broad shoulders, and looked to be in his early thirties. He introduced himself to Andy as Constable Anthony Zeb, fitness and firearms.

"Nah, ten bucks on Foster *and* Awad. No way will they let someone come back here alone," another instructor said. She had dark hair tucked neatly under her cap and was somewhere in her mid-forties. She put her hand out to Andy. "Sergeant Leslie

Manitou, APS," she said, identifying herself as part of the Applied Police Sciences team. "Les, when the cadets aren't around."

Andy shook her hand and gave her own name. The last instructor, a quiet man in his late forties named Sergeant Dave Meyers was just introducing himself as another APS team member when they heard boots on gravel. Andy recognized Cadets Hawke Foster and Michael Awad from their profiles. Andy had read Foster's file carefully as it was thicker than the rest. He was from Vancouver, and his black hair, light brown skin, and slanted, almond-shaped eyes showed his First Nations heritage. His file didn't mention any band affiliation. Foster was, not so ironically, a product of the BC foster care system, landing finally with a family at the age of fifteen that would become his home. Andy watched him run, swift and controlled, in unison with his partner, twenty-eight-year-old Michael Awad from Montreal.

The two cadets stopped in front of the assembled instructors, unsure who to address.

"You have a question, cadets?" Constable Zeb said.

"Yes, Constable! We need the keys to the bus, Constable."

Constable Zeb pulled them out of his pocket, handed them to Foster, and the two immediately ran back down the path.

"Pay up," Les said to Zeb cheerfully after the cadets had disappeared.

"Put it on my tab."

Andy watched the exchange, making continual assessments of the people with whom she was going to be spending the next few weeks.

"Betting on cadets is an age-old Depot tradition," Trokof said, seeing Andy eyeing the two instructors. Again, Andy couldn't help but be surprised by the note of a Newfie accent.

"Did you ever bet on me?" Andy said, not quite able to control the fear that she was being insubordinate to a senior officer. Some things about Depot never actually left your psyche. Which was the point, of course.

"Of course, I did." He seemed surprised at the question. "Sergeant within ten years, you made me a hundred dollars."

"Happy I could help."

"Don't lie, Sergeant Wyles. You and every other cadet wished me dead more than once."

Andy shrugged, still smiling. "Somewhere around the six thousandth push up, probably." Andy looked at the only person she hadn't been introduced to, the civilian medic. She was hunkered down in her jacket even though it really wasn't that cold. Trokof followed Andy's gaze.

"Sgt. Wyles, this is our on-site medic, Melanie Stinson. Ms. Stinson was a last-minute substitute as the medic Lincoln had originally assigned strained his back and had to pull out."

Andy shook the woman's hand. It was a limp shake, the kind that always made Andy angry for some reason.

"I've already requested a replacement," the medic said, pulling her sleeves back over her hands. Andy took an instant dislike to her.

"Good. I'll look forward to it," Andy said and turned away. She added it to the list of things to worry about. As the instructors wandered around camp and checked out the cabins, Andy focused on the next twenty-four hours. The only agenda today was set-up. Tonight, Andy intended to talk with the instructors about the schedule. Tomorrow would be inspection and drug testing, both a requirement for the first twenty-four hours. Andy had already decided to kill two birds with one stone. She would drive the samples to the lab in Vancouver, have a face-to-face with Finns to get that checkmark out of the way, and talk to Lincoln about getting a replacement medic soon. Things were already too tenuous out here without a disgruntled team member pulling everyone down.

The trampling of gravel announced the cadets' arrival, each one carrying a pack or a box, most more than one. Cadet Greg Shipman, aged twenty-six, a tall, stocky farm boy from Alberta ran with a guitar case bouncing against his back. Andy shook her head, amused. He'd better find somewhere to stow it or it would be gone. Camp was mayhem, cadets doubling between cabins, dropping bags, yelling instructions. Cadet Prewitt-Hayes's voice was the loudest. Andy watched them all listen, argue, compromise, and, finally, fall in line. With ten men and six women in this troop, Andy knew part of this challenge was to decide how to divide up the cabins. To her surprise, the women all bunked in one, taking over the cabin that was marginally bigger than the others. The men divided up the rest.

Andy checked her watch. "Troop 18, you have nine minutes," she called out.

Trokof walked over to her side, looking like he was marching even when he wasn't. "Want to see something interesting?" he said under his breath. Andy nodded, curious. "Watch this."

He marched over to one of the men's cabins and immediately started yelling. "Cadet Foster, who gave you permission to remove your hat? I didn't, Sgt. Wyles didn't, Constable Zeb certainly didn't. Are you thinking for yourself, Cadet Foster?"

Foster had stopped what he was doing, jammed his hat back on, and stood at attention. "No, sir!"

"Then give me twenty-five, Cadet Foster. And keep your uniform clean, or it will be another twenty-five!"

Andy winced internally. Twenty-five push-ups on wet gravel would suck. But as she watched Hawke Foster drop to the ground and begin his push-ups, Andy heard 'twenty-five' being yelled out, echoed around the camp. Every member of Troop 18 was down on the ground, giving twenty-five push-ups. Instructors routinely gave a whole troop behaviour modification, or mod-b as it was commonly known, for one cadet's transgression, but an entire troop taking one cadet's punishment when they weren't ordered to was pretty unusual. As soon as they were done with their push-ups, the cadets went right back to work as if nothing had happened. Andy caught Trokof's eye. Interesting hardly covered it.

Andy heard footsteps behind her as Sgt. Manitou approached. "Every time?" Andy said.

"Every time," the other sergeant confirmed. "Zeb tried to out punish them, kept giving them push ups every time they did someone else's mod-b. They collapsed trying to keep up, which is when we took away their blues."

"They didn't care?" She remembered the shame in having your kit taken away, the mix of sympathy and ridicule from the other troops.

"Oh, they cared. Some more than others. But it doesn't stop them. Nothing does."

Andy thought she detected a note of respect mixed in with the frustration. Troop 18 certainly had gotten to their instructors. Again, Andy felt the tug of a challenge. *You won't punish it out of them, you won't force it out of them, you won't trick it out of them,* Andy reminded herself.

"So, what's for supper tonight, Sarge?" Les said to Andy good-naturedly. She seemed very happy to be here.

"I'll be cooking for the instructors tonight," Andy said. "Troop 18 is fending for themselves, but they're on mess duty after this. I figure instead of the Sergeant Major's Parade in the afternoons, they can do camp clean up, haul water and garbage and make food. We'll keep them busy," Andy promised.

"I believe it," Les agreed, looking around. "This place is great. Couldn't ask for a better vacation spot."

Andy raised her eyebrows.

"I've got four boys aged seven to fourteen at home. This, my friend, is a vacation."

Andy laughed and, for some reason, thought of Kate. She didn't try to track anymore what triggered thoughts or memories of her. It didn't matter, really. Andy let the pain of missing Kate settle on her chest. And as she checked her watch and called out time to the cadets, Andy didn't bother trying to stop thinking about where Kate was right now and what she was doing. She wasn't here, that's all Andy knew. She wasn't here.

Chapter Four

Andy manoeuvred the Yukon carefully down jammed, foggy Vancouver streets. It had taken her almost seven hours to get here from Clearwater, even though she'd been on the highway before sunrise. Fog had settled in the farther she got from the mountains, turning into the kind of day where there was no hope of it burning off. You just had to slog your way through it and hope it moved out again overnight. Andy was annoyed: at having to leave so early, at the medic for making her life difficult, at the constriction of being forced to check-in, at the sixteen urine samples she was now delivering to the lab, clear the other side of town from Headquarters. As Andy dropped off the Styrofoam container with the orange-lidded cups and filled out the requisite RCMP paperwork, she called Finns' secretary and left a message saying she'd be closer to two than twelve for their meeting. Then she got back into the Yukon, glad to be rid of the samples, and fought her way through sluggish traffic to Headquarters.

The first night at camp had gone fine, the cadets burning their food on the too-hot camp stove, and the instructors happily digging in to Andy's simple chicken burgers and cold potato salad. Andy and Les had shared a cabin, Andy appreciating the other woman was easy going and funny but didn't feel the need to fill every moment with chatter. Early this morning, Andy had left a note for Kurtz and Tara along with one of the two-way radios on the porch, asking if she could stay with them in the main house tonight, knowing she'd probably get in late. Kurtz and Tara owed her nothing but they wouldn't turn Andy away.

Andy cursed at the traffic and continued to ignore the blinking light on her cell phone as she'd been doing since getting back into range early this morning. She didn't want to talk to anyone, and if Finns was calling to yell at her for being late, she couldn't get there any faster. Looking around at the dismal surroundings, peaks of buildings lost in fog, windows reflecting back nothing but grey, Andy thought she truly hated this city sometimes. It was cold, wet, damp, depressing, and, in the right light, unrelentingly ugly.

She did a second run around the block of 37th and Heather, waiting for a spot to open up outside of Headquarters. One finally did, and Andy didn't even bother to take a breath or compose herself. She just grabbed her file and her phone, jammed her hat on her head and shrugged her shoulders against the damp bite of the wind. As she was crossing the street, she heard her phone ring but silenced it irritably without looking at it. Ten seconds later, it beeped a message and another five seconds after that it signalled a text, then another. Andy cursed under her breath and called it up. Jack.

Don't ignore me. Need to talk.

Headquarters came into view as she thumbed out a quick text to her partner. *618?*

This was their personal distress signal, which had come in handy more than once. Right now, Andy was using it as her own code: if it's not important, fuck off.

More like 617 and a half. Call me.

Andy crossed the street, pushing the speed dial for Jack's cell phone. "What is it, Jack?"

"Where are you, Wylie?" Jack said nervously.

"Just heading into Headquarters, why?"

"Okay, I just found this out now, and I don't know everything that's going on but…but I think it's going to be fine. In fact I think it's going to be better than fine."

Andy let him ramble, barely paying attention as she caught the heavy doors of the familiar glass building and went inside. The large, open lobby was full of civilians looking lost or annoyed mixing with officers in uniform looking busy or bored. It was much warmer in here, and Andy used her free hand to unzip her storm jacket as she made her way through the crowd. Then she froze, every muscle in her body locking down, her heart thudding to a stop before doubling its pace, her brain frantically trying to make sense of what she was seeing.

"Jack..." she said into the phone, her voice carrying no weight. He still babbled in the background. "*Jack*," she said more forcefully, her eyes never leaving the two figures descending the stairs. "Does this have anything to do with Kate?"

"How did you know?"

"Because she's walking down the stairs with Finns right now."

"It's going to be okay," Jack said quickly. "Call me later." And then he hung up.

Andy pushed disconnect on her phone and clenched it in her palm. She was unable to move. Andy scanned Kate, the way she moved, the expression on her face, her achingly familiar silhouette. She noted a new hollowness in Kate's cheeks, framed by her red curls caught in a twist at the back of her neck. She was wearing an unfamiliar winter jacket, army green with a hood lined in orange fleece.

They were at the bottom of the stairs now, Kate smiling politely at something Finns had just said. Turning towards the front doors, Kate shifted a black backpack on her shoulders. They were now only twenty feet away. Andy felt her heart give a painful jerk in her chest as Kate faced her dead on. Everything about the way she moved made Andy hurt. As if she could sense it, Kate scanned the busy reception area until she saw Andy. Kate looked her up and down, her brown eyes locking on Andy's. Andy read her expression: happiness, relief, but above all, caution.

What does that mean? Andy wanted to yell. She wasn't sure, so as Finns and Kate approached her, Andy commanded her body to meet them half way and she did the only thing she could think of in that moment. She slammed her guard up, hard. She became still, quieted, tense. Andy forced everything she was feeling into a small ball and clenched it in her stomach. She'd unpack it later.

"Sgt. Wyles, I was beginning to think you'd gotten lost."

Andy forced herself to pay attention to the gritty, annoyed tone Finns was using.

"I'm sorry I'm late. The fog has almost shut down the city." Her voice had so little inflection, Andy knew both Finns and Kate could see right through it.

"Well, you picked a hell of a day to be late and a hell of time to decide to find some work-life balance and not answer your phone for three days, Wyles." Andy thought she could hear a note of nerves in the annoyance. But Andy didn't have time to think it through because she'd become distracted by the ghost of a smile on Kate's lips. *God, Kate's lips*...It took every ounce of willpower Andy had to drag her eyes away.

"What's going on here?" Andy couldn't stand another second of talking about the weather and her tardiness.

"Sgt. Wyles, I'd like you to meet the newest civilian member of E-division. Dr. Morrison has just finished signing the papers with Superintendent Heath." Finns did not sound impressed.

This didn't make sense. None of this made any sense.

"Part time, but permanent," Kate added. The sound of her voice made the clenched muscles in Andy's abdomen tremble slightly. It had been so long since she'd heard that voice, the slightly mocking tone, so often at the edge of laughter. Kate wasn't looking at Andy, though. She'd turned her body, angling it away. Andy couldn't help but be thankful. Talking to her was so much easier when she didn't have to see her face straight on: her pale skin, the light flecks of colour in her brown eyes.

But as Finns kept talking about Heath overriding Finns's objections, a sudden thought hit Andy hard in the chest. Kate had moved on purpose, either because she found it just as hard to be this close or because she was trying to make it easier on Andy.

Both answers threatened to undo her entirely and only Finns's harsh voice brought her back.

"Sgt. Wyles, are you listening?"

"No," she said honestly and tried very hard not to see Kate suppress a smile.

Finns sighed, muttering under his breath. He made sure Andy was looking him dead in the eye before he spoke again. "Dr. Morrison will be joining your team, replacing the Depot medic who has requested a transfer out. My objections have been overruled by Superintendent Heath." Finns seemed to scrutinize Andy for any reaction to this announcement. But by this time, Andy was numb, barely able to process. "Do you have any concerns about this?"

Yes. "No," Andy said quickly, ignoring the voice in her head.

A very long pause. Andy studied Kate in her peripheral vision, aware of every time she took in a breath or shifted her weight.

"Fine. You will have to put up with your current medic for the next two days as Dr. Morrison won't be arriving until Monday morning. Do you have any questions?"

Yes. Is Kate coming back to me?

"No," Andy said again.

Kate checked her cheap, black plastic watch. "I should get going, I'm almost late," Kate said, addressing Finns. Andy felt rather than saw Kate pull in a breath as she turned toward Andy. "I'll see you in a couple of days," she said quietly, holding Andy's eyes for a moment, then two, before she shifted her backpack again and walked away. Andy looked after her as she moved through the crowd, pushed open the glass doors, and disappeared into the fog.

"Sgt. Wyles, tell me now if this is going to be an issue," Finns said, his voice strained. "I'll fight Superintendent Heath on this decision. He seems to think you two are some sort of dream team."

We were.

"But you are my priority, not Dr. Morrison. So I'll ask you again. Is this going to be an issue?"

Andy looked him in the eye. "No. Can I have two minutes?"

Staff Sgt. Finns sighed. "I'll be in my office."

Andy barely waited for him to finish the short sentence before she followed Kate through the glass doors. She controlled her pace and fought the urge to look down at her chest where it felt like her heart was beating on the outside, not in. There, just around the building, Kate was looking down, searching through her backpack, the back of her neck exposed.

"Kate!"

Kate turned toward the sound of her voice, and Andy could see that look of relief again. And something else, something else that had always been there but Andy could never quite name. Whatever it was, it made Andy feel warm. Andy was standing in front of her now, in front of Kate. *Kate*. And she was at a complete loss.

"Can I drive you to work?"

An utterly inadequate question, of course, after fifty-three days apart. But Kate's expression said she was still being cautious and Andy took the signal as a warning, warmth or not.

Kate smiled and held up a bicycle helmet which Andy had seen but not registered.

"Thanks, but I've got my bike. My therapist told me I had to start exercising."

Kate was seeing a therapist. She was exercising. She was working at the ER and with the RCMP. She smiled at Andy like it was the most natural thing in the world. Andy collected every piece of evidence, still unsure exactly what she was investigating.

"I tried to convince her that back-to-back traumas counted as cardio, but she was having none of that."

Andy heard the laughter in Kate's voice and more than anything she wanted to be able to laugh with her or at the very least to hear her laugh again. But instead, the smile was fading on Kate's lips, replaced by that same cautious look. And something else. Resolve, Andy decided.

"This isn't how I planned this, Andy. I really didn't mean for this to be an ambush," Kate said softly. "I've been trying to call you since last weekend." Andy watched her fidget. "I didn't even know you were capable of turning your phone off for three days," she said, her smile tentative this time.

Andy stood perfectly still, searching for something to say or ask or tell. Nothing came to mind. All of her attention was focused on a curl that had escaped from the twist at Kate's neck and was brushing Kate's jaw. God, she wanted to reach out and tuck that curl behind Kate's ear, like she had a hundred times in the past. Kate checked her watch again, and Andy knew she had to say something.

"You'll be up in Clearwater on Monday?" Andy said, her voice carrying none of its usual weight. It didn't even sound like her.

"Yes, in the morning. Staff Sgt. Finns says I need to be on-site, is that right?"

Andy nodded, not quite able to believe she was having this casual, work place conversation with Kate, standing in the parking lot at Headquarters. "Check in at the main house, and they can radio up to camp for me."

"Okay," Kate said softly, keeping her eyes on Andy. That look had always twisted inside Andy, made her heart pound loudly in her chest. "I should really get going. I took all three weekend shifts from Craig so I could head up next week."

"Then I'll see you Monday." Andy's body warmed at the thought of knowing she'd see Kate again in less than seventy-two hours.

Kate smiled and settled the pack on her back before climbing on her bike. One last look at Andy, and then she pushed off and pedalled away. Andy watched Kate disappear into the fog, hearing the unseen traffic on the road and the muted conversations between invisible officers. Andy gave herself one last minute to look longingly, pathetically after her. For someone who had spent her whole life pursuing strength, Andy could not explain how she had fallen for someone who made her feel so incredibly, wonderfully weak. Andy took a quick, sharp breath, shook her head, and went back inside to try to convince her supervisor this was not going to be the disaster he so obviously feared.

It took a lot of convincing. Andy was distracted for the first half of their meeting, pacing Finns' small office. She was still dissecting Kate's words, Kate's expressions, her motivations. In her head, Andy followed Kate from Headquarters to Vancouver East Hospital, worrying about her biking in the fog. She was considering calling the ER, thinking she could check in with the desk clerk to make sure Kate had arrived safely when Finns's voice intruded abruptly.

"Enough, Wyles! Pull yourself together."

Andy stopped in her tracks and took a moment to try to consider what Finns was seeing right now. It wasn't pretty, that was for sure. Andy sat heavily in one of the chairs, clasped her hands together, breathed in slowly once, let it out slowly once. *Control, control, control.* "Sorry, sir."

"Don't be sorry, just focus. Tell me what's going on with your Camp Depot. I've got a report to write for the COs. Thank God they can't see you right now. They're nervous enough as it is."

This brought Andy up sharply. No matter what was going on with Kate, no matter how important, she couldn't do anything about it right now. And this was a promise she'd made to Lincoln, so she had no choice but to honour it by giving it her undivided attention. "Okay, what do you need to know?"

"Start with the location. Any safety issues or concerns?"

Andy focused and gave Finns all the information he and the COs needed to know. Andy talked and Finns took notes, occasionally stopping to ask a question or clarify a point. After half an hour on the basics, Finns wanted to know about the cadets themselves.

"First impressions," Finns said, when Andy objected that she'd barely spent any time with them. "What do you see?"

"They have a leader, Cadet Prewitt-Hayes, but my gut tells me someone else or possibly more than one person is influencing the group. They're very in tune with each other, and from what the instructors are telling me they've been like that from the beginning. The death of their troop mate somehow cemented that bond."

"Similar backgrounds?"

"Not at all," Andy said. She'd wondered the same thing. "Foster kid, college kid, high school drop-out, varsity athlete, second career, small engine mechanic, farmer…"

Finns held up his hand. "I get the picture, thank you, Sgt. Wyles."

Andy grinned. "They click, that's clear. They look out for each other, they have the exact troop mentality of brotherhood and sisterhood that Depot works so hard to build and maintain. They should be the shining example of everything Depot tries to create in a troop."

"But they're not," Finns said pointedly.

"They're not because they're hiding something, and, at this point, they will go to any lengths to maintain that secret."

"Including the threat of having their contracts revoked," Finns said, and Andy nodded. "I don't get it, Wyles."

"Lincoln was right. You have to see this troop in action. They read each other's minds, it's uncanny." Andy was thinking of the troop as they made supper in the mess hall the night before. They seemed hyper aware of each other, even when joking around about making a meal. Andy had expected the stress of trying to keep a secret with that many people would result in every member looking out for the others, watching to see who would crack. But it was so unconscious with this group, Andy wasn't sure they were even aware of it.

Finns eventually capped his pen and gathered his notes, lining them up neatly with his desk ledger. Andy checked her watch. Almost four o'clock. If she left now, she'd get back to the B&B before midnight, assuming the fog had dissipated.

"Okay, that's good for now. Superintendent Heath himself will be up sometime the middle of next week for inspection. I'll warn you now, whether you're in his good books or not, he's going to need to have something to take back to the COs."

"He can take back anything he wants, but I'm not going to push the troop just so he has something to put in a report. The TO himself gave me the go ahead to run this thing as I see fit, so that's what I'm going to do," Andy insisted stubbornly.

Finns held up a hand. "You're wasting your breath, Wyles. I'm merely pointing out that Superintendent Heath will want more than the basics and a tour of the camp next week. Lincoln trusts you're on the right course and so do I." Finns stopped and cleared his throat. "I also trust you will know when to call it quits if things start to head south. Either with the camp, the cadets, the instructors, Dr. Morrison, or yourself. I'm trusting you know when to call it a day."

Finns held her gaze and Andy sat still, withstanding the scrutiny.

"Yes, sir." She considered herself warned.

"Good, then go. Get back to camp."

Before she was even at the stairs, Andy had her phone out, calling into her voicemail. Eleven voicemails, seventeen texts. Most of those were Jack, most of them today. She was almost back at the Yukon by the time she heard Kate's message. Her voice was nervous, hardly like Kate at all.

"Hi, Andy, it's me. It's, uh, Monday. I've been trying to get in touch with you for a couple of days. Maybe you're screening…" Andy heard Kate stop and take a breath, then plough on. "Anyway, there's something I wanted to talk to you about. Well, of course there is, there's about a hundred and sixty five thousand things I want to talk to you about, but one of them is time sensitive. So…I'm hoping you'll call me. I'm at home tonight." A long pause, nothing, then a click to end the message.

Andy replayed the message three times, sitting in the cold Yukon. She barely noticed. She was trying to decode Kate's words, her tone, the glaring uncertainty in her voice. How could she be uncertain? How could Kate not understand Andy had ached for her every second she'd been gone? It suddenly seemed like a very good idea to start the engine of the truck, drive over to Van East and sort this out right now. Tell Kate she loved her, pull Kate into her arms and hold her, to protect her from anything hard or uncertain or painful.

No.

Andy glared out the windshield, her jaw tight, her shoulders strained. No. She'd run interference for Kate too many times. Andy had tried to coax, encourage, give space. She'd tried so hard to find the right words, and failing that, to not say anything at all. None of it had helped. In the end, she'd watched Kate turn in on herself. She'd become diminished and far away. Andy clenched the steering wheel with one hand, a flash of hot anger rising up from her stomach into her chest. She couldn't help it as all the things she'd said and done wrong lined themselves up in her head. That was the uncertainty in Kate's voice. Andy couldn't stop herself from thinking she'd help put it there.

Andy recognized the feeling of being stuck, the mental loops of self-loathing and doubt. Then she remembered Finns's words, the warning and the command to pull herself together. Turning the key in the ignition and setting the heater to high, Andy jammed her phone in the hands free unit and dialled her partner. Maybe it was time for some of Jack's unending optimism.

❖

Andy listened to the pounding of seventeen pairs of feet behind her, surprised at how little noise this many people could make in the forest. She was leading Troop 18 on an early morning run and the air was damp and cold, the kind that worms its way under your clothes and sits on your chest. Didn't matter. Andy knew she would be warm in ten minutes as her bright green running jacket trapped the heat against her body. She was angling them up into the mountain, aiming for a look-out she'd found her first morning alone up at camp. The fog had eased off in the night, settling into a more typical December damp, but at least now the view was clear.

A muted yell reminded her Constable Zeb was pulling up the rear of the troop. Andy's hand reflexively went to the radio strapped to her waist, her thumb flicking at the power button to make sure it was on. No code came through, so she figured Zeb was encouraging Cadet Petit to hustle it up the hill. It was Saturday morning, the cadets' own time even out here at Camp Depot. So the sixteen troop members, including the plodding powerhouse Bertrand Petit, were on this run of their own volition. When Andy had shown up in the quad this morning and announced she was leading a run if anyone was interested, she wasn't surprised when the entire troop had joined her in their matching navy blue jogging suits twenty minutes later.

As she ran, Andy considered her drive back from Vancouver the night before. She had arrived back at the main house just before midnight, as expected. She'd spent two hours on the phone with Jack while she was driving, listening to all the information he'd managed to dig up from his various sources.

Apparently Kate had asked to meet in Superintendent Heath's office ten days ago. Heath's appreciation for Kate saving his granddaughter's life had included the promise of a position with E-division if she wanted it. Apparently she did. Andy tried to sort through that with Jack: arguing, listening, rationalizing. And in the end, she had to admit, hoping. It wasn't a very comfortable place to be. As she drove the last few hours in silence, Andy wasn't sure how long she could navigate the pitfalls of hope. Two more days, she reminded herself. Just two more days.

The clearing came into view, and Andy slowed her pace, listening to the troop behind her do the same. Foster and Awad had run right behind her the whole time, and she could tell they itched to go faster, to lengthen their strides until they were flying. They were runners—not joggers, not fitness buffs, not even simply athletes. Andy recognized two people whose bodies and minds were built to run, not unlike herself. They hadn't broken rank, though, staying in line behind Andy as she kept an even, slow pace.

The last fifteen feet to the look-out had to be climbed with fingers wedged into wet rocks and toes mashed up against the smallest ledges. Andy went up easily and stood at the top, offering a hand if anyone needed it. Foster was next, and he climbed it easily too, his dark eyes revealing very little as he stood on the other side of the path, offering his own hand up to his troop mates. Andy stepped back, receiving the message loud and clear. If anyone was going to help the troop, it was going to be from within. As Andy watched various cadets reach out for the last boost over the rocky ledge, it confirmed for her everything she'd been thinking about this troop of cadets.

Andy took a sip of water from the bottle at her waist, holding it in her mouth until it was warm enough to swallow, hoping to avoid a stomach cramp on the way back to camp. She stood back and watched the cadets exploring the outlook. Angela Hellman, the varsity athlete from Ottawa, and Michael Awad were egging each other on in friendly tones, daring each other to climb up to the next outcrop while Hawke Foster silently and easily scaled the ledge.

A few cadets sat with their legs dangling over the edge. Petit's massive frame dwarfed the young Newfie girl, Shandly. Between them was Jacob Frances, the fourth generation RCMP recruit. Andy surveyed him carefully, intent on watching those cadets who had yet to make an impression. Cadet Frances was one of these, and Andy found this curious. He was the oldest recruit at thirty, just a few years younger than Andy.

After reading his file, she'd expected the man to be cocky and very sure of his place among the troop. Both his age and his pedigree seemed to point him toward a leadership role within this group, but that didn't seem to be the case. Andy studied him. His head was shaved, adding to the impression that he was very thin, though his broad shoulders made Andy think of someone lean and tough. But other than his build, Andy found him to be flat. He melded seamlessly into the background of this small troop. In fact, she couldn't remember actually having made eye contact with the cadet. He was also one of the slower members of the troop, always at the back of the pack with Petit. Andy had to wonder if this was another show of the pack mentality. No cadet left behind.

The rest of the troop milled about in small groups, sitting and chatting, ribbing each other as only people who have spent an intense four months together can. Cadet Prewitt-Hayes stood off to the side, chatting with two other cadets, both from Ontario. Every now and then, the right mark would look up and scan the troop, accounting for each member. Zeb and Andy were included in this scan as if they couldn't be trusted to not separate one cadet from the pack. Andy wasn't stupid. She knew that tactic wouldn't get her anywhere. But she was interested in shaking things up a little.

"Who's up for a race on the way back down?" Andy called out to the cadets. "Losers make breakfast for the winners."

Andy watched as they tested this suggestion, as if looking for the trap. They surveyed each other with quick eye movements.

"Petit better be on the losing team," said Greg Shipman, the farm boy from Alberta. "He's the only one who can cook." The rest of the troop seemed to relax a little at these easy words. Andy guessed she had just found one of the main influences on the group. Not a leader, but a human litmus test, a mood indicator for the recruits.

"I'll try to slow down, just for you guys," Petit answered drily in his rough Quebecois accent.

"Constable Zeb, you take half the troop back down the path we came up on. I'll take the other half on the rest of the loop." Andy pushed the empty water bottle into her belt and turned her back. She was halfway down the steep, rocky outcrop before she heard anyone behind her. She knew it was Foster without having to look. That kid seemed to want to be constantly on the move.

At the bottom of the ledge, Andy watched the troop descend and divide themselves into two groups. It should have been a simple rough divide of people with some friendly teasing, talking smack across enemy lines. But they were strangely silent as they grouped themselves between Andy and Zeb. Almost grim and uncomfortable at being separated.

"I like my coffee black and my bacon crispy," Andy called over to the other team, pretending she wasn't scrutinizing and drawing conclusions about the troop's every move. "Let's go!"

Andy didn't run full out, too aware of the varying levels of fitness of the eight recruits at her back as well as the uneven terrain. But it did feel good to let loose a little, to run instead of plod along in formation. Still, she could feel Foster breathing down her neck like he wanted to fly. Nearing the halfway mark back to camp, Andy looked over her shoulder and caught his eye.

"Take them in, Cadet Foster," she said and moved to the side, giving him room to take the lead.

Andy saw the look of surprise in his eyes, but then he caught sight of the open path and surged ahead, leaving Andy and the rest of the troop to pick up their pace.

They were, in fact, the first group in, already cooling down in the quad when Zeb led the other eight, winded cadets out of the forest. Sure enough, Petit and Frances were trailing behind. Andy made a mental note to check out their physical requirement exam results. It wasn't a team effort, and she was curious how Frances had scored on that. Maybe his role in the troop was to keep Bertrand Petit from falling too far behind.

The other instructors joined them for breakfast, the kitchen cabin slightly smoky from the overcooked bacon. It actually felt like camp, the troop's earlier hesitation gone as they pushed at each other, demanding breakfast of the losing group. Only the medic, Melanie Stinson continued to look annoyed, picking at her scrambled eggs with evident distaste. Andy couldn't wait to stick her on the first bus out of Kamloops on Monday morning.

Andy wrapped her fingers around the china cup of strong coffee and watched the cadets. Right now they seemed perfectly typical, no red flags, no cause for alarm. The losing group rolled their eyes as they served the winning cadets, Petit flipping bacon and sausage onto plates, Prewitt-Hayes with two jugs of juice refilling glasses, her usual look of intensity present even for this small job.

Andy turned to Sergeant Trokof, the only man still impeccable in his uniform on this Saturday morning. "What's on the agenda today?"

"The cadets have been given the option of going into Kamloops, bus leaving here at one o'clock and leaving town again at nine. Anyone not on the bus will have to walk back, a good hour and a half run, I believe. Cadets have been warned they will be searched leaving and coming back again."

Andy looked down the table at the other instructors. "I was talking to Kurtz and Tara last night, and they're saying we should take turns getting a night off from camp. One of us can stay down at the main house, get fed and have a good night's sleep. Any takers for tonight?"

"If they have a bath, I will say yes to that," Les said, happily biting down on a triangle of toast.

"A bath and a hot tub," Andy said.

"And no kids?"

"Not one."

"Cheers," Les said, holding up her coffee mug before taking a sip.

The instructors watched as the medic pushed back her plate and left the camp kitchen without a word.

"Did you talk to the TO about finding a replacement?" Constable Meyers said in his quiet, assured voice. "Ms. Stinson says she's more of a city person. She's unhappy being in the middle of nowhere."

Andy swallowed a hot sip of coffee before answering. "She won't have long to wait. Dr. Kate Morrison will be joining us Monday morning."

This name clearly meant nothing to the men in the group, though Andy caught an openly surprised look from Les Manitou. Andy let the awkwardness twist in her stomach so it wouldn't have to show on her face. At least she liked Les.

"I take it she will be an improvement on our disgruntled medic, then?" Trokof said.

"Definitely. Any bets on who's going into town today?" she said, quietly enough that the troop wouldn't hear.

"All of them," Zeb and Les said together.

Of course, Andy thought to herself, as the instructors gave each other knowing looks. Of course it would be all of them. Andy took another sip of coffee, letting the conversation angle off on another tangent. She wished Kate was here right now, so that they could pass each other significant looks. Kate could just read her mind as she'd done so many times before, knowing the trajectory of her thoughts without having to say anything out loud. Andy wondered if that could possibly have changed in the last few months, wondered if anything had changed. Or everything. That thought was impossible, and Andy swallowed it with the last dregs of hot coffee. Impossible.

CHAPTER FIVE

By late Saturday afternoon, Camp Depot was quiet. Andy stood outside the mess cabin and surveyed her surroundings as she'd done the first night. She mentally checked off the list of tasks they had accomplished today: water tank filled, garbage secured, wood piles re-stocked. Before they'd left for their excursion into town, the cadets had even hacked at the edges of the crumbling basketball square and bent the hoop back into its original shape.

As evening slowly descended on the quiet camp, Andy offered to walk Les down to the main house for her night off, telling Trokof she'd be back in time to make them dinner. He waved her offer away, saying he had a book and a fire and would make himself some tea and toast when he felt hungry. Andy pulled her hat on and zipped up her jacket, shaking her head as she and Les started down the path in the afternoon light.

"Strange to know he's actually human, isn't it?" Les said conspiratorially as they made their way through the trees. The air was cool and damp. Rain had threatened all day but never materialized.

"Yes," Andy admitted.

"Kind of rocks your whole universe, knowing the drill sergeant has tea and toast on a Saturday night," Les added, and

Andy laughed with her. Les's dry, near constant humour reminded Andy of Kate.

They walked in companionable silence, listening to the crows and blue jays above them fly hurriedly across the sky, as if sunset had caught them by surprise.

"What do you think the cadets are doing right now?" Andy said, curious about her impression of the troop.

"Same thing we did on our Saturday night off, probably," Les shrugged. "Drink beer and talk incessantly about life after Depot."

"Do you think so? Do you think they talk about their medal ceremony day and where they'd like to be posted around the country? They could barely stand to be divided into two groups for a twenty minute run this morning."

"I don't know, Andy. This troop has got me stumped. On paper, they're like any other troop through Depot. Some are bright, some are fit, some are naïve. They were devastated when we lost JT. We were all devastated." Les's voice wavered slightly. "Yes, they were different after losing their troop mate. But we expected that. What we didn't expect was the silence and the lies. Something's going on with this troop, something…destructive." She stopped again, shook her head in evident frustration then looked up at Andy. "All I know is that they're fiercely loyal to each other, and it would be a shame if we lost the whole troop."

They continued through the rapidly darkening woods, the combination of wet moss and loose stones forcing them to pay attention. Once they were down the wooded slope and on more even terrain, Andy picked up the thread of conversation again.

"Every group has a weak link. Who is Troop 18's?"

"Fitness? Petit. Academics? Tie between Awad and Russo. Following orders? Foster. Confidence? Shandly. Firearms? Frances."

"Wait, Frances? Really?" Andy knew it was a stereotype to assume that because Jacob Frances had RCMP genealogy, he was automatically a good marksman. Still, she was surprised.

"According to Zeb, that boy is shaky as hell."

"Nerves?"

Les frowned at the question. "Maybe. Talk to Zeb about it. Some days Frances is top of his game. Others he looks like he wished he'd never heard of the RCMP." Les gave Andy a sudden, sidelong grin. "Although I can still remember days at Depot when I felt like that. Jesus, that was a rough six months."

Andy thought back to her own Depot days with Troop 36. It had taken them a couple of weeks to gel, to feel like a troop of cadets instead of thirty-two individuals jockeying for position. By the end of the twenty-four weeks, they were tight. They knew each other's strengths and weaknesses. You couldn't hide from your troop mates. And by the time they were given their postings, you knew you could work with any one of them, even those you secretly felt relieved about when their postings sent them to the other side of the country.

"Does anyone not get along?" Andy said, thinking of the three cadets, Marchiori, Trace, and Bollinger who she had prayed she wouldn't be posted with. All of them were large, slightly dim, macho guys who detested the fact that anyone knew they even had weaknesses.

"No, not as far as I know. Foster's a bit of a loner, but even he's never far from the group. The two who dropped out early, Creighton and Tenley, I would say they never really fit in. But they were only in it for a few weeks."

"What about the two who got caught with drugs?"

"Tight," Les confirmed. "One of them, Mercier, was a real clown. Everyone loved him. Jessup was young, same as Shandly. More of a follower, I'd say."

"And how did the troop react when Mercier and Jessup had their contract removed? What happened?"

"We talked to them individually about what they knew, we talked to them as a group, and then the drill sergeant went at them for a good hour after that. Troop 18 was stoic. They showed us absolutely nothing. It was…" Les paused, as if trying to find the word. "It was almost creepy. If we thought they were tight before then…"

Another silence, each sergeant lost in her own thoughts as they kept walking, damp night air settling on their faces in a fine layer of barely-there mist.

"Lincoln thinks it's drugs," Andy said into the silence.

Les immediately shook her head. "But they're all clean, and why would they risk selling? Or if someone did, why would they continue to risk it? And why would everyone else risk getting kicked out just to protect someone else? It doesn't make sense."

Andy silently agreed with Les. But too much evidence pointed to drug use or some kind of drug distribution to disregard it.

"When are the results in from the last drug test?" Les said.

"Not until Monday, and we'll have to take the next round into Kamloops by Wednesday," Andy said as they rounded the last bend out of the trees. Down below, the main house shone its diffuse, warm light. A line of three hydro poles lit the path to the edge of the meadow, the rest of the surrounding grounds gradually deepening into darkness. Andy realized she was going to have to borrow a flashlight from Kurtz.

"I know it's none of my business and I really shouldn't ask," Leslie said tentatively. "The camp doctor arriving on Monday, Dr. Morrison…I thought I understood that you two were together?"

Andy kept walking as uncertainty and elation pounded through her stomach. Thirty six-hours. Kate would be here in thirty-six hours.

"I shouldn't have said anything," Les said apologetically, twisting her hands together in a nervous gesture.

"No, it's fine," Andy assured her. "If I had a simple answer I'd give it to you." She was thankful they were walking side by side in the near dark, and she didn't have to control her expression. "How do you know about Kate?" Andy said, desperately wanting to drop the subject but still curious.

Les laughed lightly. "I've had more than one paper on you in the last few months, Sergeant Wyles. My 'Diversity in Policing' unit mainly. Cadet Shandly has managed to reference you at least twice. I came across Dr. Morrison's name with yours when I was fact checking."

Andy shifted this unexpected piece of information around in her head. She also had a thought about Cadet Krista Shandly, but she shelved it for the moment. They finally hit the gravel path and rough, slick rocks gave way underneath their boots. Andy pushed open the wet, metal gate that led out of the meadow.

"Maybe you should stay at the main house tomorrow then, so you're here when Dr. Morrison arrives," Les said, her tone matter-of-fact.

They were at the house, and Andy looked up into the brightly lit windows of the huge kitchen. Kurtz was stretching up to a high shelf, pulling down a bottle of wine. Looked like it was going to be a good night. Andy thought about being here Monday morning when Kate arrived. She already felt restless, anxious, distracted.

"Maybe I will," Andy said, stopping at the bottom of the stairs and facing Les. "Thanks."

Andy left Les with Kurtz and Tara, waving away the offer of a glass of wine before heading back into the near night. Turning back the way they had just come, Andy hiked alone back up to camp, a hissing lantern in one hand, the crescent moon beautiful and useless in the evening sky.

Much later, alone in her cabin with the fire hot and bright, Andy sat at the rough table in her worn basketball sweatshirt with the troop files spread out in front of her. The cadets had arrived back just after ten o'clock and had lined up for inspection with the air of people who had nothing to hide. According to Zeb and Meyers, the day had gone smoothly with no apparent incidents. The cadets had divided into groups and shopped, eaten fast food, and had a few beers. Most had probably called home to check in on family, talk longingly to boyfriends or girlfriends, reassure that two months really wasn't that long. It was, of course. Andy knew exactly how long two months apart could be.

Andy yanked the sleeve of her sweatshirt down until it sat right on her shoulders, thinking about how many times Kate had worn this sweatshirt, pushing up the too-long sleeves. She took a moment with the thought, comforting in its memory. Then, ridiculously, she checked her watch as if she could hurry the time until she saw Kate again. The lack of knowing made Andy crazy. She wanted to know if Kate was okay, why Kate had signed on with the RCMP, what Kate had been doing the past two months, what she was thinking and feeling and whether or not Andy would ever again see her covertly stealing Andy's favourite sweatshirt.

Andy shook her head and looked down at the files on the table. Just as she was sifting through the now familiar information, trying to find something new or relevant, Andy thought she heard the grinding noise of boots on gravel. She froze, listening past the crackle of the fire and the light wind against the windows. Camp had been quiet for a good hour by now, the cadets driven into their cabins by the cold rain that had moved in. Andy kept listening and for a long time, nothing. Then again, she heard it farther down toward the road.

Andy silently pushed back her chair and moved to the front door, easing the door against its frame to limit the creaking. Her eyes automatically moved to the area beyond the orange pool of light from the hydro pole. She couldn't see anything out of place, no hint of movement or irregularity of shape or shadow. Andy considered going to the cadet cabins and waking up the troop for roll call five hours early. But she didn't, remembering it was still the weekend. Technically the cadets didn't need to check in until Sunday night at eleven. Still, Andy scanned the area one last time before walking back into her cabin, thinking that tomorrow morning the cadets would be met with a surprise inspection. They'd overturn the entire camp to see what they could find.

❖

All sixteen cadets stood in the quad area with Andy as Trokof, Zeb, and Meyers went through each sleeping cabin, classroom, and the kitchen. There was really no such thing as private property at Depot, and that clearly extended to Camp Depot. Andy sat at one of the picnic tables, her hands wrapped around a mug of coffee, her third since getting up with the sun this morning. She watched the cadets move around the clearing, most of them still groggy with sleep, having been awoken by Trokof yelling at them to clear out. No one was allowed back into the cabins until inspection was complete. Andy was the only one who had a coffee and the cadets circled around her, drawn to the smell.

They were clearly nervous. As they'd exited their cabins, pulling on sweatshirts and jackets against the cold, they'd automatically sought each other out with their eyes. It had been their own version of roll call. *Yes, we're all here, no, none of the cadets defected overnight.* Cadet Prewitt-Hayes, her eyes sharp even at this early hour, still seemed to count her sheep every few minutes, constantly on alert. Andy found this interesting. It seemed a protective gesture, almost maternal.

"Cadet Prewitt-Hayes," Andy called out, her tone friendly.

"Yes, Sergeant?" Her eyes were cautious, which was fair as Andy had just singled her out. More interesting was that every other cadet sought out Andy, then Tracey, then each other.

"Do you have any siblings?"

"Yes, Sergeant," she said, clearly taken by surprise.

"And are you the eldest by any chance?"

A genuine smile from the cadet. "Oldest of seven. How did you know?"

Andy returned the smile but only shrugged, taking a sip of her coffee.

The cadets did not relax with this friendly exchange, still seeking each other out for reassurance. Andy wished she could see a pattern in who they looked to most often, but she still couldn't. Other than the obvious shepherding of their marker,

Prewitt-Hayes, the response seemed almost automatic in all of them.

Andy watched as Michael Awad sat at one of the tables instead of pacing like the rest. The group shifted subtly, a ripple effect as the two youngest cadets, Shandly and Harper, went to sit at another table, still talking, still yawning. Then Shipman joined Awad, punching him lightly on the shoulder, saying something under his breath that made him smile slightly. It was all perfectly natural, and yet none of it was. Their behavior was too choreographed, too carefully constructed. Almost as if their goal was to have none of the cadets stand out or get noticed except for their chosen leader. Troop 18 took uniformity to a whole new level.

Trokof emerged from the women's cabin and called for Andy. The cadets all froze, decidedly not looking at each other as Andy left her seat and crossed the silent quad to Trokof.

"Two things," Trokof said immediately and quietly when Andy approached. "Men's cabin, around five hundred dollars. Women's cabin, same thing. All twenties, like it just came out of the bank machine."

Andy considered how this fit with Lincoln's concern that the troop was selling drugs to make some extra money. But if so, where were the drugs? And who were they selling to?

"What else?" The money wasn't technically an infraction, just incredibly suspicious.

"We found this in the kitchen, stashed at the bottom of the potato bin." Trokof handed her a folded and dirty piece of ordinary lined paper. Her back to the cadets, Andy unfolded it and scanned the neat printing. It seemed to be a chart of some kind, with the numbers one to thirty one on the left margin and two incomplete columns of numbers. There were no headings or measurements to indicate what the numbers were comparing.

"Homework?" Andy said.

Trokof shook his head. "Not that Constables Zeb or Meyers recognized."

Andy scanned it again, noticing only some of the columns were filled in, notably those between the numbers five and twelve. *A calendar?* Andy wondered. *Tracking what?* She looked back to Trokof, not able to pull any other meaning from it.

"Do you want to ask the troop about it, or do you want me to yell at the troop about it?" Trokof said.

"I'll ask and when they don't answer, you yell," Andy finally said, allowing the smallest hint of a smile. Ten years ago, she would have said it was impossible, but she actually liked Sergeant Albert Trokof.

"Done," he said briskly, falling back into his drill sergeant role.

Andy took the paper, walked over to the quad and watched as the cadets assembled without being asked. She held up the paper.

"Anyone want to explain why this was carefully hidden in the kitchen?"

Sixteen pairs of eyes were trained on her, and not one of them blinked. Andy continued holding the paper, letting it lift and flip with the damp morning breeze. She waited, watching to see who would shift first, who would break the unasked for rank. The strangest silence had settled on the camp. It was heavy and nervous, but Andy let it stretch longer and longer until the troop had no choice but to move their tensed muscles and maybe take a deeper breath. Angela Hellman shifted her weight to her back foot, and Andy's shooting guard instincts kicked in, reading it as defensive. Greg Shipman blinked but kept his eyes above Andy's left shoulder, as if she wasn't holding anything. Krista Shandly waited until she thought Andy's attention was somewhere else then flicked her eyes to Tracey then back again. When the young cadet's gaze centered back on Andy, she was met with a long, drilling look Andy held until it was beyond uncomfortable. Krista blushed and dropped her gaze. Andy continued to look at the troop, noting the strained set to Hawke Foster's shoulders, the drawn blankness of Jacob Frances's face.

"Okay," Andy said finally, after the silence had lasted almost five minutes. She held the paper out to Trokof, now at her shoulder, never once taking her eyes off the troop.

Andy had expected Sergeant Trokof to immediately start yelling. He didn't. Out of the corner of her eye, Andy could see him looking down at the paper. The troop seemed confused also and the level of tension increased again.

"Cadet Prewitt-Hayes, step forward please," Trokof said, his voice almost friendly. A ripple of near palpable tension rolled through the group as their right mark stepped forward, away from the protective circle of her troop. "Tell me what this is."

"I don't know, Sergeant."

"Don't know or won't tell, Cadet Prewitt-Hayes?" Trokof said, finally looking up from the paper.

"I don't know, Sergeant," Prewitt-Hayes said again.

Sergeant Trokof said nothing for a minute, then he handed the piece of paper back to Andy. She folded it along the creased seams and slipped it into her pocket. Sixteen pairs of eyes watched it disappear, though no one seemed especially concerned. This information, whatever it was, must exist elsewhere, Andy decided. Sergeant Trokof had clasped his hands behind his back, and Andy could hear him pulling in a lungful of air, his barrel chest expanding until his uniform strained at the buttons. Andy couldn't help tensing her body, aware of what was coming next. When he finally started yelling, it was almost a relief.

Sgt. Trokof yelled for ten minutes, an impressive litany of abuse, both general and individualized. He managed to pull in the long, proud history of the RCMP, the current political climate, and the tenuous but deserving future of Canada's oldest police force. He focused on the individual cadets, trouncing their weaknesses, telling them how worthless they were with his words but contradicting that message with the depth of his understanding of their character. Andy was impressed, though she stood impassively through the entire heated monologue, surveying the cadets in front of her. She couldn't help but notice the tension had eased even though no one had moved. They could stand together and be abused all day, no problem. And when Trokof ended his diatribe with a punishing fifty push-ups and a long list of camp tasks to be accomplished by roll call the next morning, Andy noticed relief rippling through the troop. Push-ups they could do, yelling they could handle, menial labour was no problem. As Andy and Trokof walked away, she couldn't help thinking that Troop 18 had just won. Again.

CHAPTER SIX

Musket the old Lab gave a long, dramatic sigh as Andy scratched his damp, doggy-smelling head. Andy grinned at him as his tail thumped slowly and happily on the porch floorboards.

"You've got a friend for life," Kurtz said, watching the dog's now-closed eyes.

"He's a good boy," Andy murmured.

"Came with the place," Kurtz said dismissively, though Andy knew damn well she loved the dog. "Tara says we paid half a million for the dog, and they threw the house and lot in for free."

Andy laughed quietly and continued scratching the dog's ears. It was late Sunday afternoon, and Andy had hiked down to the main house for her overnight stay, taking up Les on her offer of being here when Kate arrived in the morning.

"How are things going up there?" Kurtz said, leaning on the railing, looking back at her former junior officer. She and Tara were expecting a group sometime in the next hour, so Andy said she'd help act as lookout, ready to play host to the weary travellers.

Technically, they were no farther ahead, but she hadn't really expected to be only four days in. "So far, fine."

"That doesn't tell me anything, Wyles."

Andy gave a small laugh. "The troop is settling in, as are the instructors. They're starting up class tomorrow after roll call to get the cadets on a somewhat familiar schedule." Andy shrugged. "I'm still watching and waiting, information gathering." She then proceeded to tell Kurtz about the inspection and the piece of paper with the seemingly random assortment of numbers. As Kurtz processed this information, Andy reviewed her mental note to call Jack tomorrow after she'd driven the medic into Kamloops. She'd taken a picture of the paper with her camera phone and texted it to him as soon as she got to the main house, wanting to know if he could run some kind of search to glean some meaning from it.

"So really, nothing yet," Kurtz said finally.

"Like I said." She took it as a statement of fact, not criticism. She did think about Superintendent Heath arriving in three days, knowing he wouldn't be quite so blasé about the lack of progress. He would want evidence, facts, a culprit. Something to put into a report. Andy shrugged it off and didn't let it settle on her. She had too many other things to worry about right now.

"So what's your plan for Kate?" Kurtz said, looking out over the balcony. Kurtz had said very little when Andy had explained to her and Tara who would be arriving to take over as camp doctor in the morning.

Before she answered, Andy dug her fingers deeper into the wet fur of the old Lab. Musket sighed contentedly. "No plan."

Kurtz looked at her and Andy met her eyes, waiting for the next question or challenge or, worse, advice. "Watching and waiting? Information gathering?"

"Something like that." Andy heard the hard note creep into her tone. She swallowed it. "I haven't really talked to her in two months, Kurtz. I have no idea why she's coming up here."

Kurtz's blue eyes drilled into Andy's. "To be with you obviously, you dumb shit."

Andy's laugh was bitter and short. She clenched her jaw and shook her head, not saying anything. Kate didn't need to join the RCMP to be with Andy. That didn't make any sense.

The guests arrived twenty minutes later, two gay couples from Vancouver needing a pre-holiday respite. The men were rowdy and raunchy, instantly changing the mood inside the B&B from quiet and restful to loud and boisterous. Andy helped them in with their luggage and talked with them in the living room as Tara brought in warm appetizers and Kurtz poured wine. She took the few good-natured jokes about her height, her occupation, and the sly questions about the things she could do with handcuffs.

As the conversation moved away from her, Andy started to feel restless. She glanced out the window at the late afternoon light, trying to decide if she had time for a run. Her brain needed it, not her body. But if her heart was going to continue constricting strangely every time she thought about Kate arriving here tomorrow morning, she might as well put it through a workout.

Andy excused herself from the room, telling Tara she'd be back in time to help with dinner. She changed into her running gear up in the small blue room with the antique quilt folded neatly under over-stuffed pillows. Andy felt better as soon as she stepped out the door. She stretched only briefly, knowing this wasn't going to be a long run. She started up the gravel pathway, pushing open the metal gate into the meadow and lengthening her stride only until she was comfortable and her body moved with the efficiency and ease that made her relax. She let her thoughts slip into an almost meditative space.

Andy and her team had grudgingly attended a mandatory professional developmental workshop a few years ago. The focus had been on mental health, the COs needing to show they were taking care of their officers and were aware of the high divorce rates and the reported and unreported cases of depression and anxiety. So they had a full day on mindful meditation, coping with anxiety, and anger management.

One of the speakers had walked them through a very simple meditation exercise that didn't require music or yoga mats or even closing your eyes. It involved a personalized mantra of sorts—whatever you needed to tell your brain to allow it to relax. Give it permission to think or not think, to allow your thoughts to wander, to become distracted, and even to become lost.

Andy had struggled with that exercise. It went against every cop instinct she had to be alert, to pursue facts, to think with purpose and reason and logic, so she'd practised on her run in the morning, in the shower, driving in her cruiser, at her desk. And slowly she'd mastered the art of removing herself from herself for five minutes. She'd found her thoughts were clearer, sharper, and more in focus after. Calmer.

This was Andy's mindset as she ran back down toward the main house, her muscles loose and warm, her thoughts easy and unrestricted. As she picked her way down the darkening path and out into the meadow, she looked up briefly to see the first stars just beginning to show themselves in the blue blanket sky. Then something caught her eye near the gate, a movement of white against dark, a flash of pale, exposed skin. A figure detached itself from the fence and stood on the path, hands shoved into pockets.

Kate.

Andy's body caught up to her brain, and she stumbled, knees locked, the muscles in her thighs and calves tightening as if they suddenly no longer wanted to support her body. A few more uncontrolled steps down the path, then Andy stopped abruptly, the most un-athletic movement she could remember making in a very long time. She really didn't care.

Kate walked up the path toward Andy, her movements slow but purposeful. Andy had nothing, no thoughts, no ability to think or move. Kate stopped a few feet away, close enough for Andy to see the expression on her face, though she couldn't see the warm brown of her eyes in the darkness. Kate was looking at Andy like she had outside Headquarters just a few days before, her expression a combination of relief, resolve, and caution.

Andy waited, her instincts warring with each other. To touch Kate, to hold her. To throw her guard up, ward off whatever this was. To speak first, to not speak at all. To repeat the last words Andy had said to her before she left two months ago. *I love you, Kate.* Andy kept her mouth closed, breathed in and out. And she studied Kate.

Her face had lost the slight, soft roundness of a few months ago, the hollowness of her cheeks emphasizing the sweet shape of her mouth. She was wearing a green winter jacket, the orange liner in the hood the only colour still visible in the rapidly descending dark. Kate held Andy's eyes, shifting slightly, like she wanted to take a step closer to Andy, but she stopped herself. As Kate moved, Andy heard the creak of stiff denim and noticed the new jeans Kate was wearing. She'd lost enough weight that she'd needed to buy new clothes, something she hated.

A cold wind suddenly gusted up from behind Andy, making her rock slightly onto her toes. The chill went right through her sweatshirt and danced uncomfortably across her skin as she just managed to stop herself from shivering. The wind had picked up Kate's loose hair, twirling it around her face until she lifted an impatient hand to push it away. Andy became suddenly aware of how long they had been looking at each other.

Over the last fifty-five days, Andy had not allowed herself to picture their reunion. She had not considered what they might say to each other or how it would feel. Even still, Andy could not imagine they would have gone this long without touching. Not if Kate was coming back to her. This time Andy did shiver, the cold settling suddenly and quickly over her entire body, the feeling of dread making it so much worse.

Kate seemed to notice Andy shiver. She blinked, gave her head a small shake, and lifted her chin. "I thought maybe we should talk," Kate said, her voice almost too soft to hear. Andy watched her swallow, could almost hear her pull in a bigger breath as she tried again. "Before I start tomorrow, I thought we should talk."

Talk, yes, Andy thought, but she could only manage a nod of her head and another shiver. The wind wasn't letting up. Kate's eyes narrowed in concern. Andy thought her heart would break.

"Is there somewhere we can go? It's freezing out here," Kate said.

Andy looked back toward the house where the warm, inviting glow of the windows spilled over into the yard. No privacy there. Without attaching any thought to it, Andy glanced over the meadow where they were standing, the path branching off to the right, the small cabin set amongst the trees.

"Yes, follow me." Andy hated the sound of her own voice. It was commanding, falling back into the safety of her sergeant role. As she and Kate walked together down the short path, Andy also hated the distance between them, the empty air, the cold anger that now stirred in her belly. The silence seemed heavy and endless.

The cabin was small with a wide front porch that looked out over the meadow. The wood siding fit solidly and imperfectly, creating a natural look that blended in with the forest at its back. Andy walked up the steps first and opened the screen door, knowing Kurtz and Tara left it unlocked. The room was dark and cold, and Andy had to grope around the inside wall, hitting the switch and waiting for the eco-friendly lights to come on. Andy held the door for Kate, carefully avoiding touching her as she passed. Still, Andy was unable to avoid feeling the warmth, the sparked heat of familiarity and desire that shook through her.

The cabin was open-concept, a queen size bed in the far corner, positioned under a small window, its patchwork green comforter stiff and new. A sitting area with a plush love seat overlooked the front porch. The right side of the cabin was half gleaming eat-in kitchen and half woodstove, its polished glass pane showing an already stocked wood pyramid, ready to be lit.

Without a word to Kate, Andy went to the woodstove, her shoes squeaking wetly on the wide wood floorboards. She opened the wood box and added a few pieces of kindling, more to give her hands something to do than anything else. She struck a long wooden match against the cylinder box and the flame at the tip dimmed, diminished then finally caught on a dry sliver of wood.

Finally satisfied the flame had caught, Andy stood and faced Kate. Kate was framed by the window, her arms wrapped around her torso. Andy said nothing, stood perfectly still, and waited.

"It was selfish of me not to give you the chance to say this was a bad idea," Kate said, fidgeting with the sleeve of her jacket.

"I called Heath just to find out about his offer, but he only gave me three days to decide about joining the RCMP…" Kate's voice was light and jumpy. She looked down at the floor like she was re-listening to what she just said. "Every day of the last two months has been selfish." Her voice was low, and Andy recognized her self-recrimination. "Somehow, I thought ambushing you twice in the same weekend was a good idea."

Andy couldn't let this go. She had to make something clear. "I'm glad you're here, Kate," she said, trying to keep the nerves out of her voice.

Kate's brown eyes softened at the words, though she wrapped her arms even more tightly around her body. It was an unconsciously protective gesture, and Andy could not figure out what this all meant. Confused and frustrated, Andy waited.

"I wanted to come back with a plan, to have things sorted out and decided. To have made some decisions about my life completely on my own," Kate said, her eyes on Andy. "I never imagined finding someone like you. When I did, when I fell in love with you, I trusted you to know and understand things about myself I didn't share with anyone. About losing my sister, my career, my sexuality. You seemed to have this incredible capacity to carry it all, and you seemed to do it so easily."

Kate stopped again, and Andy knew by the way she lifted her chin slightly, the way her voice shook that Kate was fighting back tears. "So I let you carry it all. But that left me with so little, I got lost. And getting lost wasn't even the worst part. Because then I started to worry about how much more lost it was possible to get and how long I was going to expect you to carry around all the crap that I refused to deal with." Kate swallowed. "And I thought about how long until you would have become angry with me, until you lost your patience. Until you decided I wasn't worth it."

Andy shook her head, jaw tight, hands clenched into fists at her side. She felt the locked ball of anger in her stomach start to slowly spread through her body. It wasn't aimed at Kate, but it could no longer be contained. Andy shook with it, trembled slightly as if with cold, though the fire was now beginning to warm the room.

Kate smiled sadly. "I know what you're thinking. That it's not possible. That you would never have grown tired of me or impatient. But did you ever think it was possible I could walk away from you? I didn't."

A long silence. Kate seemed calmer, as if talking to Andy was making it easier to breathe. Andy's tension had only increased, her back and shoulders tight with strain.

"I know why you had to leave," Andy said.

"I did have to leave. I was a mess. After I left you in Hidden Valley, I stayed on my mother's couch for three days and cried. Then she kicked me out. She told me I was upsetting Tyler, and if I had any intention of ever pulling myself together enough to deserve you, I should go back to my apartment, go back to work, and maybe seek some help to sort through some significant issues."

Andy very much wished she could smile, even a little, at the lecture Kate had received from her mother. She could picture it clearly, Marie's stern practicality masking the maternal worry. She could picture Tyler watching from the corner, his eyes brown and wide like his aunt's, taking in everything like he always did.

"So that's what I did," Kate said. "I spent all my time either at work or at counselling. I wasn't very good at counselling at first." She smiled, and Andy felt her body go numb. God, she loved that smile. "Well, that's an understatement. I was shockingly bad at it. But I kept going. It was important." Kate lifted her head almost defiantly, as if daring her to confirm it or deny it.

Andy said nothing, didn't move, barely breathed. Uncertainty and doubt pounded through her body with every kick of her heart. She couldn't be sure if this was a confession or an offering, a picture painted of where Kate had been and where she was now, to see if it would be acceptable. As if anything about Kate could ever be considered unacceptable. Andy felt a tremor in her stomach. Too much anger. Undirected, diffuse. She'd had enough. She needed to know.

"Do you still love me?"

The words were out of Andy's mouth before she'd really had the time to consider them. Her heart beat rapidly, and Andy had that sensation again that it was visible and exposed. But Kate did not hesitate with her answer, though her eyes were soft and sad and her voice was very, very low.

"Yes, Andy. I love you very much."

Elation, relief, fear.

"Then why are you standing so far away?" Andy didn't even try to keep the desperation out of her voice.

Kate dropped her arms to her sides and slowly closed the distance between them, stopping just in front of Andy. Andy's body reacted as it always had to Kate standing this close to her, heat and warmth and desire and gentleness and intensity. Always.

"I need something from you," Kate said steadily, holding Andy's gaze.

Anything. Andy wanted to say it out loud. Her brain shouted it, her diaphragm tightened, throat constricted. Breathe, control, breathe. She said nothing, letting her eyes ask the question. *What?*

"I need you to forgive me."

No. Andy felt the wave of anger crash against her barrier of control. No, not forgiveness. She had nothing to forgive. Andy looked at Kate hard, letting the anger diffuse around her, as if Kate was an island to be protected.

"No." Andy said it very quietly and very firmly.

"Yes, actually," Kate responded calmly. "You're angry at me, or you should be. And I know I just made you wait two months, and I know it's unfair. But I refuse to wait six months or a year for you to accept that you're not only angry at me but you *should* be and you *can* be."

This was wrong, so wrong. Andy's body shook with the overwhelming intensity of her anger. She would do anything for Kate, was ready for anything. But this...not this. It went against every protective instinct she had ever had about Kate. Andy understood the resolve now and if she thought about it, she understood the uncertainty. Not knowing if Andy could or would forgive her. Kate was waiting her out, holding still, stubbornly not backing down. Andy had never been with anyone who understood her so well, who could stand up to her like this and absolutely refuse to give any ground.

"Do you know what the hardest part about the last two months has been?" Kate said quietly. She stood so close, Andy could feel the brush of breath against her neck. "Knowing you were blaming yourself. Knowing I was getting help and support and you were walking around punishing yourself for something that wasn't your fault."

And so quickly Andy *was* angry at Kate. Very angry. How could she? If Kate knew her so well, how could she do this to her? Andy lifted her hands and gripped Kate's face. Her touch was not gentle, soft, or reassuring. But she needed to hold her there, to direct the torrent somewhere.

"Fine. I'm angry. I'm angry you didn't listen to me. I'm angry you ignored me for months before you left, that you brushed off any suggestion I ever made to stop for one fucking moment and just *think* about what you've been through. I'm angry you lied to me for so long about how you were really doing. I'm pissed off about every time you told me you were *fine*."

Andy's voice was getting progressively louder, her hands clenched tightly around Kate's face. Kate didn't even try to look away. "I'm angry you would even *suggest* I wouldn't do anything for you, that I could ever decide you weren't worth it. I know why you had to leave. I know you needed time, but I'm furious that you let me walk around for fifty-five days not knowing *anything*. And I'm angry..." Andy stopped and swallowed the hard ball lodged in her throat. She could feel Kate's pulse and the muscles in her face tremble. She knew with absolute certainty Kate was stopping herself from crying. Andy felt the fight start to ebb and her voice dropped. "I'm angry because the last time we made love, you only did it to hide from me."

Kate did cry now, the tears filling her eyes and spilling over down her cheeks, running down Andy's fingers. But she didn't look away, didn't contradict any of what Andy had just said. Even so, Andy could hear her thoughts. *From me, Andy. I was hiding from me.* And suddenly the anger was gone. She felt empty, depleted, and she dropped her hands. "And I forgive you. For all of it." Andy gave it to her, not enough energy left to wonder how Kate had taken from her the one thing she thought she wouldn't have to give. Not knowing if she'd just given Kate permission to leave or stay.

Kate closed her tear-filled eyes and collapsed into Andy's arms. Andy automatically caught her, sliding one hand around her waist, reaching the other up into Kate's hair drawing her in until they were pressed together. The heat between them was real, intense, having nothing to do with their layers of clothes or the now crackling fire behind them.

Andy could feel Kate's arms around her, Kate's breath on her neck where she'd buried her head, the length of her body pressed against Andy's. They stood very still but not even long enough for Andy to actually believe Kate was here in her arms. Kate pulled back slightly, but she only dropped her hands to Andy's hips, using them as leverage to shift her body upward, searching for Andy's lips with her own. Andy lowered her head and kissed Kate, her heart beating the familiar, rapid-fire rhythm that always accompanied Kate's touch. As the kiss deepened, as Kate's hands pressed against her lower back, Andy couldn't help wondering if her lips had always felt this soft. Had kissing Kate always felt like she was spinning so wildly, so willingly out of control?

Yes, yes, yes.

Andy and Kate kissed exactly like they had just spent the last fifty-five days apart. Kate dug her fingers into Andy's hips through the light fabric of her running gear as she tried to pull Andy in closer, trying to defy physics, to occupy the same space at once. Andy held Kate tighter, her lips never stopping the rhythm of their kiss, leaning Kate back slightly in her arms, shifting her weight so they were balance and counterbalance. Kate pulled back just for a moment, caught Andy's eye and something passed between them, something Kate was trying to tell her but then they were kissing again and Andy didn't have to think, no room for questions. She could feel everything Kate was trying to tell her with her kiss. Love, relief, and that same warmth in her chest. Andy knew what it was: belonging. Desire, for both of them, always. And as Kate wound her fingers around Andy's neck, she felt something else. Promise.

Andy froze, a cold line of uncertainty shooting up through her belly. Kate must have felt it. Her eyes flew open, her hands dropped to her sides, and she shifted her weight abruptly until she was standing on her own. But she didn't move away. Andy, holding perfectly still, had enough presence of mind to be grateful for that. Kate waited, both of them breathing hard, Andy not entirely sure what had just happened. Promise. Andy hated the cold twist of doubt in her stomach, the look of sadness in Kate's eyes. But apparently she needed something from Kate, too.

"If it happens again," Andy started, her voice coming out harsher than she intended, sounding loud in the small cabin. "If you start to feel lost. What will you do if it happens again?"

A spasm of pain crossed Kate's face, and Andy waited for Kate's familiar, automatic reaction of shrugging off the impact, discarding the hurt without processing it first, and finding the easiest, most direct route past the discomfort. It never materialized. Andy watched as Kate took a breath then let it out slowly.

"*When* it happens again, Andy," Kate said quietly, like a confession. "I'm fighting over a decade's worth of bad habits here." Another breath. "When it happens again, I'll tell you. And I'll do whatever it takes to deal with it."

A wild, surging hope filled Andy's chest. All she'd ever wanted to hear was that Kate was looking out for herself. That she cared enough to *try*. That at least some of the energy Kate expended on everyone around her could be turned inward also.

Andy held still, trying to order her chaotic, scattered thoughts. The uncertainty and doubt were gone, replaced by joy and outrage. Words piled up in Andy's head, confessions of love and wanting. A lecture. Cursing.

Andy put her hands to Kate's face again, so gently this time, thumbs brushing along her cheekbones. "I love you, Kate." She had so much more to say, but Andy wasn't sure she could get it out. "I love you, I love you…"

Kate made a small, almost desperate sound in the back of her throat, her brown eyes filled with tears again. She touched her fingers to Andy's lips, and drew a line down her jaw, her throat, to the back of her neck. Then she gently pulled the elastic from Andy's ponytail, twisted her fingers into Andy's tangled hair and sighed as if she'd been waiting a very long time to do that. Andy felt the pads of Kate's fingers against her scalp, and she remembered the first time Kate had touched her like this. Desire sparked like a struck match, and Andy was kissing Kate again, tilting her head back and kissing down the long line of her throat, up to her ear, tugging at her ear with her teeth. She heard Kate drawing in her breath, could feel her fingers in her hair, down her neck, Kate drawing the line of her collarbone under her sweatshirt.

Andy groaned, dropped her hands from Kate's face, and pulled roughly at the zipper of her jacket, opening it with one hand and pushing it off Kate's shoulder with the other. Kate tugged at the bottom of Andy's sweatshirt, her hands just as insistent. Andy lifted her arms as Kate pulled it and Andy's t-shirt off over her head without missing a beat, the smallest, sweetest smirk on Kate's face. Andy's touch was rougher than she intended as she pulled off Kate's shirt, loving the way her red hair fell back against the bare, white skin of her shoulders.

Andy bent down, one arm behind Kate's shoulders and the other behind her knees, and she lifted her off the ground. Kate gave a shocked cry and looked at Andy, her brown eyes still wet from crying. Then she leaned her head back against Andy's bicep and laughed and oh, that laugh did something to Andy. Something cracked and broke free.

Andy lay Kate on the bed and unlaced and pulled off Kate's boots one by one. She kicked off her own shoes at the same time, watching a now-silent Kate. The trace of laughter was still in Kate's eyes, in the smile that played about her lips. It made Andy want to smile back and kiss Kate until she had to stop and catch her breath.

As she bit Kate's neck and ran her fingers very slowly up the inside seam of those new, hated jeans, Andy still had room for the anger. Part of her wanted to pause, to stop, to hold herself just above Kate and wait to figure out what this was. The other part of her, the part that slid her hips over Kate's at just the right pace, just the right angle until Kate let out the most erotic moan, knew that stopping was next to impossible.

The fire behind them blazed hot as Andy ran her hands over Kate's body, relieved that her body felt this familiar, and the sound of Kate's breath catching in her throat, the arch of Kate's body against hers was so much the same. Andy slid her hands down over Kate's shoulders and chest, trailing her thumb lightly over her breast then across her ribs, the smooth skin of her stomach and, finally, the rough, stiff fabric of her jeans. Anger surged again, and Andy twisted the fabric in her hands, wrenching it against Kate's hips. And Andy kissed her hard, kissed away the question in Kate's eyes, kissed her like she was never, ever going to let her up for air. But Kate didn't resist, taking on Andy's challenge.

Andy explored Kate's body like it was new, like she couldn't anticipate which touch would cause Kate to moan, bite her lip, arch her back, or close her eyes. And every time Kate did, Andy felt the heat in her own body kick again, and her desire seemed limitless. Tenderness gave way to urgency, and Andy tracked Kate's breathing as it increased, the movements of her hips pressing, reaching. Andy stalled, stopped, started again, feeling the groan of frustration low in Kate's throat. Andy smiled down at her, telling Kate with her eyes this was just the beginning.

Andy pushed back suddenly until her feet hit the floor, digging her fingers roughly at the button and zipper of Kate's jeans and yanking them forcefully down. Kate's whole body slipped a few inches down to the foot of the bed. Kate was naked in seconds, and Andy felt uncertainty for the first time. She wasn't going to be able to resist Kate for much longer, to fight the urge to take her hard and fast, feeling every muscle in their bodies straining for the same release.

Andy clenched her jaw, balled up the jeans in her hands and felt the anger compete with her desire, felt them mix in her belly as she threw the jeans across the room. Without warning, Kate sat up and pulled at the waistband at Andy's hips. Andy stepped out of the last of her clothes. Triumph was in Kate's eyes as she pulled Andy against her. Again, Andy allowed Kate to think she had a moment of control. She didn't.

Kate pulled Andy's head down to kiss her. She dropped her hands down, fingers trailing over Andy's thighs, tracing their own invisible seam up and up. Andy stopped breathing and clenched the muscles in her stomach against the wave of desire that threatened to undo her entirely. Kate seemed to know, and her lips twisted into a smile as they kissed. A mistake, that smile.

Andy's need for Kate had always been overwhelming, but never like this. Andy picked up Kate again and almost threw her down on the bed, this time following her down, their bodies seeking a familiar, frantic rhythm together. Kate gripped Andy's hips with her thighs, her arms tight around Andy's neck. The urgency in her body was palpable in the thrust of her hips, the shine in her eyes, and the low sounds in her throat. Close, so close.

Andy broke Kate's grip on her, one hand on her hips holding her down, the other stretching Kate's arms above her head, pinning her. Andy let the minute stretch, waiting for Kate to protest or resist. She didn't. She took it, fighting back with her lack of fight. Andy had to smile, the kiss to Kate's throat turning into a bite on her neck, leaving her love-marked and out of breath.

Andy suddenly released Kate's hands and repositioned herself above Kate, not touching her anywhere except where her long hair fell across Kate's chest as she looked down at her. She had expected Kate to pull her down and had been ready to resist, tensing the muscles in her core. But Kate held still, looking up at Andy for so long that Andy began to feel the muscles in her shoulders and arms start to burn. A small tremor shook Andy, and she wasn't sure if it was fatigue or need. Kate raised her hand and touched Andy's face very gently, lovingly, from her temple, down to her cheekbone then finally drawing one finger across Andy's lips. Kate's whole body shook, trembling with the weakness of wanting.

"Andy." Kate's voice was a whisper and somehow she managed to turn her name into a statement of love and understanding and need.

Kate's voice, her touch, the look in her eyes, finally broke something in Andy. With a defeated groan, Andy lowered her head and kissed Kate long and hard. She didn't stop her body from pressing against Kate, didn't resist anything, no more choreographed torture, no more punishment. Andy felt Kate's hands on her hips, the press of their skin together, hot and slick, the taste of her lips, the sound of Kate's voice in her ear. They were heat and fire, they were uncontrolled, seeking out each other's pleasure as they strained for their own release. Kate's breathing came in short, sharp gasps, her whole body moving upward. Every movement was doubly magnified for Andy, reading it in Kate's body, feeling it in her own. Muscles tensed, voices silenced, thoughts abandoned as every sensation in their bodies urged them onward. Kate reached it first, her head thrown back, her whole upper body arching off the bed. Andy wasn't far behind as Kate rocked her into an ecstasy she had almost forgotten her body was capable of.

CHAPTER SEVEN

A ndy woke disoriented. Her body tensed as she took in details in rapid succession: cold outside the blanket, muted rain against the roof, dawn lighting the open room of the small cabin. And Kate asleep beside her, face turned away, red curls in chaos over her pillow.

Andy breathed, stilled her body, and slowed her mind. She felt a peace settle over her, a feeling she only associated with waking up to Kate in bed. She'd missed that feeling. God, she'd missed it. Andy watched the shallow rise and fall of Kate's back as she breathed, her arms under the pillow, her body pressed down into the bed. When Kate slept well, she slept hard.

Andy fought the urge to stroke Kate's back with her hand, to press her palm gently between her shoulder blades and feel the soft warmth of her skin. She would let her sleep for now, simply content to have Kate here. As that realization sunk in, surging joy spread up through Andy's chest. Her heart stuttered, and she smiled to herself. Kate was back. Different, yes. A little. But not in her smile, not in the way she looked at Andy or the way their bodies reacted to each other. Not in the way she loved Andy. That had not changed. Andy felt peace, contentment. She never wanted to lose her again.

Very slowly, still conflicted about waking Kate, Andy moved her hand toward Kate's back, letting it hover over the warmth of her skin. She held it there for a long time, then very slowly pressed her palm against her back. Andy always felt instant warmth and this rapid-fire rhythm of her heart when she touched Kate. Kate stirred beneath Andy's hand, a deeper breath, a slow stretch of her spine, and finally she turned her head on the pillow and opened her eyes. She blinked a few times and smiled sleepily.

"Andy."

Kate said her name like a statement of fact, undisputable and solid. Andy ran her hand very lightly up Kate's spine, feeling her body slowly waking up.

"Good morning," Andy said quietly, happily.

They looked at each other for a long time, neither in any hurry to talk or move, listening to the very light patter of rain against the roof as it dripped off the tree branches. They were cocooned, and it felt so much like their cabin in Montana that Andy was briefly, wonderfully disoriented.

Kate stretched her whole body, this time from the tips of her fingers down her neck, her spine, hips and legs and right to her toes. Then she let out a long breath and turned on her side, sliding her hand on Andy's hip, skimming her fingers over the scar.

"So, do you happen to have any coffee?" Kate said, her eyes shining.

Andy laughed. No hesitation, no worry, no need to hide. She just laughed. "Sorry, no coffee," she said. "If you really need to wake up, we could go for a run." Kate made a face, and Andy laughed again.

"My attitude towards exercise hasn't changed that much," Kate said, burrowing in closer to Andy. "Therapist recommendations or not." Andy felt Kate's body stiffen just slightly, then relax again as if she'd considered worrying then remembered she didn't have to. They both held still, letting the fifty-five days catch up to them and acknowledging with the morning light that things had changed.

Andy touched the tips of her fingers to the soft skin under Kate's eyes. It was impossible not to touch Kate. Andy loved the reassurance of her presence, the thrill of familiarity. Kate smiled and propped herself up on one elbow, long red curls spilling through her fingers. Andy was aware that time was passing, the sun climbing higher outside the window. Nothing else seemed important. Nothing could compete with Kate in her bed, telling her where she'd been the last two months.

"Does it bother you that I was able to talk to someone else? That it wasn't you?" Kate's forehead wrinkled slightly, the worry causing her voice to dip. Andy tugged gently on one of Kate's curls, wrapping it around her fingers. "That depends," Andy said. "Was she cute?"

Kate poked her in the ribs, making Andy laugh.

"No, she wasn't cute." Kate shook her head. "Isn't. I'm still seeing her." Andy heard a question in Kate's voice now, an uncertainty. It was the same tone she'd had when she left the message on Andy's phone, the same tone as the night before, telling Andy that she wasn't better yet, that she was still working on it. Andy wished she could reassure Kate, explain how relieved she was to hear Kate was able to open up to someone. Andy smoothed the wrinkle on Kate's forehead with her finger, trailed her hand down Kate's face, and was rewarded with a look of contentment.

"I'd rather be your partner and your lover than your therapist, Kate," Andy said.

As a cop, the word partner meant something different to her. The word girlfriend had been sufficient in the past, but it had never been quite right with Kate. And for the first time in two months, Andy allowed herself to hear in her head the word she wanted to use. *Wife*. That's the word that fit, that adequately summed up how she had always felt about Kate.

Andy didn't say this out loud, though. It was too soon. Kate was barely back, and Andy was too conscious of not pushing, of not crossing the line. Instead, Andy shifted her arms around Kate and pulled her in closer, thinking it didn't seem possible Kate would ever be close enough. Kate slid her hips over Andy's in the easiest, most familiar way and caused a slow, hot sensation to spread through Andy's core. With her dark red hair creating a curtain around them, Kate leaned down and kissed Andy, very slowly and gently. Andy could feel Kate's lips curl up into a smile as they kissed, like her own joy was impossible to contain. Andy knew exactly how she felt.

A light but insistent knock at the door made them both freeze. "It's probably Kurtz," Andy said as Kate slid off, covering herself with the blanket.

Andy pulled on her cold sweatshirt and running pants, her feet chilled against the floorboards. With a quick glance back at Kate, who was mostly hidden by blankets, she opened the door. Tara stood on the porch in a bright yellow slicker, her long braid tucked back under her hood. She smiled knowingly and held out a basket when Andy opened the door.

"Thought you two might be hungry," Tara said as Andy took the heavy basket. She could feel something warm against the tea towel draped over top. Tara also pulled out Andy's radio from a large pocket in her jacket. "And your radio started squawking about half an hour ago. Kurtz broke into your room to get it. And just so you know, the cabin isn't booked until New Year's, so feel free to stay. Just let me know, and I'll stock the kitchen."

"Thanks, Tara," Andy said gratefully.

Tara left again without another word, her dirty boots thumping across the porch. Andy closed the door and carried the basket over to Kate who sat up with the blankets tucked under her arms. Andy handed her the basket and knelt in front of the fireplace, shifting the still hot coals and adding a small piece of wood. Kate sorted through the basket, giving the occasional exclamation of surprise.

"Oooh, biscuits. They're still warm! And I'm guessing this is coffee. And some jam and butter. Here's cream and a little sugar. This is amazing."

Andy finished with the fireplace and found two mugs in the kitchen cupboards. She poured them each a cup from the silver thermos, adding cream and sugar for Kate and keeping it black for herself. She handed over the mug and watched Kate sipping and sighing contentedly. Andy gave a silent prayer of thanks to no one in particular for the simple pleasure of watching Kate take her first sip of coffee in the morning.

Sitting on the bed at Kate's side, Andy broke open a warm biscuit, spread butter on both halves then held up the jam, waiting for Kate's nod of approval before spreading it on and handing it over. Kate bit in happily and closed her eyes, savouring each bite. Andy prepared another and handed it over before making one for herself. They ate silently, contentedly, until the static squawk of Les's voice on the radio interrupted their breakfast in bed.

"Camp Depot to Sgt. Wyles. Andy, you around?" Les seemed calm enough, no note of urgency in her tone. But as Andy picked up the radio, she felt the weight of responsibility settle back on her shoulders. She remembered she had a job to do. They both did.

Andy pushed down the button as she spoke into the radio. "Wyles here. How's camp, Sgt. Manitou?"

"All cadets accounted for. And instructors, for that matter. Our camp medic, however, is itching to get the heck out of Dodge. Any thoughts on your ETA? She's hoping to make the ten thirty bus out of Kamloops this morning."

Andy stood up from the bed, rummaged on the floor until she found her watch. 8:37 a.m. They could make it if they hurried. "Tell Ms. Stinson to be packed and ready to go, we'll be there in forty-five minutes."

"We?"

Andy smiled at Kate. "Dr. Morrison arrived last night. I'll bring her up to camp with me."

There was a long pause, and Andy wondered why the sergeant was taking so long to respond. "Sorry, Sgt. Wyles. I believe your transmission cut out. I'll tell the medic you'll be here in time to get her on the noon bus out of Kamloops. See you in a few hours. Camp Depot out."

Andy shook her head, put the radio on the bedside table, and picked up her coffee. Kate seemed to have eaten enough, and was sitting up in bed. She looked fully awake and alert, her brown eyes bright and full of questions.

"So, tell me about the cadets," Kate said, wiping crumbs from her fingers and taking a sip of her coffee.

"What information have you already been given?" Andy said, hedging.

Kate summarized the background of the troop as a whole, the cadet's tragic death, the money, the question of drugs, and the troop's unique ability to close rank. "But I don't know much about the cadets themselves. Staff Sgt. Finns only said your role was to get to the bottom of what was going on. Mine is to make sure everyone remains healthy and uninjured. And I assume my presence is also insurance against future lawsuits." Andy had always appreciated the way Kate could see past any bullshit, right to the core facts of a situation. "So, are you going to tell me or what?"

Andy thought about it. "No," she said and laughed at Kate's expression. "But for a good reason. I don't want to bias you, I want to know what you see without my impressions. Does that make sense?"

"Yes, I guess it does," Kate said grudgingly. "But I'll need to see their files, their medical information. How about I see each cadet individually, do a baseline physical, and read the relevant information then? If we do that today, I could give you my first impressions tonight and you can fill me in on the rest."

"Yes, but let's make it a team meeting tonight with you, me, Sergeant Trokof, and the three instructors. We haven't had the chance to sit down formally, so let's do that tonight."

Kate suddenly looked nervous, and she put down her coffee cup and leaned forward. Andy could see the long arc of her naked back down to her hips, but she concentrated on the expression on Kate's face, noticing with an ache in her chest the way Kate stopped when she tried to work through whatever she was thinking by worrying the ring now gone from her left hand.

"How is this going to go? How do we work together?"

"The way we always have," Andy said steadily.

Kate immediately shook her head again, like she was frustrated she couldn't get the words out properly. "But I did it badly, navigating our relationship and everyone else while we worked together. It was one of the things I just left up to you."

Slow, slow, think. "And yet you signed a permanent contract with the RCMP," Andy said quietly. To her surprise, Kate grinned.

"I know, ass backwards isn't it?"

Andy couldn't help but smile at the expression on Kate's face. But she didn't comment, waiting for Kate to explain.

"I realized I needed to start making actual decisions about my life, no more coasting. And I knew I needed to think about the choices I had and what I *wanted* to do with my career." Kate hiked the blanket up higher on her body. "I liked working with the RCMP, but I wasn't ready to leave the ER. When Superintendent Heath gave me the flexibility of part time, it seemed like the perfect fit. But I knew I had to make the decision not knowing if you would take me back."

"So right now you're wondering if we walk into camp in an hour holding hands?"

"Exactly," Kate said, clearly relieved.

"Here are my thoughts, let me know what you think. We don't hide our relationship but we certainly don't flaunt it. I figure if Staff Sergeant Finns wouldn't make out with his wife at the office, why would I?"

Kate tilted her head back and laughed, a delighted sound that echoed off the walls of the cabin. Andy shifted in close to Kate, slid one hand around the back of her neck and kissed Kate's throat.

"But just so you know, it's going to be next to impossible not to touch you. You, Dr. Kate Morrison, civilian consultant with the RCMP's E-division, are going to be the most incredible distraction."

Kate had her eyes closed, and her whole body shivered at Andy's touch. "But we can do this," Kate said, somewhat breathlessly. It was both a question and a statement.

Andy pulled back and waited for Kate to open her eyes. "Yes," she said simply.

Kate's brown eyes sparkled. "Then we should probably get going. I'm on probation for the next three months so we better put on a good show."

Andy gave Kate one last kiss, leaving them both breathless. "We always do."

❖

When they arrived, camp was quiet. They could hear the low rumble of voices coming from the meeting hall, and Andy recognized the even, steady pitch of Constable Meyers's instruction. It was raining steadily and it wasn't supposed to let up for the next few days, according to Kurtz. She'd driven Kate and Andy up to camp, wanting to check out the state of the temporary road and make sure there was no risk of wash-out during this soggy, wet season.

"The instructors are probably in the kitchen," Andy said to Kate. Wood smoke mixed with the smell of wet pine, wet rock, and burnt toast as Andy pulled open the door .

"Good morning, Sgt. Wyles," said Sergeant Trokof. Impeccably dressed, he sat ramrod straight with a triangle of lightly blackened toast and a coffee in front of him. Zeb and Les were also at the table, Les looking through a stack of marking, Zeb peering down the cracked barrel of a 12-gauge shotgun, its bright orange stock identifying it as a non-lethal or bean bag round. Andy had to assume the medic was hiding in her cabin.

"Everyone, this is Dr. Kate Morrison, civilian consultant with E-division and our new camp doctor." Andy didn't stop the swell of pride at introducing Kate to her new team.

Kate stepped forward and shook hands with the instructors. As Les sat down again, she shot Andy a quick, questioning look. Andy just smiled and Les gave a subtle thumbs up, grinning.

"How are things going this morning?" Andy said, dropping Kate's medical kit next to the door and taking a seat. Kate sat across the table, her expression open and curious.

"We did roll call at six this morning, ran them in the rain, which they hated, and then gave them ten minutes to dry out. They've been in the classroom ever since," Zeb said, twisting the barrel of the shotgun in his hands, looking annoyed. "These fucking things are going to be the death of me," he grumbled, untwisting it again and peering closely at the grooved threads.

"Constable Zeb," Trokof admonished, putting down his coffee.

Zeb looked up, confused. "What?"

"That's unacceptable language with ladies present."

Andy, Les, and Kate looked at each other, amused.

"Really, Sergeant?" Les said. "To which 'lady' might you be referring?"

Trokof looked between the three women. "Well, we don't know Dr. Morrison, do we? We should be showing her our best side, even out here at Camp Depot."

Kate shook her head, a perfect, mischievous smile on her face. "There are a lot of things you can call me, Sergeant Trokof, including Kate. But I'm afraid 'lady' isn't one of them."

Les laughed out loud, smacking the top of her pile of marking with her palm. Zeb grinned and even Trokof managed an amused shake of his head.

"Well, let's just keep our language in check, shall we? We are peace officers, and we have an obligation to maintain a sense of duty and decorum at all times." Sergeant Trokof paused, and then he dropped his voice, the Newfie accent once again emerging. "Even when we don't fuckin' want to."

Andy gave a shocked laugh at hearing Sergeant Trokof, the toughest bastard at Depot, dropping the f-bomb. She caught Kate's eye and grinned.

Just then the door to the kitchen cabin opened and Constable Meyers walked in. Andy quickly introduced Kate, and he shook her hand politely.

"I've given the cadets a quiz," Meyers said in his quiet, assured voice. Andy wondered if anything ever worked the man up. He had the most even temperament of anyone Andy had ever met.

"Aren't they going to cheat?" Kate said to the tall officer as he poured himself a coffee and sat down.

Meyers shrugged. "It's a warm up quiz, doesn't count for anything. So I gave them five minutes to cheat, then they're on their own."

Andy checked her watch and saw it was just after ten. She was going to have to leave soon to take the still-missing medic into town.

Trokof noticed her check her watch. "What's the plan, Sgt. Wyles?"

Andy looked around the table, the members of her new team looking back at her expectantly. "Are the cadets in class all day today?"

"All day," Les said.

Andy indicated Kate with a quick nod of her head. "Dr. Morrison would like to do a physical on each cadet. We're going to set up the spare cabin as an examination room. If you could release the cadets from class one at a time to see her, we should get through the whole troop by the end of the day. Then tonight, I'd like to have a team meeting, gather impressions and information and see where we stand with Troop 18."

Trokof and the instructors all gave their agreement. Kate shifted in her seat and leaned forward, waiting for a nod of approval from Andy to speak.

"I just want to clarify one thing," Kate said to the group, her voice quiet and confident. Andy knew not everyone could address a room full of uniformed cops and have the assurance their opinions mattered just as much. It was one of the things

Andy had always loved about Kate. "It's been made clear to me by Chief Training Officer Lincoln that a physical exam is a requirement of the cadets. If they refuse, they could have their training agreement cancelled."

Kate waited for any questions before carrying on. "Normally, when a patient walks into my exam room, I automatically assume a doctor-patient confidentiality agreement, both ethically and legally. The cadets have, to a degree, waived that right, so any information I gain which is pertinent to their mental or physical performance level or that I believe makes them unfit to continue their contract, can be shared with this team."

Andy rolled this piece of information around in her head, trying to see it from all angles, to figure out the advantages and disadvantages of what Kate had just shared. There was no question that Kate was right. She would know the legal boundaries of this better than anyone else in the room.

"This isn't new to the cadets, I take it," Les said, her expression thoughtful.

Kate shook her head. "No. They would have signed something to that effect when they accepted the contract at Depot. But I will make it clear to each cadet as they walk through the door today, just so there's no confusion. I am not their family physician. Information shared with me may not necessarily be kept confidential."

"But then they're less likely to admit anything to you," Zeb said, frowning.

"True," Kate said. "But ethically, I need them to understand the situation. And besides, it doesn't exactly sound like this troop would willingly give me any information, confidentiality agreement or not."

She was dead on as usual and Andy saw that none of the instructors opposed this statement.

"So then will you be willing to also share your impressions of the cadets, Dr. Morrison?" Sergeant Trokof said.

Kate smiled at Trokof. "I'll be happy to share my personal observations on who is compliant, who's a pain in the ass, that kind of thing."

Tension eased out of the room a little as Kate skilfully smoothed over any snags, creating a sense of team and trust and absolute confidence. Andy felt her heart kick and suppressed a foolish grin of pride. She had always loved to watch Kate at work.

Meyers checked his watch and lifted his mug to drain his coffee. "Five minutes is up," he said, then he checked in with Andy for any last minute directions.

"Class and physical exams are what we're focusing on today," Andy said. "I'll take the medic back into Kamloops, and I'm guessing I'll need to get groceries, so give me your requests now. Then tonight, let's say nine o'clock, team meeting. Questions?"

Andy surveyed the room, checking for any signs of dissent or disapproval. As the team broke up, back to their individual tasks, Andy caught Kate's eye, and she knew with absolute certainty what that look was. Together, Kate's eyes said. We're back together.

CHAPTER EIGHT

I still say he's hiding something."

Zeb stubbornly repeated the same message about Cadet Foster for the last ten minutes. It was after eleven, the gas furnace of the kitchen hummed and rattled as it warmed the cabin where Andy, Kate, Sergeant Trokof, and the three instructors were meeting. Andy shifted her annoyance to the background and forced herself to give Zeb's strong opinion the same weight as everyone else's, no matter how much she disagreed.

"He's so quiet, but you can tell he's itching to talk back," Zeb continued, though no one offered a contrary opinion. They'd already tried and Zeb refused to listen.

Andy had assembled the troop's files, and they'd been going through the cadets one by one, offering opinions and insights, seeing where their observations overlapped or jarred. So far it had been pretty straightforward, Andy encouraging the team to offer what they were thinking without coming to any conclusions or making definitive statements about the cadets as individuals or the troop as a whole. But as soon as they'd come to Hawke Foster, they had disagreed instantly.

"But he's not talking back. He's following orders like he should," Les said, her tone showing that her patience was wearing thin. "Just because it's clear he's got some attitude underneath that, doesn't set him apart from fifty other cadets at the training academy right now."

Zeb shook his head, his mouth set in a hard line, but he didn't say anything. Andy was confused at his strong reaction. Zeb didn't seem to dislike Hawke, but he did seem mistrustful. Andy wondered if shades of prejudice coloured Zeb's opinion of Cadet Foster. Andy waited to see if anyone would offer anything into the silence, but the team seemed to have all said their piece.

"Dr. Morrison, may we ask your opinion?" Sergeant Trokof broke the silence, turning everyone's attention to Kate. She'd been generally quiet through the whole discussion, occasionally offering an insight or asking a question. Andy wasn't the least bit surprised at how focused an opinion she already had of each cadet, how well she was able to pinpoint a characteristic or a personality trait, even though she'd only spent at most twenty minutes each with them.

"You've all read his file, I assume." Kate looked around the assembled group who all affirmed the assumption. "Then I can tell you that Hawke Foster's medical file supports his cadet file. Given his difficult history in the foster care system, I imagine Constable Zeb is right. Foster probably has a lot of secrets."

The group was quiet, digesting Kate's words. Even Zeb seemed taken aback at Kate's quasi-agreement. Hawke Foster's case file read like a thousand files Andy had seen of young offenders. But Foster's had two differences. At the age of twelve, he had testified against a former foster parent who was brought up on charges of physical abuse. The man was eventually sent to jail. And the second difference was that she was looking at his file because he was in the process of becoming a peace officer, not a criminal. So yes, Foster probably had a great deal to hide, but that didn't mean it had anything to do with the situation they were currently investigating.

Andy was just opening her mouth to drive this point home with Zeb when the sound of a door slamming across the quad caught her by surprise. She only had time to quickly check her watch—twenty minutes after cadet lights out—when the shouting started. Meyers and Zeb were the closest to the door, Meyers reaching it first and swinging the door wide. Andy followed quickly, hearing the rush of feet behind her.

Her eyes took a moment to adjust from the bright lights of the kitchen cabin to the diffuse orange light from the hydro pole. She heard sounds of a struggle, fighting, more screen doors being slammed as cadets poured out of their cabins, all watching the two figures grappling at the far side of the quad. Andy squinted as she tried to figure out who and what she was seeing.

Andy clearly saw Greg Shipman's face as he straightened up, then reached down and across the back of whoever he was wrestling with, grabbing the man's shirt and pulling, hockey jersey style. His opponent went low and grabbed Shipman around the legs, lifting him in a dump tackle. Shipman landed flat on his back in the wet gravel with a sharp grunt.

Meyers reached the pair first, placing himself between the attacker and Shipman, who had rolled over onto his side on the ground, but made no other move. Meyers had his hands out and used his tall frame as a barrier, moving whoever it was backwards. Zeb knelt down beside Shipman and Andy, seeing the cadet's eyes open, figured he was fine and continued to advance on his opponent, who Meyers had steered back and away from the group of wide-eyed cadets standing in a nervous circle.

It was Foster.

Andy followed Meyers as he continued to separate Foster from the rest of the group, the cadet walking backwards, his hands clenched in fists at his side, his eyes locked at a seemingly random point over Meyers' shoulder. Meyers stopped and let Foster take a few more steps back, then looked at Andy. She took a step in, letting Foster register her presence and take a few more steadying breaths. They could hear voices in the background: Andy sorting through Trokof's harsh commands, Les's neutral directions, Kate's soothing assessment. Andy waited, but of course Foster offered nothing into the silence, his posture remaining tensed.

"What happened, Cadet Foster?" Andy said.

Hawke Foster looked up at Andy and met her eyes for one brief moment before looking back over Meyers' shoulder. It was long enough for Andy to see his raging defiance. *This is what Zeb sees*, Andy thought to herself. His defiance seemed to be deliberate, an odd kind of control.

"Answer Sgt. Wyles, Cadet Foster," Meyers said quietly, an edge of authority to his tone but completely lacking any kind of threat. Andy kicked her estimation of the man up a notch.

"Shipman and I had a disagreement," Foster said, his words precise and neutral.

"A disagreement about what?" Andy said, knowing he was going to give the least amount of information possible without being insubordinate. It was a good trick Andy had used often enough herself, but she had no intention of letting him get away with it.

"Music," Foster said.

Andy caught Meyers's eye in the dim light. Music.

"Cadet Foster, do you really expect me to believe you and Cadet Shipman risked being kicked out of Depot for conduct unbecoming of a cadet over *music?*"

Foster tensed. It was barely noticeable, just a tight line of his shoulders and chest under the thin grey t-shirt. It could have passed for a shiver of cold, but Andy knew better. Foster cared very much about his place in this troop, in becoming an RCMP officer. Again, she stored it. Again, she waited.

"I asked you a question, Cadet Foster, and I expect an answer."

"We had a disagreement over music," Foster reiterated, and this time it sounded beyond neutral. Rote.

Andy gave him an absolute look of disbelief, staring him down, waiting for him to shift or blink or fidget. Foster unfocused his eyes and remained perfectly still. Andy had a grudging respect for Hawke Foster. She recognized a good defence system when she saw one.

The gravel crunched behind Andy. She didn't turn to see who it was, but she caught the light scent of her shampoo as Kate joined them, standing between Andy and Foster, angled slightly towards the cadet. Foster reacted with a quickly controlled startle, like he had not anticipated anyone being anywhere close to his side in this. Kate gave Andy a questioning look, and Andy gave her assent to speak to the cadet.

"Are you hurt?"

Hawke looked at Kate, blinked, then flicked his eyes to Constable Meyers.

"You may answer the doctor when she asks you a question, cadet," Meyers said.

Hawke shook his head. "I'm not hurt," he said, his voice an unemotional monotone.

Kate waited, but Foster offered nothing else. "Do you know where to find me if you need to follow up?" she asked.

Clearly Hawke Foster was not used to neutrality, let alone an offered kindness. Another controlled flinch, a knock to his defence system. Andy wanted to smile. Kate had that effect on people.

"Yes, Dr. Morrison."

"How's Shipman?" Andy said, deliberately allowing Foster to hear the question and Kate's answer. Andy watched his reaction out of her peripheral vision.

"Fine, just winded." Andy read her expression and saw she wasn't keeping any information back.

Foster quietly shifted again and straightened slightly. Andy turned, her instinct twigged, just in time to see Shipman and Foster pass a look between them. Andy caught Foster's questioning look, Shipman's slight shrug of a reply. This didn't seem like two people who had just been fighting.

Diversion, thought Andy and she turned her body all the way, scanning the quad, trying to count the cadets in front of her. Many of them were moving, talking and regrouping, crossing the quad to talk to someone else. Very few were still, though their movements were slow. Too slow, deliberate. Choreographed. Andy couldn't track the cadets easily enough. Les looked up and caught Andy's searching look.

"Roll call, Sgt. Manitou," Andy called across the quad.

"In formation, Troop 18!" Les called out loudly, and the cadets instantly began to fall into two neat lines in front of her.

Foster hesitated and looked to Meyers.

"Formation, Cadet Foster," Constable Meyers said.

Meyers followed Foster as he hustled back towards his troop. Andy hung back with Kate, watching, waiting to figure this out. As the troop gathered in formation, she saw who was missing. Petit.

Just as Les was about to say something to the cadets, the door to the kitchen opened and Petit walked out holding a half-eaten banana. He paused comically at the sight of his troop in perfect formation before him in the quad. The screen door slammed loudly behind him in the tense silence.

"No need to line up for me, friends," Petit said.

No one laughed, though Andy caught Shandly nervously biting her lip. Sergeant Trokof stepped forward.

"Cadet Bertrand Jean-Pierre Petit," Trokof started, his voice drippingly friendly. "Would you be so kind as to inform myself, your instructors, Sgt. Wyles, Dr. Morrison as well as the rest of your assembled troop as to exactly what you were doing in the kitchen after hours?"

Petit stared at Trokof like he hadn't understood the question, then he looked down at his banana then across to his troop. They stared back at him silently.

"I got hungry?"

"Are you asking me if you got hungry, Cadet Petit? Or are you telling me you got hungry," Sgt. Trokof said, his voice implying he had unlimited patience. Everyone present, except possibly Kate standing curiously beside her, knew differently.

"I got hungry, Sgt. Trokof," Petit said.

"Well, I'm certainly happy we could accommodate your appetite so late in the evening, Cadet Petit. But please explain to me how you came to the decision to satiate your hunger instead of breaking up a fight between your troop mates."

Petit clearly didn't have an answer for this, either funny or straight. "I figured they would work it out, I guess," Petit said nervously.

"Work it out," Sergeant Trokof repeated, his voice going quiet.

"Yeah," Petit said, shifting his weight from side to side, his nerves obviously heightened. Andy tracked his gaze to Prewitt-Hayes, like she could help him out of this mess. Andy couldn't see her from this angle, but she could imagine the tense expression on her face. "Yeah," Petit said again. "Sometimes Greg's music gets on my nerves also."

Palpable tension rolled through the group. Andy had to see this for herself. With a quick look at Kate, she joined everyone in the quad, coming to stand between Petit and the rest of the assembled troop. She saw the bleak intensity on the right mark's face, then caught Trokof's eye. He gestured expansively towards the troop. *Take it*, the gesture said to Andy.

"Cadet Petit, do you share a cabin with Shipman and Foster?"

"No, Sgt. Wyles," Petit answered immediately. Andy wasn't watching him, though. She was watching Prewitt-Hayes who was glaring daggers at Petit. Andy waited. Prewitt-Hayes controlled her expression.

"Cadet Prewitt-Hayes, perhaps you would like to explain how Cadet Petit knows what the fight between Cadets Shipman and Foster was about?"

Tension, fear, nerves, Andy read all of these on every member of the troop. Frances, at the back left of the second row, even seemed to shake a little.

Prewitt-Hayes shook her head, like she was unable to speak. Trokof yelled into the silence, startling everyone including Andy, who had been half-expecting it.

"You will give Sgt. Wyles an actual answer with actual words, Cadet Prewitt-Hayes!" he roared.

"I don't know for sure, Sgt. Wyles. He must have heard it," the right mark, leader of the troop, answered in a shaky voice.

Andy considered her options. They were caught, but Andy had no idea what they were caught in. Frustrated, she let the troop suffer the silence. She followed the information backwards, thought about sitting in the kitchen, the sound of a fight, the scattering of the instructors, what she could now see as choreographed movements of the fight, the purposeful shifting of the rest of the troop, Petit coming out of the kitchen…

Drill Sergeant Trokof was looking at Andy expectantly. She gave a slight shake of her head. No more interrogation, but there would be another inspection and Andy hoped like hell this would turn up something more definitive.

It didn't. The moon had descended past its peak in the sky by the time inspection was done, the troop standing in formation the entire time in the quad, even when the rain began just after midnight. Nothing. Not a sign, not a shred of evidence, not even a piece of paper this time. The cadets were clean, the cabin was clean, and overturning the kitchen turned up nothing.

Andy passed the punishment of Troop 18 over to the instructors, heading wearily back to her cabin with Kate walking silently beside her. It was impossible not to hear Trokof raging at the troop behind them, but Andy blocked it out. She was tired, but her brain was on overdrive, thinking about Superintendent Heath arriving the day after tomorrow, trying to explain to him how this troop was continuing to defy them all. She felt annoyed, she felt worried, and above all frustrated.

As she held the door open for Kate, Andy questioned her defense of this group. It didn't make sense. She forced herself to keep her priorities straight. She was here to get to the bottom of whatever this troop was hiding, not to help individual cadets, not to get them back on the straight and narrow, not to punish them or shape them or encourage them. But it was hard. Something about this troop tugged at her. Cadet Hawke Foster, she had to admit to herself, was highest on that list.

Kate was adding some small logs to the fire, pushing them in before locking the glazed door. Andy read a similar look of concentration on her face, though Kate's was tinged with curiosity instead of Andy's frustration. Kate stood, wiping her hands.

"I don't get it," Kate said.

"Neither do I," Andy admitted, shoving her hands into her pockets, wishing the fire would hurry up and warm the cabin.

"I get that it was a diversion, that they wanted us out of the kitchen cabin. At first I thought it was a prank, like they really did just get hungry. But the way they reacted..." Kate trailed off.

"They were scared," Andy finished for her.

"Of getting caught?"

It seemed like such a simple question.

"Yes, of getting caught and all the consequences," Andy said. "But I think they're more afraid we'll uncover whatever they're protecting."

Kate tilted her head, seeming to think through Andy's answer. She unconsciously tried to twist the absent ring on her finger again. Andy's heart constricted, and she hesitated. Then she walked across the cabin, sifted through her bag by the door and pulled Kate's sister's ring out of one of her pockets. She handed it to her silently. Kate turned it over on her palm, studying the thick silver band with the simple, worn pattern. Then, to Andy's surprise, she pocketed it just like Andy had done so many times over the past two months.

"I think I'll give it to Tyler when I get home," Kate said quietly, meeting Andy's eyes.

Andy's heart lightened as another burden was lifted. It was a symbol of how far Kate had come in the two months she had been gone. For Andy, it meant Kate could let the past be the past and she could refuse to let guilt weigh her down. Andy couldn't help smiling and pulling Kate into her arms, completely overwhelmed with just how in love she was with this woman. Kate clasped her arms around Andy's waist, buried her head in her chest and they stood like that for a long time. Andy could hear the crackling of the fire, the click and hum of the hot water tank, Trokof's distant, continuous yell. But she concentrated on the sound of Kate's breathing, the smell of her hair, the incredible feeling of being held so tightly.

Eventually Kate pulled back and looked up into Andy's eyes. "They'll come around," Kate said.

"What makes you so sure?" Andy asked, wishing in that moment she had Kate's confidence.

"Secrets don't stay secrets. They can't. Even I can see this troop is working overtime to keep up appearances. It takes a lot of energy," Kate said evenly.

"But they've been at it for months. Successfully. It's like they're getting better at it, not worse," Andy tried to articulate her frustration.

"I didn't say you'd break them. I said they'd come around," Kate clarified, and Andy thought again of the mantra she'd been trying to keep in mind since Lincoln presented her with this challenge a week ago. *You won't punish it out of them, you won't force it out of them, you won't trick it out of them.*

"Tell me why you think so."

"Because you are offering them a way out. They might not see it yet because they're still so caught up in maintaining. But I saw the way you pulled back instead of going after that cadet, Petit. You saw right through Prewitt-Hayes, but you didn't attack her. You let it go, you let them remain intact," Kate said. "They trust you, I think. They'll come around," she repeated, her voice sure.

Andy shook her head, wanting Kate's confidence. But it was enough for now, that someone had it. It was enough that Kate was here with her. Andy kissed Kate lightly, even the gentlest brush of their lips making her heart hammer strongly.

"Do you have any idea how much I love you, Kate Morrison?" Andy whispered to her.

"Yes, I do," Kate said happily. "I love you, too, Andy Wyles. And I missed you."

❖

Tuesday dawned sunny, the weather seeming to agree with Andy's assessment that they needed to start fresh, move past the night's turbulence and start again. While Kate showered, Andy went to the kitchen cabin, finding Sergeant Trokof alone with a coffee, toast, and a glass of orange juice.

"Good morning, Sgt. Wyles. I trust you slept well after last night's chaos," Trokof said, still clearly annoyed.

Andy looked closely at the drill sergeant. He seemed pale this morning, drawn. She considered the possibly that at his age, the man needed more than four and a half hours of sleep. She made a note to talk to Kate when she had a minute today.

"Yes, fine thank you," Andy said.

"And the doctor? How is she faring this morning?" Trokof said. Andy, listening carefully for tones of disapproval, heard only inquiry and interest. She imagined either Les had discreetly filled in the other instructors, or they'd drawn their own conclusions as Kate and Andy had disappeared into a cabin together last night.

"Kate's good, she should be joining us in a minute," Andy said, meeting Trokof's eyes. She felt the brief awkwardness of her personal life and her work life colliding, but she navigated it with confidence, knowing others would be looking for her cue in how to respond. "She's trying to figure out this troop like the rest of us," Andy added, shrugging. She pulled two clean mugs off the tray and poured herself and Kate a coffee before walking them carefully to the table across from Trokof who was shaking his head.

"Christ almighty, this troop is starting to piss me off. Part of me wants to tell the CO coming up tomorrow to just get rid of all of them, cancel all their training agreements and damn the consequences. It's what they deserve after the shit they put us through last night." Trokof was clearly angry now, the early morning sun streaming through the cabin windows apparently not having the same effect on him as it had on Andy. She didn't offer her own opinion. Her contrary views seemed unnecessary. But Trokof looked across the table at Andy, as if sensing her disapproval.

"You don't agree, I can see that much," he said, drilling her with a long look.

"No, I don't."

Trokof didn't answer, but he did shake his head again before taking a fierce bite of his toast. Andy took a sip of her coffee, waiting for Trokof to add in his next two cents as she wondered idly what Kate would want for breakfast this morning.

"Tell me why I'm wrong," Trokof said suddenly, putting his toast down and picking up his coffee. Andy noted that his hand shook slightly, and she wondered again about his health. Or maybe it really was just anger.

"I think your opinion this morning is based more on frustration than anything else. I've heard the way you talk about this troop, I can see how well you know these cadets. Having all of their training agreements revoked is the last thing you want." Andy said it all in a very matter-of-fact tone, watching Trokof carefully. He didn't say anything at first, then he lowered his coffee cup and passed a hand over his eyes.

"I just..." Trokof started then paused, lining his spoon up with his plate, angling the handle of his white china mug so it sat directly perpendicular to the edge of the table before trying again. "I just worry about what we're teaching them," he said finally.

"What do you mean?"

"I know that Depot isn't the real world," he said carefully. "I know that you and every other cadet who have passed through Depot in the twenty-two years I've been there forgot at least three quarters of the shit we drilled into you mere minutes after we handed you your medals." He looked at Andy who gave a small grin, offering no objection. "And I know every cadet whines about how they're not going to use drills and deportment when they're out on the streets chasing bad guys, enforcing the law, upholding the peace, and everything else they want to learn to be Mounties."

Andy could detect no note of bitterness in the man's tone, though given the length of time and energy and the sheer number of Mounties in training he must have seen over the years, Andy wouldn't blame him one bit for being bitter. "But I know what my role is. I know I am trying to teach the cadets to *listen* for once in their young lives, to be able to follow an order with efficiency and precision, and to trust in the people around them so explicitly it becomes an unconscious thought. I may not have spent much time on the streets as a peace officer, but I know enough to believe to the depths of my Newfie soul that those ideals and skills *are* necessary out in the real world."

"I wish you'd been able to explain that to me as a twenty-three year old," Andy said, smiling respectfully at her former drill sergeant.

"Would you have listened to me?"

"No, probably not."

"Exactly," he said, taking another sip of coffee. "So I worry about what we're teaching this troop. They keep getting away with,"—he waved his hand above him, etching frustration and futility in the air—"*something* and we keep punishing them to no effect and they carry on, day by day getting closer to the moment where we shake their hands, hand them a medal in their red serge, and send them off. So what have we taught them, Sergeant Wyles? What skills and ideals are the cadets of Troop 18 taking out into the so-called 'real world?'"

Andy had no answer, but she realized she had underestimated Sergeant Albert Trokof. He was not showing the simple frustration of this troop getting away with lying yet again. His concern for the troop went much deeper. Andy rearranged her thoughts and assumptions quickly, sorting through Trokof's views and judgements and landing on his final question. She still had no answer, so she posed her own question.

"What is the best case scenario outcome for this troop?"

Trokof seemed surprised by the question, and he leaned back in his chair, the sunlight from the window slanting in a bright, diagonal line across his uniformed chest. He was just about to speak when they both heard Kate coming in from outside. She was wearing jeans and a dark blue fleece, her damp hair caught in its usual twist at her neck. Andy's heart gave a small, joyous kick at the sight of her, then a bigger one as Kate smiled at her before turning to Sergeant Trokof.

"Good morning," Kate said, giving her warmest, pre-coffee smile. "Am I interrupting? I can come back."

Trokof waved a hand at the seat in front of him. "Please, sit. Your Sergeant Wyles has just posed a question as to what I see as the best possible outcome for this troop."

Kate took the seat and picked up her coffee, giving Andy a quick smile of thanks before taking her first sip. As Trokof reordered his thoughts, Kate also gave Andy a look, raising her eyebrows slightly and giving the smallest shrug of her shoulders. Andy knew she was reacting to Trokof's possessive and assuming use of the word 'your.'

"The best possible outcome would be if it is discovered that whatever the troop is hiding is a minor transgression only. The appropriate punitive measures would be put in place and Troop 18 can get back to their regularly scheduled cadet training program. Realistically however, I know that's probably not the scenario we are dealing with. In that case…" he paused, sighed, and finished the sentence. "In that case, I guess damage control is the best possible outcome."

"Damage control," Andy repeated, waiting for Trokof to complete the thought.

"Yes, that we have to release the fewest possible cadets. And when I say damage control, I mean limiting the impact on both the RCMP and the cadets," he said, looking across the table at both of them.

Before Andy had time to comment, she heard more footsteps outside the door. Les entered first, holding the door for Meyers and Zeb who followed her into the kitchen cabin. Andy noticed both Les and Meyers also exhibited the same signs of being up late with the troop: haggard expressions and an automatic bee-line to the coffee machine percolating on the counter. Zeb, however, seemed utterly unaffected. He was full of energy, standing by the door, rocking on the balls of his feet then back down again. He looked like he would drop and give fifty push-ups if only someone would give him the excuse.

"What is our delinquent troop up to this morning?" Trokof said, taking his frustration down to a level of mere annoyance. Andy guessed he didn't like to show how much this troop was wearing him down in front of the other instructors.

"Ran them through a modified PARE this morning," Zeb said, almost gleefully.

"Bet they loved that," Andy said, watching the young constable.

Zeb grinned wider. "They were as quiet as kittens," he said. "I think maybe we're finally getting to them."

Les balanced a coffee and a plate of toast as she sat down next to Trokof. Once her breakfast was safely on the table, she looked up at Zeb and snorted in disbelief. "Either you're naïvely optimistic or totally off your rocker, Zeb," Les said.

A spasm of anger crossed over Zeb's face. He hid it quickly with a gruff response. "Neither," he shot back. "I just think we're starting to crack this group. Bringing them out here was a perfect plan," he added, with an appreciative nod to Andy. She said nothing, knowing no part of her plan had ever included 'cracking' the group. Andy quickly jumped into the conversation, seeing Les just about to offer her own retort to Zeb. Bickering was going to get them nowhere.

"Are the cadets in class today?" Andy said.

"Supposed to be," Zeb answered before anyone else could respond. "But I think we should use the day. It's sunny and dry."

"What were you thinking, Constable Zeb?" Trokof said in his formal way. Andy considered Lincoln's reasoning for wanting the drill instructor out here at Camp Depot. Decorum and structure, he'd said. Andy understood now and appreciated Lincoln's forethought.

"Either defence class up on the basketball court or target practice just at the edge of the forest. Or both," he added. He looked around the room at the other instructors, as if remembering he should include them. "Anyone else want them?"

Les waved away the offer. "They're all yours," she said, and Meyers nodded in agreement.

"Wyles?" Zeb said, almost mocking.

Andy ignored his tone. "I'll shadow the troop today if you don't mind," she said, her tone a firm, professional neutral. Zeb shrank only slightly then squared his shoulders and gave a nod of assent. Not that he really had any choice. Then he turned to Kate.

"Dr. Morrison? Want the troop for anything today, or should I just point them in your direction if one of them gets a boo-boo during hand-to-hand training?" Zeb's tone now dangerously danced the border from mocking to offensive. Andy heard the implied, though probably unintended, insult and felt her hackles rising. She slowly turned to Zeb, taking the time to school her features and take a breath so she didn't bite his head off. But before she could say anything, Kate had interceded.

"Sure, I'll take them," Kate said, her voice calm and assured. She turned away from Zeb, ignoring his look of surprise. She directed her next question at the drill instructor. "The cadets do some kind of first aid training, I take it?"

"Yes," Trokof said, sounding amused. "They have an in-class component, and they also come across first aid situations in the scenarios we run."

"I'd be happy to run them through some scenarios this afternoon," she said, then turned back to Zeb. "If that fits with your plans, Constable Zeb?"

"Sure thing, Dr. Morrison," Zeb said, his tone drifting back down towards respectful. Andy wanted to shake her head. She couldn't quite figure out Zeb. He seemed like a kid with ADHD, but one who had learned some skills and could hide it. But sometimes it caught up to him.

There was a brief, awkward pause.

"Come on Zeb. I'll give you a hand setting up the targets," Meyers said, draining the last of his coffee and standing up. Andy gave him a brief, grateful look as he walked by, and Meyers acknowledged it with an almost embarrassed dip of his head.

Once they'd left, Les let out a long breath. "Sorry," she said to no one in particular, "I know I shouldn't bait him like that. I just hate energetic people on a morning that I'm dragging my ass."

"Especially before your first coffee," Kate added, laughing.

"Exactly!" Les grinned, taking a sip of orange juice to wash down her toast. She made a face and put the cup down. "Ugh, that tastes awful. Did the cadets make it?"

Trokof looked down at his own empty juice cup. "Yes, I think so," he said. "Tastes fine to me."

"I think for a lot of reasons, I should stick to coffee," Les said, and Kate laughed again.

Andy watched them have a casual conversation over their coffees though she tuned it out quickly, walking back over the last half hour, sorting details and ideas in her head in an attempt to keep up with the rapidly shifting scenario she found herself in. After a moment, she felt Trokof watching her. He still seemed pale, but his shoulders were set.

"We all need a bit of patience, it seems," he said to Andy quietly.

Yes, Andy thought to herself. That summed it up entirely. They could all use a bit of patience.

❖

Andy didn't spend the day shadowing the troop like she'd hoped. Instead she spent it mired in the details of running a camp: garbage disposal, water purification, taking laundry down to the main house, fiddling with the portable printer connection, a running toilet in one of the cabins, and the endless task of keeping enough food in stock to feed this many hungry adults. She checked her voicemail while she was in cell range at the main house, confirming that Superintendent Heath himself would be descending on Camp Depot tomorrow sometime in the early afternoon.

Then she was back up to camp with cleaning supplies, fresh bed linens, and empty recycling buckets. Andy didn't mind the menial work. She'd known what she was getting herself into when she'd presented this offer to Lincoln. Still, she felt disconnected from the instructors and the cadets for most of the day. Finally, with her list of jobs diminished and the late afternoon sun at her back, Andy walked up behind the cabins where Kate had already begun running the cadets through some first aid scenarios.

Kate had broken the troop up into four groups of four, each with at least one cadet badly imitating an injured person. Andy gave a small wave to Kate, who was standing side by side with Les, having an ongoing conversation while they surveyed the activity. Kate returned the greeting and Les waved Andy over. But Andy shook her head and instead sat on a damp, old log that had obviously served as bleachers for this run down court. She wanted to survey the troop. Watching them interact, Andy could sense a quietness that had been missing in the past few days. Maybe because this wasn't really a class or because Kate was a civilian, but as Andy watched the cadets, none of the tension or hyperawareness was present. Maybe Zeb had been right, Andy thought as she listened to Kate calling the troop back together. Maybe this was really working.

"Okay, I think that's about as much as we can do without fake blood and bandages," Kate said to the cadets.

"Or without breaking someone's leg to see what it looks like," Shipman said, making the other cadets laugh.

"Or that," Kate agreed with a slight roll of her eyes. Andy watched as Kate's expression became serious. She could sense a question coming, some kind of test. "How do you know if someone is injured?" she challenged the cadets.

"Blood and bones," Shipman called out immediately, still angling for a laugh from his troop.

"Yes. But what else?" Kate said patiently and pointedly. The troop was silent, taking in Kate's shift in mood.

Les jumped in. "As a first responder, you'll need to know the signs. Even if you won't be treating anyone, you have to know what to look for to call in to EMS or at the very least to put in your report later."

"Signs of shock," Prewitt-Hayes said decisively, as soon as Les had finished talking.

"What does that look like?"

"Disorientation, acute anxiety, lack of response to stimuli…"

"Yes," Kate interrupted, "but what does that *look* like, Cadet Prewitt-Hayes?"

Another silence, the troop looking at Kate with curious eyes. She had them stumped.

"Let me try it another way," Kate said, glancing around the group. "What did the people around you look like after they walked out of the tear gas test?"

The cadets immediately started talking over each other, giving descriptions of physical symptoms, expressions of pain, what it looked like when someone was having difficulty breathing. All cadets went through the OC or pepper spray test in week seven of their training program. Andy still vividly remembered the burn that instantly took over her entire head; her throat, nose, mouth, eyes all streaming with tears and mucous as her body tried to rid itself of the toxin. Kate had done her homework about the cadet training. She wouldn't have expected anything less.

"Right," Kate was saying as Andy tuned back in. "So some injuries are easy to identify. We instinctually understand what pain looks like on another human being. But some are more subtle and shock is one of those." Kate paused. "Here's another question. How do you know when someone is well?" She motioned to the cadet closest to her to step forward. "How do you know Cadet Frances is well?"

A quick, tight anxiety rolled through the troop. Andy could see it in a small sidestep, a drawn breath, an uneasy look. Tension. Andy controlled the urge to walk around to where Kate and Les stood so she could see better. Something had happened, some shift, something the troop didn't like. Singling out one cadet? Is that what spooked them? Andy watched silently, cataloguing all her questions.

"If I may say so, Dr. Morrison, I'd say that Frances kind of looks like shit, actually," Greg Shipman said, his jocular tone breaking the strained silence. Kate looked at him, annoyed, then she turned to Frances as if seeing him for the first time. Andy watched Kate give him a quick assessment.

"He's right," Kate said. "Are you not feeling well, Cadet Frances?"

Frances shook his head, held his hand to his stomach in a terrible pantomime. "Something I ate," he mumbled. Andy noticed he was pale, and his hand shook.

"Me, too, I think," Petit said, almost immediately. "Something we ate. Shipman, you're on clean up from now on. No more cooking."

Kate scanned the big man, and Andy knew full well she was attempting to see past their admitted symptoms, to make her own assessment of their illness or wellness. "Then I suppose you should head back to your cabins," Kate said evenly, talking to both Petit and Frances. "Anyone else?"

Silence.

Les checked her watch, and then she pointed at the two supposedly sick cadets. "We're almost done here. Both of you can go."

Petit and Frances left the circle, decidedly not looking at the rest of their troop as they passed, Andy noticed. They had to walk right by Andy on the way back down to the cabins. Andy kept her eyes on them. Frances acknowledged her with a quick, polite dip of his head, Petit mumbling 'sergeant' under his breath as they passed. Andy considered following them down but instead she listened to Kate wrap up her session.

"The list of shock symptoms can be completely contra-dictory," Kate was saying. "And it could mean absolutely anything. A victim of stabbing could have a lacerated kidney but still be telling you his life story before he felt any pain. The human body has an incredible capacity for pain given the right circumstances and the right levels of adrenaline. If there's even a chance someone's been injured, you need to watch for it. Keep them talking, keep asking questions, watch their body language. A body can compensate for injury. It automatically takes whatever action it needs to protect itself. There are signs, you need to watch for them." Kate paused and looked out over the assembled troop of fourteen cadets. "Any questions?"

Andy was surprised she'd asked, figuring Kate would sum up and release the cadets. The sun was already beginning to set behind the mountain, and the temperature was rapidly dropping.

"Does it always know?" Shipman blurted out the question with none of his usual jovial swagger.

"Does the body always know what?" Kate said calmly, though Andy could tell by the way she asked that she already had an idea what Shipman was getting at.

"Does the body always know when something's wrong?" Krista Shandly filled in the question.

"No. Not always." No one said anything else, but no one moved either. Andy could tell they couldn't get there on their own. Kate seemed to know the help they needed. "What are the symptoms of cardiac distress?" she asked the cadets quietly.

The troop knew. Of course they knew. They listed in great detail the signs of symptoms of a variety of cardiac episodes.

Kate nodded each time someone gave a response, and she began tracking their answers on her fingers, starting over again once they got past ten. Finally they'd given as much as they could, and Kate didn't wait. She asked them the next question. The one that Andy anticipated by now.

"Did you see any of those things on Cadet Justin Thibadeau before he died?" Kate said, her voice understanding but also not letting this go. She would follow it through, she would answer their questions. Even the ones they hadn't said out loud. "In the weeks or days or even minutes before he went down during your training exercise, did you see any of this?" She held up her hands as reference.

Prewitt-Hayes answered for the group. "No."

"No," Kate confirmed, dropping her hands. "You wouldn't have seen it because Thibadeau wouldn't have felt it. Cardiomyopathy is sudden, and twenty percent of the time it results in instantaneous death. As you all had the misfortune to witness."

The group was silent, sad. Andy watched them intently, waiting for the moment they would shrink back into each other, forcing a barrier between themselves and the rest of the world. After a few minutes of silence, Andy had to conclude either it hadn't happened or she hadn't seen it.

Kate looked up at Les. "I think that's good for today," she said quietly.

Les addressed the troop. "Go get ready for dinner, cadets," she said, sounding more maternal than instructive.

Each of the cadets nodded silently and respectfully at Andy as they passed on their way back down to the cabins. Andy, Kate and Les followed silently. Andy didn't want to have the cadets overhear their conversation. It would have to wait.

The mood at camp that night was sombre. As Andy expected, Petit and Frances didn't join them for supper but neither did Shipman or Hellman or Awad. Andy watched as Kate made the rounds through the cabin, asking questions about the absent cadets. But the troop had closed rank again, and Kate got very little beyond the reassurance that they were all fine. Dinner was quick, the cadets leaving as soon as they had finished eating and cleaning up. The instructors offered each other what little insight they could. Andy couldn't help thinking that they were missing some piece. But they couldn't reason this out, and no amount of logic could be applied to make this make sense. So the instructors took the troop's cue, everyone turning in early, lost in their own thoughts.

It wasn't until roll call the next morning that Andy understood the extent of the troop's quieted mood. The troop lined up dutifully and nervously in the pre-dawn light. But only fifteen cadets answered roll call. Cadet Greg Shipman was missing.

CHAPTER NINE

A ndy hiked into the foggy morning, five silent cadets shadowing her movements on the slippery trail. It had taken only minutes to verify that Shipman wasn't anywhere in camp. Trokof had grilled the cadets, but they knew nothing. They looked miserable and stressed, Petit and Frances now not the only ones who could pass as sick. Foster said he'd heard the door of the cabin sometime after midnight but hadn't really thought anything of it. He figured Shipman was sneaking out for a smoke after a long day. Foster had gone back to sleep and said he hadn't known Shipman was gone until roll call.

Foster was at Andy's heels now, and his tension was palpable. He and the four other cadets in Andy's search party—Hellman, McCrae, Awad and Mancini—took turns calling Shipman's name, hearing it swallowed by the fog in the low areas or disappearing up into the sky as they crested the next series of hills. Initially, they had heard Meyers's team as they also called out for Shipman, but that had been over an hour ago.

Andy pulled the radio out of her belt and called Meyers. Nothing. She checked with Les who had taken a group in the other direction, down past the main house. No sign. Zeb had taken Andy's Yukon and was slowly making his way down the highway into Kamloops. He didn't have a radio, so Andy had to call Trokof who was waiting by the phone at the main house.

Kate was alone at camp, hoping he'd show up there. Nothing from any of them. No one had heard a thing.

Andy shoved the radio back into her belt and tried to quell the mounting concern that had moved from her stomach and up into her chest. She thought about the quick team debrief they'd had right before breaking up into teams. Shipman had seemed no more or less sombre than the rest of the troop when he'd last been seen. He'd given no indication that he was suffering or depressed or that he was considering quitting. Shipman was just gone.

"Does Shipman have a significant other?" Andy said to the cadets over her shoulder.

"A girlfriend back in Alberta. She's a teacher, I think," Cadet Chris Mancini offered, stumbling a little on the loose rocks, as if talking and walking at the same time was troublesome.

"Have they been fighting recently, do you know?"

Mancini shrugged his shoulders, kicked at a rock and dug the toe of his boots into the hard-packed mud in an attempt to gain purchase. Andy looked briefly at the other cadets, but no one seemed to have anything else to add. She tried to temper her annoyance. Pushing would get her nowhere. Troop 18 had made that perfectly clear.

"You tell me then, why do you think Shipman would take off? Best guess," Andy said to the cadets trudging behind her, wondering how they would take this question. It could be seen as concern, or prying or an offer of betrayal.

No one spoke for a long time, the silence only broken as Awad called out Shipman's name into the fog.

"Today could be rough," Foster said in his low, clipped voice. Andy wondered if he ever spoke in full sentences or explained what he meant without having to be asked.

"Why?"

"JT's birthday," Foster said, his mouth set in a grim line, his body held rigidly still. He looked near Andy, but not at her.

Andy silently berated herself for missing this detail.

"He would have been twenty-five, is that right?" Andy said. Shandly nodded, the crease across her forehead telling Andy she was struggling not to cry. Worried as she was about the missing cadet, about the CO arriving at camp anytime, about what the hell this troop was hiding, Andy's heart still went out to the sixteen surviving cadets of this fractured troop. She knew how death could shape you, how absence could be an all-consuming void. Sometimes the most significant shaping stemmed from how one chose to fill that void. Troop 18 had each other.

"I didn't know Cadet Thibadeau, so I won't tell you how to honour his memory," Andy said to the miserable cadets in front of her. "But I'm going to guess that having all of Troop 18 together today would help whatever it is you're going through."

Shuffling of feet, boots against rock, shoulders shrugged against the damp wind off the mountain.

"Let's keep looking, then. We'll take the path up to the lookout then complete the circuit back down to camp."

They continued their hike, Andy and Foster climbing up the wet wall of rock to check the look-out. No sign of Shipman up here, and fog blanketed the valley as far as they could see. As they made their way back down the circuit, Andy's radio went off, and Sergeant Trokof asked for her to check in.

"Go ahead, Sergeant Trokof," Andy said into the radio, walking back down the path toward camp. She hoped like hell he had something.

"Superintendent Heath has just arrived."

Shit.

Andy thumbed the button on the radio. "He's aware of the situation?"

"Yes, sergeant," Trokof replied in a tone that let Andy know Heath could hear their two-way conversation loud and clear.

"If you could ask Kurtz to drive him up to camp, we'll be back down within half an hour."

"Copy that, sergeant," Trokof said awkwardly, obviously not used to the tools of field work.

Heath was already in camp when Andy and her team descended through the back field. He was standing in the middle of the quad with Kate, Trokof, and Meyers, who had arrived back empty-handed with his own search team just a few minutes before. Andy dismissed her team, and told them to go get some breakfast. They'd likely be heading back out again if the fog lifted. She joined the roughly assembled group in the quad, attempting to read anything other than fury in the commanding officer's lined face. That search came up empty, also.

"Superintendent Heath." Andy acknowledged him respectfully, deciding if he wanted to open this thing up and cause a scene, they might as well get it over with now. The sooner the better, so they could get back to their search. Superintendent Heath was a tall man, the kind who was thin without ever really having been in shape. His eyes were grey and cold as he looked at Andy and attempted to keep the vaguely disgusted look off of his face. Didn't matter, she'd seen it before. And the feeling was mutual, but the difference was Andy refused to let it show.

"Less than one week into this little Depot adventure, and you've already lost a cadet, Sgt. Wyles," Heath said, his voice seething. This would come down on him, among others. And Superintendent Heath was a man who guarded his reputation closely.

"Cadet Greg Shipman failed to report at roll call approximately four hours ago, sir. Three search parties have spread out over the perimeter, and Constable Zeb, one of the Depot instructors, is covering all the roads into Kamloops. Shipman was last seen just after midnight by one of the cadets," Andy said, thinking Heath probably loved having an excuse to dislike Andy again. Owing Andy for her part in saving his granddaughter's life last fall had probably given him an ulcer.

"Sergeant Trokof here mentioned that you haven't put a call into the local RCMP unit. May I ask why?" His voice was a condescending sneer, and Andy felt the muscles in her back tighten in annoyance. She could also see Kate shove her hands into her coat pockets as if she'd just repressed her own defiant response.

"Yes, sir. A missing person's report wouldn't yet be valid, and I couldn't quite figure out how to word a person of interest report with the Kamloops detachment that left Depot free of any questions." She paused, letting Heath weigh the words, seeing how they were balanced in his favour. "I intend to call them in if Cadet Shipman doesn't appear in the next two hours," she said after it was clear Heath wasn't going to add anything. Andy needed Heath to know she wouldn't put the cadet's safety and well-being above a bad public image.

"Is there anything else I need to know about?" Heath's eyes bored into Andy's. She didn't flinch, it made sense. Her boss's boss was pissed. Shit rolled down hill.

"Yes, actually. A detail came to light just a few minutes ago." She turned away from Heath to address the rest of group. She could read tension and defiance in Kate's eyes, a diminished awkwardness in Trokof's rigid stance, and a worried steadiness to Meyers. "Today would have been Justin Thibadeau's twenty-fifth birthday. I don't know if it's connected or not, but it could explain Shipman's mindset and his unexplained absence this morning."

"I thought they seemed different today," Meyers said quietly.

"And have you asked the rest of the troop where Shipman is? Someone must know something," Heath demanded, apparently not happy he was being left out of the conversation.

"Yes, sir," Andy said. "They were questioned by Sergeant Trokof this morning. The cadets know nothing of Shipman's whereabouts."

"And you trust them?" Heath said, incredulous. "The troop is here for the simple reason that they are a group of manipulative bastards who aren't to be trusted. And you believed them?"

Trokof's posture changed, from rigid, silent attention to anger. He started to speak but Andy cut him off.

"Yes, I believe them."

"I want to talk to Troop 18. All of them. Now," Heath said. He tugged at the sleeves of his uniform, clearly dismissing everyone.

Andy indicated with a jerk of her head that Meyers should get the cadets from the kitchen cabin, giving a quick nod to Trokof and Kate that they could go. She'd deal with Heath on her own. Without another word to Heath, Andy pulled the radio out of her belt and called Les to find out where she was with her team.

"We'll have the whole troop assembled in ten minutes," Andy said to Heath after she'd checked in with Les.

I opposed this," Heath said to Andy, not acknowledging what she'd just said. "I told the rest of the COs that this was only going to make a bad situation worse. And so far you are proving me right, Sgt. Wyles. Find the cadet, turn this thing around, get to the bottom of this, and for fuck's sake find out something I can report on to show that you're making some kind of progress." He walked away across the quad, not even giving Andy a chance to speak.

Anger seethed in Andy's belly. Standing alone, she let it run its course, snaking up through her stomach into her chest and muscles until she could breathe it out again. Heath wasn't the most pressing issue. The troop's transgression wasn't even the pressing issue. Cadet Shipman was still missing and needed to be found. Right now, that was her only focus. Andy walked down the gravel road away from camp and radioed in to Kurtz down at the main house, asking her to switch to a private channel.

She had to smile as Kurtz poured expletive after descriptive expletive through the small two-way radio, giving her opinion of Heath and his boys club mentality. She called him an asshole, a dinosaur, a prick. Andy agreed and felt better having listened to Kurtz vent. But only for a moment. She asked Kurtz to call Zeb and have him continue his search around Kamloops and to check in every twenty minutes. If Shipman hadn't been found in the next two hours, he was to call into the local detachment for support.

Nine minutes later, the fifteen members of Troop 18 stood silently in three rows in the quad. The instructors and Kate stood near Heath, none of them turned towards him, none of them even wanting to look at him. Andy felt slightly sick as the worry gnawed at her, annoyed they were going to stand around and listen to a useless, enforced, and self-aggrandising lecture from Heath instead of continuing to look for Shipman. She flicked the radio on her belt and hoped like hell that Zeb could find some trace of the missing cadet in town.

"Where's Cadet Shipman?" Heath said to the troop, his voice pitched to carry, his tone relaying exactly what he thought of them. Beside her, Andy saw Trokof sway slightly, rock on his toes then back again, before planting his boots firmly in the ground. He didn't move again through the interrogation.

The troop didn't move in response to the question—not a boot out of place, not a shiver in the wind, not a blink. Troop 18 fought back the only way they knew how.

Getting nothing, Heath moved on. He pulled a list out of his pocket and scanned it before looking back to the troop.

"Cadet Awad," he called out, reading from the top of his list. "Where is Cadet Shipman?"

"I don't know, Superintendent Heath," Awad called out his response, not breaking formation.

Heath immediately went down to the next cadet on his list. It didn't take long for him to go through the entire troop, each cadet answering exactly as the one before. Andy clamped down on her frustration, refusing to check her watch to verify how much time they were wasting on this effort.

Heath put away the paper, seemingly satisfied with the response he'd just been given.

"Thank you, Troop 18, for confirming for me that you are a group of useless little shits who are willing to lie to their superiors. Reading the file from the Chief Training Officer, I had suspected as much, but having my opinion validated is reassuring to say the least."

Andy felt the tension rip through the group, but not the cadets. They were used to threats and intimidation. The instructors, however, all held themselves rigidly in check, each reacting in their own way to Heath's accusations. Andy had a moment to be thankful Zeb wasn't here. She couldn't be sure if he would have reacted to this with full agreement or protective denial. Either way, it would have been difficult to keep him quiet. Andy caught Kate's eye again, her mouth set in a grim line, her hands shoved deep into her pockets. Kate was pissed.

"You might think you've got this whole thing worked out, that you are smarter than me and smarter than your instructors. But I'll tell you none of you will survive five minutes outside of Depot with this kind of attitude and this kind of history." He said it with every nuanced threat he could manage in his voice and his body language. "No one will coddle you. No one will care about what you went through at Depot because every one of those bastards have been through the same shit. You aren't special, and you damn well aren't ready to be Mounties. Right now, Troop 18, all I can say about you is that you are an embarrassment."

Heath turned to the instructors. Andy had no doubt he was including every one of them in that accusation of embarrassment.

"Regardless of when Cadet Shipman is found, I will be recommending to the Chief Training Officer that his contract is immediately revoked. And let me be perfectly clear—"

Superintendent Heath never got the chance to finish the sentence. A ripple of noise came from the cadets, and Andy stepped around the still-speaking superintendent. The troop had broken formation, all turned toward the gravel road that led out to the highway. Cadet Greg Shipman stood there, still wearing his civilian gear, a past five o'clock shadow darkening his face and circles under his eyes making him look like he'd been up all night. He looked weary and uneasy, but as everyone turned to look at him, he squared his shoulders, dug his shoes into the gravel, and stood resolutely at attention. Andy felt relief flood through her, and it wasn't just seeing Shipman alive and in one piece. As she watched him compose himself, even tired and scruffy, he put the effort into looking like a cadet. To Andy, this meant he wasn't quitting. He hadn't left the troop. Apparently the rest of his troop felt the same, because Andy heard the whispered relief ripple out behind her.

All of that stopped as Superintendent Heath started walking toward the lone, unkempt cadet, his face a mask of barely checked fury. Andy knew he had no power to release Shipman from his cadet training contract, but she wasn't sure if Shipman knew that. Heath passed the instructors, keeping his eye trained on the cadet, but Sergeant Trokof stepped in front of the furious CO, subtly and effectively cutting him off. Trokof's face was blank, but his walk was purposeful, even angry. Andy couldn't be entirely sure where that was aimed right now. She wondered if Trokof himself knew.

"Cadet Shipman, where the hell have you been?" Trokof yelled, his deep voice booming across the quad. Before Shipman could respond, Trokof added a caution. "A complete answer is necessary. All the information your miniscule brain can come up with. I want to hear it, Constables Meyers and Manitou want to hear it. Sgt. Wyles and Dr. Morrison I'm sure would like to hear it. And you can see we have a Commissioned Officer with us today, and I am positive Superintendent Heath will demand an explanation as to your whereabouts. So a complete answer, Cadet Shipman. Where have you been?"

Shipman scanned the assembled crowd with bloodshot eyes running over his troop, glancing briefly at the superintendent's unsympathetic expression before moving to the more neutral looks from his instructors and Kate and Andy. Shipman took a breath.

"I couldn't sleep last night, so I came outside for some air. Took a flashlight, found the highway and just kept walking." Shipman called it out like he'd rehearsed it, presenting the facts as neutrally as possible. "I…" Shipman started again, then stopped, glanced quickly at his troop and back to Trokof. He licked his lips nervously. "Today is JT's birthday. It's…hard. But I should have been back at camp in time for roll call this morning."

Trokof seemed taken aback, like he hadn't actually been expecting a complete answer. The facts, the timing, and the reasoning all scanned for Andy. They added up and made sense. Still, there was such a huge potential for loss here...taking a walk and risking losing his place in the troop. Losing a career, something he'd been working so hard to accomplish. All for one very bad day.

"Cadet Shipman, you have twenty minutes to make yourself presentable, then I want you to get checked out by Dr. Morrison. I will be conferring with Chief Training Officer Lincoln to decide your future with the RCMP." Trokof said this all with very little inflection. Andy wondered if this was it. If Shipman had finally broken Trokof and what she was witnessing right now was him giving up on Troop 18.

Shipman hesitated, waiting for his signal to be released.

"Now, Cadet Shipman. Go now."

Andy felt a small wave of unease slip through her stomach as Shipman hustled to his cabin with only a quick glance at his troop. This isn't how she wanted this to end. They needed more time. She needed more time.

Trokof took a moment, staring at the spot the cadet had just vacated. His eyes were blank, and he seemed to sway so very slightly that Andy had to wonder if she'd imagined it. When he turned back again, he was all business, his voice sharp, his instructions precise.

"Meyers and Manitou, I want you to take the troop into the lecture hall. Dr. Morrison, if you could check over Cadet Shipman and report back on his health status. Sgt. Wyles if you could radio in to Kurtz, have her call Zeb back and then if she would be so kind as to pick us up and bring us down to the main house. We have a call we need to make."

Trokof didn't make eye contact with Superintendent Heath until after he'd completed his orders. It was the first time he'd looked at the CO with anything resembling parity. Andy saw no challenge there, no egotistical male pissing contest. Just a check, from one senior officer to another, that protocol was being followed. Trokof's gaze slipped over Andy as he walked away, his face unreadable. Andy swallowed her unease and pulled out her radio. Right now, the only thing she needed to do was follow orders.

❖

Half an hour later, Andy, Trokof, and Heath sat stiffly in Kurtz and Tara's plush living room. It was an odd assembly in a strange setting. They crowded around Heath's cellphone for their impromptu teleconference, surrounded by *Country Life* magazines and coasters decorated with pressed wildflowers. Trokof stood awkwardly, leaning down slightly when he wanted to speak, which was little. Heath leaned back in one of the armchairs, ankle crossed over his knee, one hand pressed against his mouth as he stared down Andy sitting across from him.

He spoke loudly and often, presenting his opinion of the troop in general and Cadet Shipman in particular with all the clarity and insight of someone who'd been on scene for five minutes. Andy sat with her elbows on her knees, leaning her body forward, not allowing Heath one moment to think he was intimidating her. Andy gave her opinion when Lincoln asked, sat silently the rest of the time, and hoped like hell Lincoln wouldn't be swayed by the idiot of a CO sitting across from her.

"Okay," Lincoln said, and Andy thought he sounded tired. "Okay, let's handle it this way. Have Meyers write him up for this one, which will make two flags on his file. Albert, hand out whatever mod-b you think is appropriate. And make it clear to Greg Shipman that he's on his last chance. Either he makes it through Camp Depot and the rest of training as well as his field placement without another mark on his chart or he's gone. Shipman is out of chances." Lincoln's tone was final. This troop was pushing him to his limit.

"Five hours late to roll call, and he's getting a notation in his file?" Heath said incredulously.

"He's getting one last chance, that's what he's getting," Lincoln said. "Feel free to recommend punishment to Sgt. Trokof, but it won't get us anywhere."

"You know my recommendation, Lincoln. Cadet Shipman should be released from his contract."

Silence on the other end of the phone. Andy looked up and quickly caught Trokof's eye before they both looked away. She'd been relieved to hear him adamantly, if quietly, going to bat for the cadet.

"You're too close to this," Heath said when he didn't get a response. "I don't think any of you are able to see these cadets for what they really are. Sneaky, manipulative—"

"Your opinion has been noted, Francis," Lincoln interrupted, his voice going hard. "Both formally in my report and respectfully in this phone conversation. I am taking your opinion into account, as well as Albert's and Sgt. Wyles's. We all agree. Shipman gets one more chance."

Superintendent Heath gestured sharply with one hand, leaning forward suddenly, almost lunging for the phone. Then he paused, collected himself, and spoke. "My report will reflect my opinion. You should have it tomorrow, Lincoln."

Lincoln was in the process of signing off when Heath stabbed at the disconnect button. Andy refused to show her annoyance, but Christ, she really couldn't stand this man. Heath stood, straightening out his uniform. Andy immediately pulled herself up from the chair, and the three stood silently, both Andy and Trokof waiting to be addressed. Heath turned to Trokof first.

"I have no doubt you will find appropriate punishment for Cadet Shipman, Sgt. Trokof. Your reputation in this area is well-deserved, I imagine."

Trokof bowed his head slightly in acknowledgement. Heath turned next to Andy.

"I meant what I said earlier, Wyles. Keep your head on straight and turn this thing around. If not for the troop, then at the very least to preserve your own reputation." Andy said nothing, her eye contact the only acknowledgement that he was speaking. "Personally, I'd rather not have my name anywhere near this shit storm."

With that final insult still hanging in the air, Heath left the room. Andy and Trokof stood together, listening to the CO's heavy tread on the stairs as he left. Then they heard boots on gravel, a slammed door, the hum of a car's engine, and finally tires spinning loose rocks up and over the hill. Superintendent Heath had left Camp Depot.

Trokof's shoulders slumped slightly, and he dropped into the nearest chair.

"Sometimes I fucking hate cops," Trokof said. It was so sudden and so unexpected that Andy burst out laughing. With the cadet found, Heath gone, and Trokof seeming back to his regular self, the tension was beginning to ease out of her. She rubbed her temples. Andy knew she should get back to camp, mete out Shipman's punishment, update the instructors, check in with Kate, and get the troop back on track. They all needed to put this day behind them.

"I shouldn't have said that, should I?" Trokof said.

"I'm not in Heath's fan club, don't worry." Andy wondered if she could take just five minutes and sit with Trokof before heading back up to camp. Just as she was wavering, Kurtz came around the corner with a bottle and three glasses. Without a word, Kurtz cleared a spot on the table, twisted the lid off the bottle, and started pouring. The sharp smell of scotch hit Andy as Kurtz passed the glasses around. Kurtz had always been old school with her drinking.

"To rising above the assholes," Kurtz said, holding up her glass.

"Amen," Trokof said, with evident feeling.

Andy somewhat reluctantly put her glass out, clinked with her peers, then tipped the bright liquid down her throat. She felt it burn, her eyes watered, and she knew this was pretty much a bad idea. But sometimes the bad ideas were the best ones.

"I'll deal with camp," she said to Trokof, handing the glass back to Kurtz. "Take a night off, sergeant."

Trokof shook his head. "I don't want the cadets to think I'm hiding out here, Sgt. Wyles. I don't want them to think they've broken me."

Andy considered this. "I'll tell them you're bogged down in departmental paperwork dealing with CO reports and conferring with HR and the Chief Training Officer. I'll make them think you're pissed."

Trokof laughed. "You're going to lie, Sgt. Wyles?"

"I'm quite good at it, Sgt. Trokof," she said, with a straight face. The scotch had made its way into her belly, warming her in a way only good scotch can.

"Need a ride back to camp, Andy?" Kurtz said, pouring another drink for Trokof, ignoring his feeble resistive gestures.

"No, I'm going to run," Andy said decisively. "Shouldn't take me long to get there. Need to burn the scotch out of me, anyway," she said, grinning. It felt good to have camp back to themselves. No, things weren't going well and no, she wasn't any farther ahead and yes, she had yet again pissed off her CO. But they could get Camp Depot back on track. They *had* to get Camp Depot back on track.

"If Dr. Morrison has cleared Cadet Shipman, he can be on mess clean up for the rest of the week. By himself. If he elicits help from his troop, that will count as his third mark on his file," Trokof said, his face serious. They both knew it was nothing more than a show of authority and would mean little to the cadet. Hopefully, the threat of a third strike against him would change his behaviour. And hopefully, God, please hopefully, would serve as a warning to the other cadets.

"Done. See you tomorrow. Thanks for everything, Kurtz."

Kurtz waved away the appreciation as she handed Trokof his next drink. "Don't worry about it, kid. You guys are providing a great deal of entertainment for this retired officer."

Andy laughed and left the two of them to work on that bottle of scotch, thinking maybe it was just what Trokof needed tonight.

Andy was barely past the garage, heading out to the meadow when she heard insistent honking behind her. She looked back down toward the house to see Zeb behind the wheel of the Yukon, waving at her to come on back down. Andy hesitated for only a second. She'd really wanted to run, to physically vent the tension of the day. But Zeb probably felt entirely out of the loop, and this could be a good time to try to mend fences with the young constable. Andy waved back and approached the Yukon.

"Thought the timing might work out to give you a ride back up to camp," Zeb said, reversing back down the driveway with a little less caution than Andy would have preferred.

"Thanks for thinking of me."

"Is the CO still here? Heath?" Zeb said as he paused to check for traffic on this dead stretch of road.

"No, he left about twenty minutes ago," Andy confirmed, not voicing her opinion of Heath. She didn't trust Zeb the same way she did Trokof. "Did you want to hear the details?" At his vehement nod, Andy filled him in on what had happened while he'd been wandering the back roads of Clearwater down into Kamloops. When she got to the part about the phone conversation with Lincoln, Heath's recommendation, and Trokof's punishment, Zeb shook his head in disbelief. Andy wanted to hear his opinion, totally unsure which side he would take in this. "What is it, Zeb?"

"It just seems like they're getting a lot of chances."

Andy said nothing, though her heart sunk a little. She really needed the team, the whole team, to be pulling for these cadets. And if Zeb thought Shipman should be going home...

"It's good he's staying," Zeb said quickly, as if he hadn't managed to express himself properly. "It's good he's back, it's just..." Zeb trailed off, clearly struggling to put thoughts into words. The gravel road ended, and Zeb pulled sharply to the side, next to the bus. He killed the engine and handed Andy the key. Andy took it without a word, allowing Zeb a moment to line up his thoughts.

Zeb moved in his seat, fiddling with the gear shift, locking and unlocking the doors in quick succession, leaning forward to check his parking job before finally turning to Andy. "Sometimes too many chances can fuck a guy up, you know? Make him wonder where the boundaries are. If Depot is supposed to be teaching these guys rules and limits and all that, aren't we kind of..." he waved his hands at Andy, frustrated he didn't have the words.

"Contradicting ourselves?" Andy suggested.

Zeb pointed at her quickly, his shoulders tight and high. This guy really couldn't sit still. "Contradicting ourselves. Exactly. Aren't we doing that?"

Andy gave him a genuine smile. "I think you just summed up what the entire team is trying to figure out, Zeb. Maybe we're getting it wrong, but we're trying our hardest to do right by this troop."

Zeb drummed his fingers on the steering wheel. He nodded slowly, then more emphatically.

"Let's go find something to eat," Andy offered.

Zeb grinned and they got out of the Yukon and walked back down towards Camp Depot.

CHAPTER TEN

A ndy woke to the sound of the troop gathering in the
quad: boots on gravel, a low muttering as two cadets
passed outside the cabin, the cushioned slap of a door against its
frame. With Kate curled against her side, Andy shrugged down
deeper under the blanket, thankful she wasn't on morning duty
today. Kate stirred slightly in Andy's arms, pushed her head back
into the thin pillow and slept on. Andy smiled, savouring the
feeling of being cocooned in bed with Kate, their bodies touching
at every point. She listened to the low, commanding tones of
Meyers's voice, his words blurred and indistinct. The sound of
feet in unison on gravel signalled to Andy the cadets were off on
their run. A minute later and camp was dark and quiet again.

Superintendent Heath had left four days ago. The first night
and the following morning had been almost awkward, the troop
walking on eggshells around the instructors, waiting for the next
step in punishment, the tighter restrictions, the lecture. But Kate,
Andy, and the instructors had all decided to carry on, business
as usual. Let Shipman take his punishment and stress about his
last chance. The instructors needed to move forward with the
assumption of good behaviour. Anticipating the next fuck-up was
getting them nowhere.

Kate had cleared Shipman physically, so he was now four
days into his punishment. Every meal he was on mess clean-up,

a task he clearly didn't enjoy but did without comment. He seemed no worse for wear from his night time excursion. Petit and Frances on the other hand, stretched out their sick story, Frances even losing a day in the converted infirmary. Kate said it sounded like a stomach bug, but she had no way to confirm it. She recommended a restricted diet, a day off to recuperate and heavy fluids to recover lost electrolytes. Frances was back after a day, his spirits clearly much higher but still managing to look like he'd been the one up all night, not Shipman.

Andy pulled her thoughts back to today's tasks: the list of chores, the never-ending grocery list, the urine samples Kate was going to collect and they would drive into Kamloops later this afternoon. Andy made a mental note to check-in with Finns, Jack, and her parents while she was in cell range. She wanted to update Finns, see if Jack had made any headway on the perplexing columns of numbers they'd found over a week ago. Andy also wanted to check in with her parents to see if she had a new baby niece or nephew. She also had a list of items Kurtz wanted her to pick up in town. Andy tracked it all once, then twice, making sure everything was still on her mental list.

"You're thinking too loudly," Kate said, her voice muffled by the pillow and her own sleepiness. Andy hadn't known she was awake. Smiling, Andy kissed Kate's shoulder and pulled her in closer.

"Did I wake you up?"

"Mmm hmm," Kate said sleepily, rolling over onto her back. Andy studied her face, the shape of her lips, the faint lines from the pillow on her cheek, her eyes still puffy from sleep. She was perfect. She was beautiful. "Are you thinking about bringing me a coffee?" Kate ran her fingers over Andy's face like she'd been studying it, too. "You better be."

Andy laughed, propped herself up on one elbow and leaned over and kissed Kate. It was a slow kiss, an easy kiss. It was an everything-is-right-with-the-world kind of kiss and Andy felt her own body sigh and relax. They pulled apart slowly.

"Are we going into town today?" Kate said. Andy could see her body was beginning to wake up, her brain already planning, even before her first coffee. "Is that what you were really thinking about?"

"Yes, just going over my list." Andy gave Kate one last quick kiss before pulling back the covers. Kate groaned her disapproval but got up also. As they dressed, Andy went over her list out loud, adding in a stop at the pharmacy when Kate requested it. She was running low on some basics and wanted to pick up a few things to see if she could get Frances' stomach problems sorted out.

"So it's okay that I'm leaving camp?" Kate said, her brow furrowing slightly as she zipped up her fleece. "No one will be on-site."

"The cadets are in class all day, no training exercises. It will be fine." Andy pulled her long, blonde hair back into a low ponytail, wrapping the elastic around four times and pulling it tight.

They walked in silence to the kitchen cabin, the sun climbing up over the mountain behind them, the sky a confirmed grey in the distance over town. Andy wondered idly which would win out, betting silently on the clouds. She'd lived in BC most of her life. Betting on the clouds was almost a sure thing.

The kitchen cabin was warm, Trokof greeting them with a soft good morning and Les nodding her hello while stifling a yawn behind her coffee mug. Kate brought their coffees to the table while Andy made two slices of toast for Kate and mixed instant oatmeal for herself. They had a routine now out here at Camp Depot. Everything felt familiar already.

As Andy stirred her oatmeal, waiting for it to cool, she kept herself on track and listed her priorities in her head. She didn't want to get comfortable out here. This wasn't a vacation for herself or the instructors. Certainly not for the cadets. She thought about her initial meeting with Lincoln, how she had to convince him giving the troop some space and not having any other plan was a viable approach to this dilemma. Andy was still convinced this was the best way to go but measuring their success or failure was difficult and intangible. Andy was vaguely aware that Les and Kate were talking, laughing about something over their coffees as they did most mornings. She kept thinking, following each thought to its most logical conclusion. Finally she put her mug down with more force than she intended, causing Kate, Les, and Trokof to look over at her.

Andy used the break in conversation. "Does anyone know what the weather is supposed to do later today?"

"Chance of rain this morning, clear by this afternoon, I think," Trokof offered, sounding tired. Andy looked more closely at him, wondering if it was the overhead light in the cabin or if Trokof looked a little grey.

"What are you thinking, boss?" Les said to Andy.

"I know the cadets are in class all day and Kate and I will be in town, but I was thinking the cadets could chop some wood this afternoon and get us ready for a campfire. They've had a good couple of days, let's reward them."

"Sounds good to me," Les said, picking up her coffee mug.

Andy turned her attention to Trokof, wondering what he'd have to say about a special reward for what should be some basic good behaviour.

"What are you thinking, Sgt. Wyles?" Trokof said.

"I want to see what happens when we give the cadets a chance to relax around us. We get to see a little of that at dinner, but only for half an hour or so. Let's give them some time and space and an environment where they have the chance to actually interact with each other and us."

"We aren't trying to make friends with the cadets," Trokof said slowly. "That's a mistake, I think."

Andy shook her head. "No, you're right. That's not what I meant. I…" Andy stopped, wanting to choose the right words, to make her intentions clear.

"They're starting to look to you, to all of you, to see how to act," Kate said, her hands wrapped around her coffee mug.

"This," she continued, indicating Andy's campfire idea with a nod of her head, "could be a good time to show them what it looks like to be a cop, both on-duty and off-duty, individually and as a crew. They're sort of blank slates right now."

Andy gave Kate a brief, warm smile when their eyes met.

"But they should be getting that from their peers," Trokof said, his brow still furrowed. "That's part of what Depot tries to do, pairing up newer troops with older troops. It's supposed to be similar to a sibling relationship, the older siblings protecting and guiding the younger."

Knowing Kate's history with losing her younger sister, Andy's heart ached to see that Kate needed to stop to breathe through the force of the hurt. Then Kate answered Trokof with a question.

"But do they? Has Troop 18 ever connected with another troop on that level?" Kate said, her voice even. She kept her eyes on Trokof, though she seemed very aware Andy was watching her closely.

Trokof paused then shook his head slowly.

"Never," Les said. "Troop 18 has always been on their own."

Kate nodded but didn't add anything else.

"We are what they've got right now," Andy said. "And right now we think they're doing well. Let's show them that."

Andy finished off her oatmeal as Trokof worked through the implications of their actions. He was careful, Andy knew that already. But he was also motivated to do right by this troop. He wanted to give them every chance to prove themselves without overstepping the professional boundary of teacher and student, leader and subordinate.

"Okay, we'll try it," Trokof said. "But whoever heard of a campfire without beer?"

Zeb walked in just then, catching only the last part of the conversation.

"Someone mentioned beer?" he said hopefully, heading directly to the coffee.

"In your dreams, Zeb," Les said, laughing.

In the midst of the commotion, Kate drained the last of her coffee and got up from the table, clearing her dishes to the kitchen. With a quick, almost apologetic look at Andy, she slipped out the front of the kitchen cabin. Andy sat for a moment, knowing somehow Kate didn't need her to follow, fighting the instinct to go anyway and make sure she was okay. In that moment, Andy heard her mother's voice in her head saying *trust her, Kate told you what she needed, so trust her.* Andy took a sip of her coffee, feeling the hot, strong brew in her bloodstream already. As she sat listening to the instructors talk about the day ahead, Andy realized she did trust Kate. For the first time ever in their relationship, Andy had the confidence Kate would take care of herself. And she had to let her. That was the shift: Andy had to let Kate take care of herself.

"She's very insightful, your Dr. Morrison," Trokof said, catching Andy's eye while Zeb and Les bickered good-naturedly over their breakfast.

Andy smiled at the drill instructor. "Yes, she is."

"Then the RCMP is lucky to have her," Trokof said decisively, making Andy smile again. "And Camp Depot is lucky our original medic wasn't much of an outdoors person."

Andy laughed and finished the last of her coffee before taking her plate to the kitchen. She sorted through the food stocks in the back pantry and made a few last minute changes to her list, adding chocolate chip cookies for Les and *The Vancouver Sun* for Trokof. She refused Zeb his forty ouncer of rye whiskey. Then she pushed open the kitchen, noticing the clouds had covered camp now and a very light, barely noticeable rain had begun.

She surveyed the empty camp and checked her watch. The cadets would be back in ten minutes or so and would need time to shower and change before Kate could collect the weekly urine samples. Close to an hour until they could leave, Andy estimated. Going on instinct, Andy took a walk through camp to find Kate. She forced herself to walk slowly, smelling old, wet cedar as she passed the hedges and climbed up into the clearing.

Kate was sitting on the same log where Andy had watched the cadets running their first aid scenarios. She was looking up toward the mountain where the sun was blanketed by layers and streaks of grey. Andy approached slowly, wanting to give Kate time if she still needed it. Kate turned when she heard Andy approach. Her eyes were red-rimmed and she gave a small smile. Andy sat next to her, hip to hip, and Kate leaned into her automatically. Again Andy felt a sense of relief. In the past, Kate would have been giving reassurance, not seeking it. They sat in silence, watching bands of misty rain descend over the tree line. Kate slipped her arm through Andy's, and Andy leaned her cheek against the top of Kate's head and waited.

"You're trying really hard not to ask how I am, aren't you?" Kate said, and Andy was relieved to hear a hint of humour in her voice. And steadiness, even now Andy could sense her steadiness.

"Yes." Andy pressed a kiss into Kate's hair.

"Right now I'm trying to convince myself it's okay to feel sad." Kate took a breath. "I hate feeling sad," she added, and her voice shook slightly. "Angry, self-recriminating, guilty, numb…. I can handle all those. Sad, I'm not so good at."

Andy gave her a moment, knowing she didn't need to say anything right now. She turned Kate's hand over and traced the barely visible scars on her palms with a light touch. She had always been amazed by what Kate had done to find her sister in a slum house in Winnipeg after a panicked, late-night phone call. It had been bull-headed and stubborn and entirely too dangerous, yes. But also brave.

Andy knew now what she hadn't known the first time she'd read the report in Kate's file. Kate was fiercely loyal and protective. Andy worried Kate cast that net too wide sometimes, that she overcompensated for having let her sister Sarah slip away. But that was who Kate was, and Andy had to love her for it. With that thought, Andy lifted Kate's hand and kissed her palm before lowering it to her lap again.

"Did you know she's buried just outside the city?" Kate asked suddenly. "Sarah. We brought her home. My parents couldn't stand the thought of having her in Winnipeg."

Andy did know that Sarah Elise Morrison was buried in Burnaby's Mount Forest Cemetery. She'd read it in the report. But she'd kept it to herself, knowing the story was Kate's to share. Kate tightened her grip on Andy's hand.

"Would you come with me, when we get home?" Kate said. "My mom and I took Tyler this fall, but I'd like you to come with me."

"Yes." Sometimes the shortest answers said the most.

Kate smiled, a genuine smile. It was tinged with sadness, with a level of heartache Andy couldn't really imagine. But she did smile.

"I should get set up," Kate said, standing and brushing the damp wood from the back of her jeans. "Sixteen urine samples aren't going to collect themselves," she added wryly.

Andy laughed quietly and stood also, giving Kate's hand one final squeeze.

❖

The sky cleared early in the afternoon, exactly as the weather report promised. It had seemed unlikely as Andy and Kate steadily moved through their list in Kamloops, ducking their heads against the rain. But as they exited the grocery store, each pushing a full cart, the sun shone thinly through the clouds. And when they pulled back into camp, everything gleamed brightly in the last, winter-thin rays of light.

As Andy and Kate hauled boxes and bags down the soggy path, recruiting cadets to help as they passed, Andy sensed a difference in the mood at Camp Depot. The troop was spread across the quad. Some were chopping or hauling wood, some were making their way back up the path to unload the Yukon, and Andy could hear a multitude of voices in the kitchen. It felt like

Friday, the end of the work week, everyone laid back and easy with the thought of two days off ahead of them.

Andy challenged herself to walk the fine line of engaging and participating with the troop tonight, while also remembering to observe. They were still trying to achieve an outcome and as the hydro pole hummed its way into light, announcing that another night had descended on camp, Andy felt the weight of that unknown outcome pressing down on her.

Dinner consisted of hot dogs on the fire, industrial-sized bags of chips, and veggies and dip. The cadets carried the picnic tables across the quad, forming a circle around the large fire-pit. Zeb was carefully constructing a large-based pyramid, choosing just the right size and shape of log from the pile Prewitt-Hayes brought over. A cheer went up as the first flame of fire burned through the paper and kindling and caught in a perfect orange-tipped arc up towards the pale navy of the evening sky. Andy, sitting by herself on one of the picnic tables, caught herself sending a silent prayer up with the flame. *Best possible outcome, let us see the best possible outcome for this troop.*

"May I sit with you, oh fearless leader?" Les said.

"Sure, pull up a bench," Andy said, waving at the empty tables around her. Les sat and pulled over the nearest bowl of chips.

"Kate said she'd be right out. She's pulling a branch-sized sliver out of Shandly's paw."

They sat in silence, watching the troop. Andy took a handful of vegetables as the tray was passed around, and she chewed on a thick wedge of bell pepper, thinking someone got lazy with the chopping.

"You know, I've never seen them like this," Les said, cupping a handful of chips in one palm, watching the troop.

"Like what?"

"Normal. Have you noticed that Prewitt-Hayes isn't counting her flock? That the troop is split up into at least five groups around camp right now? And they're *laughing*, Andy. Troop 18 isn't known for laughing."

Andy turned her attention back to the cadets. Prewitt-Hayes and Zeb were still discussing the fire, the young cadet attentive and interested and for the first time seemingly unaware of the exact location of the rest of her troop. The rest of the troop was scattered, some grabbing handfuls of chips, others using pocket knives to sharpen sticks for the hot dogs. Laughter came from the kitchen cabin as the cadets brought plates of hot dogs and bags of buns to the campfire. Andy felt the absence of tension, there was no heightened response as someone moved or spoke. There was no alarm. That's what she'd been sensing about Troop 18 since they'd shown up at camp over a week ago. They always resonated with a deep sense of alarm.

As Andy and Les watched the troop, another cabin door opened and closed and Kate and Krista Shandly walked down the stairs. Kate was talking in low tones to the young cadet, who somehow managed to look even younger out of her cadet uniform. They approached the campfire, and Kate stopped at the edge of the circle, obviously wanting to finish what she was saying before they got too close.

Shandly listened quietly, looking down at the ground. Then, she nodded once, meeting Kate's eyes with a shy, nervous smile. Then they both surveyed the action around camp. Shandly caught Andy and Les watching her and ducked her head, blushing. Andy allowed her thoughts about the young cadet to surface, but she held back on judgement, watching as Shandly left for the kitchen cabin and Kate came to join Andy and Les.

"How's our baby cadet doing?" Les said, wiping greasy chip crumbs from her hands.

Kate shrugged and grabbed a handful of chips, then on second thought, she shoved a carrot stick into her mouth before sitting down.

"Shandly'll be fine, just has to keep it clean for a few days. She's just starting to get that 'I'm too tough for a doctor' thing. Do you guys select for that trait or something?"

Les leaned back and laughed, banging her palm down on the table. Andy laughed too, knowing Kate included her in that cop trait. But she said it good-naturedly and even with a hint of appreciation.

The three of them watched the action of the campfire in companionable silence. Zeb was still poking at the fire, a thick, soot-covered stick in one hand. It was the first time Andy had seen him entirely focused on one thing for any extended period of time. She guessed Zeb was the type who wouldn't leave his fire post all night and would take it as a personal insult if anyone tried to mess with it.

"I'm going to see what's happening in the kitchen," Les said, standing up and grabbing another handful of chips. "Save my spot, okay ladies?"

Andy got the sense Kate had something to say but she waited it out.

"You should find some time to talk to Cadet Shandly tonight," Kate said, her words vague and her tone the kind of neutral that let Andy know she needed to pay attention.

"About anything in particular?"

Kate just turned and smiled at Andy, shaking her head a little to let Andy know she wasn't going to share.

"Fine, make me work," Andy mumbled.

Kate laughed and bumped Andy's knee with her own. Andy suddenly wished they were alone, that she could pull Kate onto her lap and kiss her from her ear down to her collarbone, until Kate's laugh became a moan. Andy shook her head and let the thought slip away as her heart returned to its normal rhythm. Kate looked up and smiled. Andy fought the urge to touch her. Friday night feel or not, they were at work.

Les made her way back over to them, and Andy had to admit she was thankful for the distraction.

"Kurtz just radioed up to camp," Les said, sitting down. "The lab called Staff Sgt. Finns's office who faxed the message up to Kurtz. All our cadets peed clean."

Andy nodded once quickly in acknowledgement, though a sense of relief flooded her body.

"Did they fax over the report?" Kate said.

"Kurtz said it's in an envelope with Andy's name on it in the front hall. I'm glad they're clean. Again. I stress out every time, wondering who it might be."

"How prevalent are steroids at Depot?" Kate said.

Les looked at Andy quickly, her mouth hardening into a line of defensiveness. Then Les sighed and looked back at the cadets jostling for position around the fire so they could cook their hotdogs.

"Not prevalent, but performance enhancing drugs have a history at Depot. A few cadets always think they can beat the system and try drugs instead of working their asses off to pass the PARE."

Andy held her silence. She'd considered the possibility it was steroids when Lincoln first told her about the case. But not enough added up and everyone in Troop 18 had passed their PARE. Andy hadn't known any cadets who used drugs when she was at Depot, but the rumours had been rampant. She'd assumed she was included in those rumours. She'd never failed at the PARE, not even during the training. That had pissed off a lot of people.

"What are the urine tests testing for?" Andy said to Kate, keeping her voice low and her eyes on the troop.

"A basic toxicology screen looks for the presence or absence of both legal and illegal substances," Kate said, her voice falling into the even, professional cadence that told Andy she was accessing the giant vault of information she was able to carry around in her head. "So it tests for over the counter-medication as well as alcohol, narcotics, anti-psychotics, marijuana, amphetamines, PCPs, barbituates, GHBs, Rohypnol…all the bad stuff. Any of that will show up in a tox screen."

"But not quantity."

"Right. Urine tests detect presence or absence. Only blood work can confirm levels of any substance detected in the blood.

And there would either have to be consent to have blood drawn for a tox screen or to declare the case emergent enough to bypass consent."

"What if I just don't want it to be drugs?" Les said. "What if I'm so afraid it's drugs that I'm overlooking something or explaining it away just so it's not?"

"Best outcome," Kate said, repeating Andy's question to Sergeant Trokof from days earlier. "What do you see as the best possible outcome for the troop, Les?"

Les didn't say anything at first, and Andy started to wonder if she was going to answer the question. If she even had an answer.

"I just want them to be happy. Even if they don't all make it through and become Mounties. I just want to know that they're happy." Les paused, looked back to Kate and Andy. "I know, I'm such a mom."

Kate laughed and even Andy had to smile. "Are you missing your kids by any chance, Sgt. Manitou?"

"They're small, messy devils, that's what they are," Les grumbled, grabbing another handful of chips. "And I miss every one of them. My husband included."

They watched as the first wave of cadets handed off their roasting sticks to the second wave, passing the inevitable jokes about charbroiled wieners and hot sausages.

"What about you two? Are kids in the plan or what?" Les said.

Andy felt her stomach tighten.

"We haven't talked about it," Kate said lightly with a small, knowing smile to Andy. Andy focused on that smile, on the seemingly sympathetic look in Kate's eyes. "But Andy's about to become an aunt again any day now," she added, smoothly diverting the topic.

Les gave a delighted sound, jumping on this piece of information with a ton of questions. Andy listened but allowed Kate to answer for her. She was too caught up in trying to figure out Kate's answer and the implications behind that look. Andy loved her niece and nephew. She loved how different they were from each other, how smart and how fun. She had been honoured when her best friend Nic and her partner Erika has asked her to be godparent and guardian to their son, Max. Andy had known him since the day he was born and was so incredibly proud that she could watch him grow up and see who that chubby, smiling boy would become.

But Andy had never wanted her own kids. She couldn't imagine it, couldn't picture how it fit into her life. She couldn't understand the compromise of work and family, how to stretch the hours in the day to do both to the standard she thought each deserved. As she listened to Kate and Les discussing the pitfalls of raising teenagers, Andy had a brief moment of panic. She really didn't know what Kate's thoughts were on having kids. This clearly wasn't the time to discuss it, but they should. Not now and maybe not for a long time. When Kate was ready.

Andy consciously switched her attention from Kate and Les back to the cadets. Foster concentrated on rotating his hot dog over the flames at just the right speed, clearly attempting to get a perfectly even char. Andy watched as Mancini, who had three hot dogs on one stick and seemed to grow quickly bored of roasting, accidentally bumped into Foster on his way to the condiments. Foster's stick dipped into the fire, coming up covered in ash. Foster's whole body changed. He went rigid with unchecked anger, his face becoming a mask of outright fury, his free hand automatically clenched into a fist, his body turning in one swift movement.

Startled by his response, Andy began to rise from her seat, thinking she was going to have to break up a fight. But Foster checked it, the change to his body so incredibly rapid that Andy had to wonder if she'd imagined the anger in the first place. Andy continued moving toward the fire, still wanting to hear the exchange between the two cadets.

"Sorry man…dude, sorry, it was an accident," Mancini was saying, holding his hands up. He'd clearly seen Foster's reaction and was attempting to placate the pissed-off cadet. Andy figured Mancini would be the type to snap if he got any push-back. But Foster had changed his attitude, his face back to neutral, his body still tight but his fists no longer ready to punch.

"Never get between a native and his hot dog," Foster said, his face still blank, his tone deadpan.

Mancini laughed nervously, like he couldn't really tell if Foster was joking or not. Foster let it stretch out before finally offering a small, sidewise grin. "I'm messing with you. Grab me another dog on your way back."

Mancini relaxed and offered Foster one of his own which started a joking, heated debate about standards of hot dog roasting. Andy, passing the cadets now, thought back to Les's comment from earlier in the evening. Everything about this exchange was normal. They were showing the typical extremes of camaraderie, the expected spikes and dips of annoyance and acceptance. The most alarming thing about Troop 18 had always been their unnatural flatness.

This is what Andy tracked over the evening, relieved she'd finally found some way to frame what was so off-putting about the way Troop 18 had been presenting themselves. The troop clustered in small groups, the boundaries between them easily morphing to grow larger or smaller as people joined and left. A few dyads had broken off, the angled bodies and rapid verbal exchange of the cadets making it difficult, but not impossible for someone else to join.

Shipman had his guitar out, strumming pieces of familiar music that floated freely across the quad into the cold night air. The instructors were spread throughout the group. Les and Kate were sitting closer to the fire now, still talking and laughing as they ate. Meyers was talking to Awad and Hellman, his movements more animated than Andy had ever seen, clearly enjoying telling his story. Zeb, as Andy had predicted, had not left the fire all evening.

Only Trokof was missing. He'd come out briefly, refused the offer of a roasting stick and had disappeared not too much later into the kitchen. The troop had changed when the drill instructor had been with them, quieter and more tense. But that was to be expected when the guy who handed out mod-b push-ups for the most minor transgression was walking around.

Andy had just decided to go check-in with the sergeant when she saw Shandly look up from the group she was talking to. Her gaze stopped on Andy, who smiled slightly, causing the young cadet to duck her head then return the smile before excusing herself from the group and walking deliberately over to the abandoned food table. Andy quietly joined Shandly.

It was cold away from the fire. Andy could feel the damp bite of the near-winter air against her face. Shandly was cleaning up, putting remnants of hot dog buns together in a bag and twisting them shut. Andy approached the table, waiting for Shandly to acknowledge her before taking a seat. Shandly's movements were quick and nervous, as if she wanted to keep her hands busy but was afraid she would run out of things to do if she moved too fast. Andy held her silence, waiting to see if Shandly would start the conversation. When it was clear she wouldn't or couldn't, Andy decided to help her out.

"Dr. Morrison thought you might want to speak to me," Andy said as an opener, keeping her body language and her expression open.

Shandly nodded and started stacking plates, trying to determine which were clean and which were dirty. After a moment, she abandoned the sorting and stacked them all together in a tall pile. Task completed and nothing left to do, Shandly finally sat down beside Andy.

"I wanted to talk to you about what it's like..." Shandly started to say, her words jumbled and soft-spoken. She took a breath, made fists out of her hands then spread them wide and clasped them together before looking up at Andy. "What it's like for you...and what it might be like for me...to be an openly gay police officer."

Andy did not congratulate herself on having guessed right. She simply let this piece of information become fact and added it to the profile she had in her head of Cadet Krista Shandly, age twenty-one from Gander, Newfoundland.

Andy considered what she wanted to say, trying to isolate exactly what Shandly was trying to get at. Until she knew, Andy decided to focus only on her own experience.

"I got posted to Ottawa right out of Depot and did my six month field placement there before getting posted to Vancouver. I've been here ever since. Vancouver is generally a gay-friendly city, and it's got a large lesbian population." Andy paused to check that Shandly wasn't bored with a personal history lesson. But Shandly seemed rapt and Andy had to wonder how many gay officers she'd had the chance to talk to. If any.

"My rookie year was the hardest. More than one asshole wanted to use my sexual orientation against me. But everyone's rookie year is the hardest, Shandly. People either ignore you or try to beat you down and show you you're not going to make it unless you toughen up, fall in line, and follow orders like a good little rookie should. I decided early on that being gay was only a weapon in someone else's hand if I let it be a weapon. And I imagine Constable Zeb has drilled into you the first rule of engagement..."

"Always protect your weapon," Shandly said, finishing the sentence quietly. Andy nodded but didn't add anything more. Shandly looked out into the dark. A burst of laughter behind them seemed to shake Shandly from her thoughts and she looked up at Andy, pushing her blunt-cut brown hair out of her eyes where it immediately fell back again. Andy had known a lot of women who had cut their hair at Depot, mainly because they were sick of push-ups every time a stray hair fell out of place and touched the collar of their shirt. Andy hadn't, she'd refused. For the first time ever, she braided her hair, pinned it up against the back of her neck, and hair-sprayed the shit out of it. Five days a week. For six months.

"So if I survive Depot and my rookie year, it might get easier?" Shandly said, still staring out into the night.

"That depends on you. And some of it depends on where you end up and where you want to go," Andy said, not willing to make any promises. Shandly didn't seem to have much of a tough shell, and being a police officer was mentally and physically exhausting work. "May I ask you a question?" Andy said and Shandly nodded shyly. "Why did you decide to become a cop?"

This apparently was an easy answer. Shandly sat up a little straighter. "I was just a kid when the planes hit the Twin Towers in New York. A couple dozen trans-Atlantic planes were diverted to Gander, so our little town almost doubled in size in half a day. Everyone was so freaking scared, no one knew what was going on, but everyone wanted to help. I went down to the airport with my parents in our van. We figured we could house a family or two. It was chaos. People crying, yelling, lining up for phones, huddled around TVs trying to get news.

"The cops were trying to organize things and keep everyone calm but most of them didn't know what to do. Then one officer found a ladder and stood in the middle of the lobby, started waving his hands above his head. It was so bizarre that eventually everyone got quiet. And he told the group that everyone was going to get news as it came in. They were setting up phones so everyone was going to get a chance to make phone calls, and they were lining up housing so everyone would have somewhere to stay and something to eat. He told them that even though their hearts were scared, they should fill their bellies and warm their bodies so they were ready when the next stage came. And the community of Gander would be there for them, whatever they needed."

Shandly stopped, seeming to realize how long she'd been talking. But she carried on. "He wasn't even the senior officer, now that I think about it. But he just figured out what needed to be done. And he totally changed the tone of this mass of people. Even as a kid I could see that. So…I want to do that, I think I'll be good at that." Shandly finished, looking back down again at her hands.

Andy had asked a lot of people this question, and she'd answered it herself more times than she could count. But Andy wasn't sure she'd ever heard a more succinct answer.

"Do you want to end up back in Newfoundland eventually?"

"All Newfies want to go home," Shandly said, but it seemed like an automatic response, ingrained. Andy didn't believe her for a second as the look she gave Shandly made her disbelief clear. Shandly seemed to flush slightly but only added to her answer. "It would be good for other kids...other girls....to have a role model, I think. I wish I'd had one growing up. Gander isn't the most diverse town," she added, somewhat bitterly.

Not a good reason to go home, Andy thought to herself. With that attitude, Shandly's best intentions had the potential to backfire.

"I don't give out advice very often, Cadet Shandly, but here's mine. Don't rush home. Go where you're posted, learn everything you can during those six months, then see what offers you get and what kind of postings are available. There are a lot of ways you can have an impact, so go and find out what those are before you make any decisions about going home. It's an opportunity. Use it."

Shandly nodded slowly. "Thanks, Sgt. Wyles. I really appreciate this."

Before Andy could accept the thanks, a roar of raucous laughter echoed around camp, and both the cadet and Andy turned around. Shipman was acting out some incident, flailing his arms above his head in an exaggerated pantomime, making the cadets and instructors gathered around the campfire laugh even harder. As she looked around the assembled group, Andy saw Cadet Prewitt-Hayes staring intensely, questioningly at Shandly. Beside her, Shandly dipped her head in acknowledgement.

"You're making Cadet Prewitt-Hayes nervous, talking to me," Andy said. A statement, not a question.

"No, she knows what we're talking about," Shandly said, then seemed to realize how that sounded, and her eyes grew round and she shrunk back slightly.

"So you cleared the topic with her first," Andy added in quietly. She tried to keep any accusation or judgement out of her tone, but she had to make clear to the young cadet that she knew how this troop functioned. She could see they had a system, even if she didn't yet know what the system was attempting to accomplish.

"We...yes, I did...but just..." Shandly stumbled over her words, clearly nervous now. Andy said nothing, just continued looking at the cadet. "It's not what you think," Shandly concluded desperately. One of the worst things she could have said.

"Tell me what I think, Cadet Shandly," Andy said.

Shandly just shook her head and looked over her shoulder, obviously wanting to escape to the safety of her troop.

Andy wasn't ready to let Shandly off the hook but then she heard a sound of hurried movement behind them. The laughter had ceased, and people were talking in low voices. Shandly was looking across the quad.

"Oh, no..." Shandly said very quietly, almost defeated. Then with a quick, blank look at Andy, Shandly joined her troop.

Andy stood also and surveyed the night time scene. The majority of the cadets and instructors were still around the campfire, many of them now on their feet looking back across the quad at the cabins. Andy saw Cadet Foster walking swiftly towards two figures moving in the dark shadow thrown by the bright light of the cabins. Even from this distance, Andy could make out Petit's hulking figure. Someone else seemed to be leaning on him. Andy started to move toward them, sensing the unnatural silence in the group, the tension stealing over Camp Depot in a thick fog.

Andy walked quickly toward the cadets, watching as Frances cursed and pushed off Petit. Foster arrived next and seemed to deliberately step in beside Frances, blocking him from Andy's view. More people advanced from the dark, forming a quieted, tense semi-circle around the trio. Petit made another grab for Frances as he keeled far to the right, but Frances shrugged it off, spitting angry words at his troop mates.

Andy finally got a proper view of the scene. Frances was swaying on his feet. He took a step forward, stumbled, and Petit grabbed the back of his sweatshirt and yanked him back and up. It would have been funny in any other situation, but not now. Not with Petit looking desperate, Foster looking furious, and Cadet Jacob Frances looking all the world like he was drunk.

Frances seemed to register Andy's presence, then slowly scanned the crowd that had assembled behind her. He paled in the harsh orange light, then he twisted in Petit's grip, took a few steps between the cabins, and threw up.

CHAPTER ELEVEN

H e's not drunk."
Kate and Andy had just joined the rest of the instructors in the kitchen cabin. Camp was quiet, the thick smell of wet ash still drifting through the cold night air. Andy had sat on the steps outside the infirmary cabin while Kate had examined Frances, not comfortable leaving her alone with the belligerent cadet. He'd quieted quickly, though, and a thoughtful Kate emerged forty-five minutes later, saying she'd like to talk to the team.

Now, Andy watched as the team absorbed the information. Zeb clearly didn't like Kate's assessment.

"Bullshit," he said. "I know what a guy who can't hold his alcohol looks like. I just want to know how he snuck it into camp."

"I have a pretty good idea what a drunk person looks like also, Zeb," Kate said pointedly. "My ER's not that far from the UBC campus, so September is always a blast." Zeb shook his head, his expression angry. Andy noted the other instructors also seemed somewhat doubtful but would take Kate's opinion as truth. "More to the point," Kate continued, "I know how a person with alcohol intoxication *acts* and Cadet Frances's behaviour was too erratic for him to be drunk."

Even Andy wondered about that statement. It didn't make sense.

Kate sighed and tried again. "Picture someone drunk. Picture them trying to *act* sober for longer than thirty seconds. No swaying, no slurring, no impairment in their ability to focus, no nonsensical outbursts." Kate paused and let the instructors make a mental image of this. "It's not possible, is it? You can't act through alcohol intoxication. Frances was perfectly fine for long stretches of time then he'd start to feel dizzy again, which is what brought on the nausea. Apparently, he's been like that all night. He was trying to get back to his cabin to sleep it off when Petit found him in that state and told him he should see me. They fought about it, which is what we all heard, and Frances insisted he was fine and didn't need medical attention."

"If it's not alcohol, then what is it?" Trokof said quietly.

"I really can't be sure without more tests. It could be something as innocuous as an imbalance of electrolytes from the stomach flu he's been fighting for almost a week, or it could be a symptom of a much more serious systemic issue."

"Or it could be drugs," Les added quietly.

"Yes. I won't rule out the possibility that what we're seeing are the effects of a different kind of intoxication."

"Then test him," Zeb said, forcefully inserting himself into the conversation again. Andy gave Kate a quick sidewise glance. She was handling Zeb's anger, so Andy suppressed the instinct to run defense for her.

"And take it where?" Kate said calmly. "It's after midnight on a Friday, and labs won't open until eight o'clock Monday morning. By which time the results would likely be invalid anyway."

Zeb shook his head angrily but said nothing more, roughly digging at a long furrow in the wood table with his thumbnail.

"Is Cadet Frances ill, Dr. Morrison? Does he need to be taken for more tests?" Trokof moved his gaze from Zeb back to Kate, looking like he could give the constable a drill instructor style lecture right about now.

"I've let Frances know I will be monitoring him daily for the next little while, and if he refuses the daily physical or misses one appointment, that will go directly to the Chief Training Officer." Kate stopped and looked around. "Sorry, I should have checked with you first. I didn't mean to go above your heads—"

Trokof waved this away. "No, you were right to bring Lincoln's name into this. We may be asked for our opinions, but it is not up to us to decide the fate of the cadets."

Kate nodded then continued. "I'll make the judgement on a day to day basis as to whether or not I think the cadet needs additional medical testing. Right now he's presenting with odd but explainable symptoms. I'll monitor him over the weekend, and if I think he's not fit to participate in regular cadet duties on Monday morning, I'll recommend he's taken into Kamloops for full testing."

Kate folded her hands on the table, but Andy noticed the awkward way she held her body, pushing herself slightly back from the table like she was conflicted about her conclusion. She was holding something back. Andy wanted to know, felt the questions pile up in her head. But she forced herself to listen to the conversation as Trokof and Meyers outlined the plans for the weekend, another trip tomorrow into Kamloops for the troop, minus Frances who wasn't cleared to go.

Kate and Andy stayed at the table as the meeting wrapped up and the instructors left one by one, yawning their goodnights. Andy could read signs of fatigue and weariness, not just from tonight, but an accumulation of a week's worth of worry and organization and decision-making. Meyers was the last to leave, closing the door quietly behind him. Andy stored the concerns for the instructors and their mental health for the moment. She and Kate were alone, and Andy had a lot of questions.

Kate was silent, though, her hands clasped in front of her, braiding her fingers together in an unconscious motion. Thinking, always thinking.

"Frances said something interesting during his examination. I didn't share it with the instructors because something is... wrong with the way he said it. And I can't figure out what it is." A few more twists of her fingers, then Kate shook them out irritably. "When I was questioning Frances about his symptoms and his recent bout of stomach issues, he mentioned that his dad was being tested for Crohn's disease."

"Ulcers?"

Kate made a wavering motion with her hands. "Basically," she said, clearly having decided that a more medical explanation wasn't relevant right now.

"Does it explain Frances's symptoms?"

"It could. His symptoms could absolutely be Crohn's disease." She paused, her brow furrowing. "It actually makes more sense for Jacob Frances to be getting tested for Crohn's now than his father. It usually comes on early."

"His father was a cop," Andy reminded Kate with a small smile. "Maybe he was one of those types that decided he never needed medical advice."

Kate returned the small smile, but she seemed to do it more to humour Andy than anything.

"What am I missing?" Andy said.

"It took Frances a long time to tell me about his father, though I'd asked about family history more than once. And when he did, he got very emotional." Kate paused, and her voice got quiet. "He cried, Andy."

"Why did he cry?"

Kate shook her head, obviously perplexed. "Crohn's can be a painful condition. It requires a change in diet and lifestyle, and it needs to be managed for the rest of the person's life. But it's not debilitating, and it's certainly not a death sentence."

"Has the topic of his father or his family come up before?"

"The first time he came in to get examined. I read in his chart that he was fourth generation to go through Depot, and I asked him about it. He seemed proud, he seemed nervous. And he changed the subject. I assumed because he's sick of being asked about it."

"Could be," Andy said. "I can ask the other instructors about that, see if they've noticed anything around Frances being sensitive about his family's past. If that's okay with you."

"Of course. But am I looking for issues that aren't even there?" Kate didn't wait for Andy to answer. "There are so many layers to what's going on with this troop, so many things that almost but don't quite make sense. I didn't share this with the instructors because I wasn't sure if I was just…making things up."

Andy gave another small smile. Kate wasn't afraid to speculate, but she always wanted her speculations to be anchored in fact.

"I've wondered the same thing myself," Andy said. "I keep having to remind myself that I can't force this. Whatever this is, it's going to have to surface by itself. And we have to keep watching for it."

Kate gave a quick nod of agreement. Then she straightened up, massaging a knot in her neck.

"How'd it go with Shandly?" Kate said, shifting gears.

"Fine. We had a good talk, I think. Did Shandly say she wanted to talk to me, or did you point her in my direction?"

"Shandly wanted to talk to you but was too shy to approach you herself. It was the first time someone has come out to me because I'm gay, I think. Or at least," Kate said, a smile in her eyes, "because Shandly felt like I have some sort of influence over you."

Andy sat very still for a moment, watching Kate. This was the first time she'd ever heard Kate refer to herself as gay. Andy didn't want to overreact, but she didn't want to under-react, either. She wasn't even sure how she felt about it. Her heart thudded in her chest, a snake of fear tearing up through her stomach. She didn't want to get this wrong.

Kate saved her. She laughed sympathetically at Andy's expression before standing up and walking around the table. Andy pulled Kate onto her lap, like she'd wanted to all night, tucking Kate's small frame into her own body until they fit just right. Until they fit together perfectly.

"I shouldn't laugh at you," Kate said, her tone contrite.

"You're one of the only people who can," Andy said, lifting Kate's hand and kissing her fingers as she said it. "I don't blame you for taking advantage of that fact."

Kate laughed again, and Andy felt the coldness leave her body. This was Kate. Her Kate. She had nothing to be afraid of. Kate leaned her head against Andy's shoulder, pressing her warm lips against Andy's neck. Andy couldn't suppress the small shiver that went through her body. Kate angled her head so her lips were at Andy's ear.

"Then should I also take advantage of the fact that we share an extremely small bed together and you somehow have the ability to be very, very quiet?"

Andy ran her left hand up the length of Kate's whole body, turning Kate's face so she could kiss her. Their kiss was long and slow, until Andy couldn't remember what cold felt like. There was only warmth. Only heat.

"Yes," Andy said to Kate, her voice a whisper. Yes.

It rained for the next three days solid. Camp was soggy and dark and dreary, and it did nothing to improve the mood of the instructors. By the end of the third day, Andy wasn't sure what was going to break down first, the nearly washed-out road from the highway or the now completely strained relationship between Zeb and the rest of the instructors. The young constable was struggling to keep his body under control. He was jumpy and irritable and cabin-fevered without the ability to get outside and burn off any of his excess energy. Andy felt for the guy. She was itching to move too, to stretch out beyond the small cabins, to feel herself moving swiftly through space and the hard impact to her muscles from a long run.

By Monday night, Andy knew she had to do something. She sat at the beat-up table by the window in their cabin, having a static-driven conversation with Kurtz over the radio while Kate sat cross-legged on the bed with a stack of medical journals. Dinner had been a disaster, the cadets burning their potatoes on the hot camp stove and filling the kitchen cabin with acrid smoke.

Zeb had made a comment which Les had taken the wrong way. Meyers had attempted to intervene in his quiet way, but Les and Zeb seemed intent on hashing this out. Finally Trokof had walked around to the two instructors and said something sharply under his breath. Les had closed her eyes briefly before looking up at the cadets who had been watching the exchange with furtive glances. Les and Zeb mended fences, Trokof had left not too long later, and Andy began thinking about what the hell she was going to do to snap Camp Depot out of this.

As worrisome as it was to have the instructors at each other's throats, even more troubling was that the three days of rain and the distraction of the instructors had allowed Troop 18 to retreat again. They had slowly, imperceptibly, closed ranks again, pulling Frances back into the fold when Kate had given the all-clear that morning. They showed up to class, they made little impression during meal times, and they followed orders without complaint. The flatness was back, the blandness was back. Troop 18 rested comfortably in their camouflage.

Andy wrapped up her conversation with Kurtz, agreeing to meet her in the morning at the highway, regardless of the weather. They would check out the condition of the gravel road and see if any of their ideas for getting the troop out for a day would come together. Andy pushed the radio into its base and cracked her knuckles, a bad habit she'd forced herself to quit years ago. She looked around the cabin. Kate's things were spread haphazardly on various surfaces, and Andy's were tucked neatly away. She listened to the muted crack and shift of the fire in the woodstove, the unending rain against the shingled roof. Andy walked to the window and looked out through the blur of rain at the soaked, deserted quad, barely visible through the sheets of water and the thin light from the hydro pole. Nothing moved, just a wavering glow from the porch lights on each cabin.

"So, what's the plan?" Kate said, and Andy turned away from the window to see Kate sitting up, folding the page over in the journal and tossing it carelessly onto the floor.

"I don't know yet. Kurtz needed to make a few calls and see what she can come up with. She seemed pretty confident we can find somewhere to take the troop tomorrow."

"Is the rain supposed to let up at all?" Kate stretched her arms above her head then relaxed with an exaggerated sigh before rubbing the back of her neck. Andy gave a small smile and walked over to Kate. She climbed onto the bed behind Kate and leaned up against the wood walls of the cabin. She pushed Kate's hair off her shoulder, found the knot in Kate's neck and worked it gently with the pad of her hand, applying a gentle but firm pressure. Kate gave a soft sigh of happiness, and Andy smiled again before answering her question.

"Rain all week, according to Kurtz, but not nearly as bad as the last few days. Kurtz and I are going to check out the road tomorrow, make sure we still have an escape route out of here."

They were silent for a long while, Andy continuing to massage the chronic knot in Kate's neck.

"I miss Jack," Kate said suddenly.

"He misses you, too," Andy murmured. "I'm mainly happy we're back together so Jack can stop pestering me."

Kate laughed quietly, Andy feeling the vibrations of Kate's laughter through her fingers.

"I'll have to take him out for lunch when we get back to Vancouver and thank him for keeping you in one piece while I was gone," Kate said lightly, leaning back slightly into Andy's touch. "And he can tell me all about my new supervisor," she added, almost as an afterthought.

Andy stopped massaging for a moment. "I thought Finns was your supervisor," Andy said, slightly confused.

"Technically, I report to Staff Sergeant Baird who oversees civilian consultants, same as Jack. But Heath made it clear all my assignments would come through Finns. So really, you and I work for different divisions, Sergeant Wyles. I'm practically fraternizing with the enemy right now."

Andy poked Kate in the ribs with her free hand, making her laugh. She often forgot that Jack didn't report to Finns. Sometimes Jack did, too. He referred to Baird as the 'forms dude,' someone he sent his stats and vacation requests to. It was a good system, though Andy didn't envy Finns's having to supervise someone else's staff. Still, she appreciated the freedom it allowed. Technically, she and Kate weren't breaking any rules being together, and they would still be able to work with each other.

"How's your schedule going to work?" Andy said, trying to figure out how Kate was supposed to work two jobs. Even part time, the workload for either was heavy. Neither had regular schedules, either could mean an emergency response.

"I owe the ER two day shifts and one night shift per week and one weekend per month. They don't really care when I get the hours in, as long as the schedule isn't affected, and there are always more hours if I want them. I'm not sure about RCMP yet. I've got an hourly rate with minimum and maximum number of hours per week. After my probation is up, Heath said he'd talk to me about a part-time, salaried position."

Andy finished massaging Kate's neck, repositioned her shirt, and pushed her hair back over her shoulder. "Sounds stressful," Andy said, deciding to voice her concerns. She played with Kate's hair, making loose braids with her red curls.

Kate seemed unconcerned. "Could be. Could turn out to be a really bad career decision. But I feel good about having made a decision. I'm actually pursuing something with some measure of forethought."

Andy didn't push. She didn't even really disagree. But Andy couldn't help but worry. Until she knew what it looked like, until she could see Kate thriving in the dual roles she'd willingly taken on, Andy was just going to worry.

"Trokof said the RCMP is lucky to have you," Andy murmured, keeping her other thoughts to herself. She felt Kate smile.

"He's a sweetheart."

Andy leaned her head back against the warm wood walls and laughed. Never could Andy have ever imagined any context in which Depot's drill instructor Sergeant Albert Trokof could be called a sweetheart.

"Do you know the kind of hell that man put me through? Thousands of push-ups, repeating drills until I had blisters, mod-b for having one stray hair out of place or my left sleeve being crooked. He was the devil in an RCMP uniform, Kate," Andy laughed.

Kate turned her body so she could see Andy's face. "And do you still think that about him?"

Andy shook her head. "No. But he's a serious hardass, Sgt. Trokof. I think he's half the reason Troop 18 is still standing."

"Camp's wearing him down, though," Kate said, her voice thoughtful. "I'm going to keep my eye on him."

Good, Andy thought, feeling a sense of relief at hearing her own concerns out loud. She felt the weight of worry shift a little, as Kate unknowingly offered to share the burden. Andy pulled Kate in and buried her face in Kate's chaos of curls. They held each other and listened quietly to the continuous rain drumming against the roof of their cabin.

To no one's surprise, Camp Depot woke to rain the next morning. Light but steady, it pattered against the window with the occasional gusts of wind. Andy woke early, dressed quietly, and kissed Kate lightly on her way out the door, getting only a soft, mumbled acknowledgement in return. In the kitchen cabin, Andy turned on the lights, lit the camp stove so it would be warmed up when the cadets showed up in half an hour or so, and started the industrial-sized canister of coffee. She didn't have time to wait for a first cup, so she grabbed a granola bar instead and headed out into the rain.

Andy shrugged into her storm coat, feeling the cold air worm its way under the thick fabric. She pulled her watch cap over her ears and tried not to let the weather affect her mood. Andy stepped carefully down the gravel path, swinging the wide beam of her flashlight left and right, checking for rivulets in the road from the rain. She saw a few but none wider than her hand.

Fifteen minutes later, Andy saw the headlights of Kurtz's truck, pulled in just off the highway so she didn't compromise the road by driving on it.

Andy pulled herself into the warm cab of Kurtz's truck.

"Morning, Andy. How does the road look?"

"Not bad. The culverts seem to be working for now. Maybe a dozen or so channels over the whole length of the road but nothing too wide."

Kurtz grunted at the news, seeming satisfied with Andy's report. She pulled a silver thermos out of the drink holder in the console, twisted off the lid, and poured something hot into a small cup. "Coffee?"

"Thanks," Andy said gratefully, wrapping her hands around the small cup and taking a sip. It was hot and strong. And spiked. "Jesus, Kurtz, what the hell is in this?"

"A shot of whiskey," Kurtz said with a grin. "What? Are you going to give an old lady a hard time for wanting to warm her bones in the morning?"

She snorted and took another sip before passing it back. "Old lady…right."

"Speaking of old lady," Kurtz said, "how's Kate?"

Andy couldn't help grinning. "Kate is good. Kate is perfect."

"You going soft on me, Andy Wyles?"

Andy shrugged, the gesture probably lost in the dawn darkness. "It's possible."

"Good, you could do with a little softening."

Andy laughed quietly and looked through the windshield into the cold, wet dark of the day. "Any luck with plans for the troop?"

"Yep. Got a good one, you're going to like it," Kurtz said with renewed vigour in her voice. Andy had to wonder what it was like to retire, to completely shift your brain from the overload of a staff sergeant job to...well, anything else really. "Put in a cold call to the Sports and Recreation at TRU." Kurtz had wanted to get the troop down to Thompson River University, just at the edge of Kamloops. "The women's volleyball team is away this weekend at CIS championships, so he said as long as someone from the RCMP signed an insurance waiver, we could have their gym time. That gives you the gym for three hours, half the pool for one, and the workout room for however long you want it."

Perfect, Andy thought. It was an ideal space where they could run the troop through scenarios or just work them hard. It wouldn't be so bad for Zeb, either. In fact, Andy figured she'd just turn the troop over to Zeb for a couple of hours and give the other instructors some free time.

"Yes," Andy said out loud, mentally working through the logistics of organizing, transporting, and chaperoning the troop. Andy asked a few questions and got some timelines, the name of the director, and directions. "Perfect. I keep saying I owe you. You're going to have to figure out how I'm paying you back."

"Stay for a few days after the troop's gone," Kurtz said immediately. "You and Kate."

Andy would love to stay for a few days, visit with Kurtz and Tara, and have some actual alone time with Kate. She also thought about her responsibilities and Kate's new schedule. She waivered.

"We'll see," Andy hedged. "I'd love to, if we can."

"Settled," Kurtz said. "But you and Kate can stay in the honeymoon cabin. I don't need to hear you two up all night."

Andy shook her head again, laughing as she pulled open the door of the truck. A blast of cold air hit her in the face, instantly cooling her body temperature. With a goodbye to Kurtz, Andy slammed the door, ducked her head, and ran the few kilometres back to camp.

By the time the troop had gotten up, done roll call in the lecture cabin, eaten and cleaned up breakfast, packed a bag, slogged their way down the road to the bus, stopped at Wal-Mart to buy swim suits, and wound their way through Kamloops until they found the compact university and its athletics complex, they ended up just making their noon hour gym time.

Everyone's mood had shifted. The cadets milled about in small, excited groups, looking like a visiting sports team in their Depot-blue workout wear. Andy signed the four-page document releasing the university from any future lawsuits as a result of the troop using their facility and put down a cash deposit on twenty locks and twenty temporary pass cards.

"Okay, Troop 18," Andy called out. "You are with Zeb and I for the next three hours in gym two, then you'll have an hour of optional pool time and exactly one hour after that, we will do roll call here in the foyer."

The troop gave murmurs of surprise. Andy had basically just given them two free hours in the middle of their week. Trokof had suggested it, and none of the other instructors had disagreed. Work them hard, he'd told Zeb, fitness and hand-to-hand practice and self-defense and drills. Work them hard, give them a chance to breathe, then ship them back to camp.

"I suggest taking advantage of the unlimited supply of hot water," Andy added just before she released the cadets. The four-minute showers had become something of a joke at camp. It was barely enough time to get clean, let alone warmed through before the hot water started to trickle off into an increasing stream of cold. Now that Kate was with her, it was really the only thing that made Andy the least bit homesick.

Once they'd each received a pass card, the cadets raced off to find the change rooms, jostling and joking down the long, tiled hallway. Andy handed out the pass cards to Zeb, Les, and Kate. Meyers had volunteered to do grocery duty today, and Trokof had asked for an afternoon of solitude. Andy had worried about this request and also saw Kate's concern, but Trokof had insisted all he needed was a few hours of quiet to re-set, and he'd be fine. Andy had backed off immediately but just before they'd left for the wet hike to the bus, Andy had seen Kate talking quietly to Trokof. Her tone had been low, her face serious, and her gestures a combination of pleading and insisting. Andy wasn't sure exactly what she had said to the drill instructor but when Kate looked up, a moment of understanding passed between them.

Andy, Les, and Kate walked the long hall to the change rooms. Les and Kate were going to use the treadmills while Andy and Zeb worked the troop. Kate was going only reluctantly, Les having to coax her with pleas of female bonding. It was the chance to watch Food TV while running that had finally won Kate over. Andy changed quickly, tied up the laces on her shoes, and pulled her long hair back into a low ponytail. As she walked down the hallway, she tried to remember how long it had been since she'd set foot in a university gym. She'd spent most of her undergrad at the UBC athletic complex: four nights a week for basketball practice, games every weekend during regular season, travelling between provinces for championships. As she pushed open the doors for gym two, Andy did a quick count to make sure everyone was accounted for. Listening to Zeb's commands echo around the gym, punctuated by short, sharp whistle blasts, Andy remembered what being part of a team was like—to follow commands, to be critically aware of where your team was on the court, to be able to anticipate your opponent's next move and see two plays ahead, adjusting and flexing your muscles to choreograph and execute a perfectly timed play. She remembered what it was like to know every single member of your team was working just as hard to achieve the same goal. As the afternoon wore on, Andy felt a new appreciation for Troop 18. She had almost forgotten to see their dedication and commitment to each other as admirable.

As they approached the three hour mark, Zeb giving them time to wind down and cool their muscles, the next group began trickling in. Andy guessed by their tall, lean bodies, their heavily muscled legs and the massive, expensive sneakers, that the university's men's basketball team had just arrived.

The troop continued following Zeb's instructions, but awkwardly now, very aware of the new audience. Andy caught Zeb's eye, and gave a quick, sharp movement with her hand across her neck, telling him to cut it short and wrap it up. Andy didn't like the way the newcomers automatically edged in on the court, the aggressiveness of their volume, their display of ownership over the space. Zeb released the cadets, reminding them they had two hours until they were to meet the instructors out front. Andy stood back and watched as they walked past the men's basketball team. They'd fallen into loose formation, Prewitt-Hayes and Petit at the front, Awad, Foster, Hellman, and Shipman forming an almost evenly spaced barrier between the basketball team and the rest of the troop. But nothing happened, and the two groups gave no acknowledgement of each other.

"Assholes," Zeb muttered under his breath beside Andy as they followed the troop back into the hallway. Andy could feel him bristling with defensive anger, his eyes darting back and forth from the door to the team behind them. The three hour workout hadn't seemed to work its magic yet. Zeb seemed more up than down.

"We're done, the troop's done. Leave it alone, Zeb." Andy had been careful to not push Zeb these last two weeks. But she needed Zeb to keep it together, and she knew him well enough by now to recognize when he needed an outlet. "Kate and Les are going to supervise the troop at the pool, so why don't you take the next few hours off? Meet us back at the bus by five."

The gym door locked shut with a metallic clang. Zeb glanced through the safety glass window.

"Okay, sure," he said, running a hand over the short bristles of his shaved head. "See you in two."

Andy found her way back to the women's change room and decided to take her own advice of a very long, hot shower. The steady stream loosened the muscles in her shoulders and neck, and the steam worked its way into her lungs, seeming to warm her from the inside out. Andy let herself lose track of time, knowing Kate and Les had the troop for now, giving herself a moment of reprieve from the weight of responsibilities that had become her everyday life at Camp Depot. Reluctantly, Andy turned off the shower, towelled herself dry and pulled on her uniform over her still damp body. She pulled tightly at the belt around her waist, feeling uncomfortably light without the holsters she'd left back at camp. Andy bypassed the hair dryers, knowing from experience that they were useless, instead twisting her wet hair up off her neck before grabbing her bag and heading out.

Andy followed the smell of chlorine to the pool, hearing shouts and shrieks echo off the tall ceilings. She looked through the large observation windows along the corridor and could see most of the troop was playing water polo. A few sat on the side, dangling their legs in the water. Andy craned her neck up to look into the stands and saw Kate and Les with their feet up on the railing, sharing a bag of cheesies from the vending machine. Andy smiled to herself and walked back to the foyer.

Finding a semi-quiet corner near the wall of windows, Andy pulled out her phone and her notebook, looking out into the dark and rainy afternoon. She checked her messages first, prioritizing the six calls from work, circling the two she would follow up with on her own, and underlining the ones she would forward to the sergeant covering her cases back in Vancouver.

Andy paused to watch the sky open up in a torrential downpour, the intense roar only minimally dulled by the layers of glass. Mesmerized, Andy watched the rain and the few unlucky people racing through it until the intensity eventually lessened. She checked the time on her phone. The cadets would be getting out of the pool in about ten minutes. Andy dialled her supervisor's number and left a message with his secretary. She controlled the urge to drum her fingers on the table while she waited.

Instead she started a list, kicking herself when she realized they should have combined today's trip with their weekly drug screen. Someone would have to come into town in the next few days for that. With the rain pinning them down at Camp, the other instructors might like the change of scenery to come into town and drop off the samples, even if it meant being responsible for sixteen mini bottles of urine.

The phone vibrated on the table, beeping importantly. Andy checked the display, saw the main line for headquarters, and picked up. Their conversation was short, Staff Sgt. Finns checking in quickly between meetings. She updated the limited information she had on the troop, reassured him that everything was fine, then signed off. Andy spun her phone in her hands. Suddenly it vibrated again and Andy saw that it was headquarters again. Curious about what Finns had forgotten to tell her, Andy pressed at the pick-up button.

"Wylie! It's me, Jack."

As if after all these years she needed the reminder. She only allowed one person to call her Wylie.

"Hi, Jack."

"I heard from Lydia that you just checked in with Finns. How's it going out there? How's the troop? How's Kate?"

Andy didn't bother asking how he already knew about a conversation with Finns from three minutes ago. Jack heard everything.

"Camp is fine, the troop is fine, and Kate is fine. She says she misses you. What's up Jack?"

"Okay…well…I hadn't really done anything with that list you faxed over to me a week ago. You did say it wasn't a priority," he added nervously, like he wasn't sure if Andy was going to give him shit. Not that she ever did. The worst she ever did was glare at him or cut him off when he started to babble or go on a tangent.

"Okay, so I decided to do something similar to a Boolean search, using the phraseology of the numbers as opposed to the specific digits. Are you following?"

"No, not at all. Skip to the part where you found something."

"Okay, the majority of the hits I got were from parenting sites and mom blogs, which I disregarded as irrelevant at first. The second highest number of hits came from horticulture sites, looking at mixtures of nitrogen, potash, and potassium and comparing those to types of growth and areas of coverage."

Jack stopped to take a loud, fortifying sip of something, probably coffee. Knowing she was in for a long explanation, Andy wished she had her own fortifying substance.

"So I spent way longer on that thread than I should have before I actually went back and looked at the specific numbers in the charts and realized the quantities didn't make sense for it to be fertilizer."

"And the context doesn't really add up either," Andy said.

"Right, that too," Jack said, somewhat sheepishly. Andy wasn't annoyed, though. She appreciated that Jack wasn't afraid to pursue an avenue that didn't make any sense at first glance. It had given them valuable leads more often than she could count.

"So you went back to the mom blogs," Andy said, knowing her partner and the way his mind worked. "What did you find?"

"Right, so two things popped up on the mom blogs. One was basal body temperature charts, daily tracking of women's temperatures to correspond to their monthly cycles to show peak periods of optimum fertility. These were sometimes then compared to various levels of hormones detected in a blood test."

"Okay…" Andy said, this explanation forcing her brain to angle off sharply in a direction she wasn't expecting. She shifted rapidly through the information, adding context, motivation, environment and plenty of her own speculation, waiting to see if something clicked. Nothing. "You said two things popped up. What was the other one?"

"The other one was more simple. It was multiple discussion threads and postings about how much acetaminophen or ibuprophen to give to infants and toddlers, and the question of whether going by age or weight was more appropriate."

This twigged for Andy. She disregarded the context of the mom sites, the type of meds, and the age. They were back to drugs. "And when you look at the specific numbers from the chart we found?" Andy said.

"This is where I'd need Kate," Jack said apologetically. "It makes sense one column is looking at days of the month and the second column is weight in kilos. The third column could be dosage, but I don't have a clue what the dosage could be and I couldn't put enough parameters in to make my searching find anything more relevant."

"So I need Kate," Andy said, scribbling notes so she could fill Kate in on the hypothesis Jack's search had just outlined.

"Of course you do, Wylie. I've known that since the day we met her."

"Very funny," Andy said, scanning her notes, making sure she had everything. He wasn't wrong. Jack had always known what Kate meant to her. He'd been able to see what Andy had been so desperately trying to ignore as she and Kate worked their first case together in Seattle. Sometimes having a partner who could see through you was helpful. Sometimes it was a pain in the ass. "Okay, I'll have Kate look at the chart with that lens. If we get a chance, we'll text you before we hit the dead zone near Camp. Anything else comes up, send a message to me through Kurtz, okay?"

"Yep. Got it. Over and out, Wylie."

Andy rolled her eyes and hit the disconnect button on her phone. She twirled it in her hands again as she scanned the deserted foyer, thinking about her conversation with Jack, eliminating nothing, adding facts as they fit or presented themselves as relevant. She became distracted by a movement in the window, a play of light against the darkness of the day. She realized it was a reflection from down the hall. Though the image was distorted by light and distance, she had a fairly good view of cadets Greg Shipman and Hawke Foster having what seemed like a heated debate. Shipman was shaking his head, looking left and right, anywhere but at Foster. Foster was leaning in, like he was trying to convince Shipman of something with the intensity of his stance. Shipman raised a placating hand but Foster slapped it away.

Andy half rose out of her chair then stopped herself. She should let them work this out. She could hear them now that she was paying attention. Foster's voice was sharp and angry, Shipman's placating. Foster gestured sharply at Shipman, tapping him in the centre of the chest. It was a provoking gesture intended to get a reaction, but it didn't. Shipman put his hand on Foster's shoulders, shook him slightly, still shaking his head. Shipman's whole demeanour screamed an almost casual acceptance of inevitability. Apparently, Foster refused to accept.

Andy's phone buzzed in her hand, and she looked down quickly. It was a text from Kate, asking where she was. Andy quickly thumbed out 'foyer' and was hitting send even as she looked up to see what was going on with Shipman and Foster. A third person showed up, his face puffy and distorted in the reflection so it took a moment for Andy to recognize the cadet. It was Jacob Frances. Both cadets were turned toward him so Andy couldn't see their expressions or guess how Frances had changed the dynamic of the argument. Frances spoke, checked his watch, shrugged, and then he punched both cadets on the shoulder and walked back the way he had come. Shipman and Foster stood still, then looked quickly at each other and followed their troop mate down the hallway.

Andy debated whether or not she should pursue the cadets. She wished one of the other instructors had seen it, so she had someone else's opinion to consider. Even Zeb's seemingly biased view of the cadets would be helpful right now. Andy checked her watch, like Frances had just done a moment ago.

Nineteen minutes until the cadets were due to check in, which meant Foster, Shipman, and Frances had nineteen minutes of freedom left, and Andy couldn't and shouldn't follow them. She sighed, checked her notes, scrolled through icons on her phone, and pulled up the picture of the chart she'd taken with her camera phone last week. Andy scanned the numbers, but there was no point. They meant nothing to Andy.

Kate and Les arrived less than a minute later, wandering down the hall, chatting quietly, laughing easily. As they approached the table where Andy was sitting, Kate looked up and smiled, and then she seemed to be scanning Andy's face, her body language, the way she held her notebook in one hand, her phone in the other. Kate's ability to read her and know when she was keeping something back had been unnerving for Andy in the beginning. It had rapidly become a lifeline for Andy, though. A necessity more than a convenience. Which was why their two months apart had been hard, of course. Jack was right. Andy needed Kate.

"What is it?" Kate said, sitting across from Andy.

"Jack has a hypothesis regarding that chart we found," Andy said quietly, aware her voice could easily carry. She quickly outlined the three hits Jack's search had isolated, allowing both Kate and Les to make their own judgements about the relevance of each. Kate asked to see the chart again and scanned it on the small screen, and then she asked for Andy's pen and notebook. Andy and Les watched as Kate sketched her own chart, putting the numbers one to thirty-one in the first column and filling in numbers beside that in the second. Reading the chart upside down, Andy figured out she was translating what they suspected was the weights column from kilos into pounds.

"If Jack is right, this column tracks daily weight fluctuations in an individual who weighs at most two hundred and three pounds and at their least, one hundred eighty-seven," Kate concluded, turning the chart around so Les and Andy could take a look.

"That's a pretty big fluctuation," Les said. "Especially since the chart only shows twelve days' worth of data.

"True. Given the fluctuations as well as the numbers we're looking at, I'd guess male. Females don't lose weight that rapidly."

"Bastards," Les muttered reflexively. "Who fits that in the troop?"

Kate tilted her head to the side. "Off the top of my head, Foster, Frances, Mancini, Awad…and I'd put Shipman in there, too, but at the heavier end. I'd say he's minimum of high one-nineties. I can double-check the cadet files when we get back to camp."

"Could any of the women fit the profile?" Andy said. She would guess no, but wanted to hear the reassurance of another opinion.

"Hellman at her most muscular would just reach into the one-eighty range. So I'd discount that possibility for now unless you get something else to suggest the profile is female rather than male."

Kate talked like a cop, building on evidence and fact, holding every nuance and suggestion as relevant until it could be definitively disregarded. Her brain naturally worked that way, sorting and isolating and scaffolding information into a cohesive whole.

"Andy…" Les said quietly.

Andy looked up. Cadets Prewitt-Hayes and Shandly had just come around the corner, talking quietly, their hair still wet from the swim and shower. Andy cursed in her head and checked her watch. Only four minutes until the cadets had to report back. Kate folded the piece of paper before slipping it into her coat pocket.

"Later," Les muttered under her breath. "Let's get the team together after cadet lights out."

Kate mumbled an agreement, but Andy was busy observing the cadets. They'd been joined now by Hellman and McCrae, Petit, and Awad. The cadets moved down the hall in twos and threes, and Andy watched them with a sinking feeling in her stomach. She saw forced casualness in the way they spoke to each other and circulated around the foyer in choreographed neutrality. The troop was attempting to pull their camouflaged blind around them, attempting to go unnoticed.

"Shit," Andy said, drawing Kate and Les's attention. "They're hiding something."

Just then Zeb walked in through the front door. He shook his head and body out like a dog, water spraying out from his jacket as he approached the table where Andy, Kate, and Les were sitting.

"Hey," Zeb said. He seemed calm and in control. Good. Who knew what the hell Troop 18 was going to try to pull right now?

Andy stood, and Kate and Les followed. "Did you see Frances or Shipman or Foster while you were out there, Constable Zeb?"

"No. But the rain's so heavy I couldn't see shit. Should I go back out? Are they missing?"

"No, they have another two minutes." She watched as more and more of the troop arrived. She lowered her voice until the instructors and Kate had to lean in to hear what she was saying. "I saw Shipman and Foster having a verbal fight about fifteen minutes ago," Andy said. "Then Frances arrived, said something, and left. Shipman and Foster followed."

"Andy...look..." Les said.

Shipman walked in through the front doors, hands shoved into his pockets, and went to stand with Petit, Awad, and Prewitt-Hayes. He didn't look at the rest of the troop or the instructors. He simply held still. While Andy was processing Shipman's suspicious entrance and body language, Foster arrived from down the hall with a wet jacket balled up under his arm. The troop shifted and made room for Foster. Andy thought of the way the troop had almost unconsciously made a barrier between themselves and the men's basketball team earlier. Right now though, they seemed to consider Andy, Kate, Les, and Zeb the threat. Andy took a step to the side and just caught the look Foster was giving Shipman. A sharp shake of his head, a warning glare. Shipman gave the smallest of shrugs and looked away.

"It's five," Zeb said tightly.

Andy began a head count.

Just as she did, the men's basketball team arrived, this time moving *en masse* down the hallway. Their noise and movement filled the already crowded foyer as they headed to the doors with their gym bags slung diagonally across their broad shoulders. Andy felt the tension immediately, and she willed the team to just keep moving. But their momentum slowed and Troop 18 mobilized.

Andy didn't see it start. She heard a raised voice near the front, a short response, then a challenging question thrown carelessly into the crowd, and a low, threatening statement. Zeb and Andy both started moving, aware of the tight tension, the restless, nervous shift of thirty people in the lobby. As Andy was trying to move her way to the front, the troop suddenly shrank back and then surged forward as a shout rose up. Andy began pulling at cadets, moving them forcefully backward and out of the way.

Behind her, Les called individual names, the warning in her tone sharp and clear. Andy was at the front now, watching Shipman fighting against Petit's hold on him, cursing and challenging one of the basketball players. He was also being held back by his teammates. By the look on both their faces, the red welt under Shipman's eye, and the bloody nose of the basketball player, they'd both managed to get a good hit in before being hauled off.

"You fucking asshole!" Shipman yelled across at the other guy, even as he was being hauled farther and farther back by Petit.

"Nice one, douche troop," the basketball player sneered, pushing his teammates away but standing his ground. It took him just a second to register Andy's presence. He seemed to calculate her height, her uniform, and her stance, and he settled for a smirk.

"What's the problem?" Andy said, keeping her eyes on the team in front of her while monitoring the troop in her peripheral vision. Shipman had finally shaken off Petit, but the large man continued to use his bulk as a barrier.

"No problem, no problem," the basketball player said, disrespect heavy in his tone. He wiped the small trickle of blood under his nose onto his sleeve. "Just a friendly disagreement." Andy didn't ask. It wouldn't do any good to hash it out in front of everyone. She could see the desk clerk talking on the phone, her eyes wide. Andy hoped this would be done by the time campus security showed up.

"Good, then you can go. All of you," Andy said, indicating the whole team. Zeb edged his way to the front of the crowd, his body tense. She really hoped he would stay out of this.

Clearly, the player did not like being kicked out of his own gym. His whole demeanour changed from disrespectful indifference to a reckless, seething mass of anger. He puffed out his chest, stretched to his fullest height, and balled his hands into fists at his side. Andy didn't try to match his postural challenge. She waited him out and stared him down.

"Fuck it," he finally said, half turning to the rest of his team. "Let's go." He picked up his bag and swung it over his head, letting it fall heavily over his shoulder. The smirk was back, not aimed at Andy this time, but over her shoulder. Andy assumed it was meant for Shipman, but she didn't turn to look. She monitored the progression of the basketball team as they made their way to the front door, a silent hostility hanging between them and the troop at her back.

Just as they reached the large glass doors, Andy saw the guy lean in and say something quietly to Shipman. The cadet surged forward, but the basketball player moved easily out of reach, laughing. Andy moved to intervene but Foster was quicker, placing himself between Shipman and the front doors, pushing Shipman back toward his troop. Zeb suddenly yelled from the opposite end of the foyer, catching even Andy by surprise.

"Troop 18, in formation!" If Andy hadn't been looking, she would have sworn it was Sgt. Trokof. "Now! I want you in formation *now!*" His voice echoed around the glassed-in foyer. The cadets fell into line, the command triggering an automatic reaction. Shipman had to be partially dragged, but even he pulled himself into position, breathing hard. The troop had fallen into four neat rows of four. Everyone was accounted for.

After a brief conversation with the instructors, Zeb loaded the now-silent troop on the bus. Shipman avoided eye contact, his normally jovial face a mask devoid of any emotion. Shandly sat beside him and spoke quietly to him under her breath, a constant monologue he didn't respond to. Andy thumbed out a brief text to Lincoln and Finns in the near darkness of the bus, Kate sitting silently beside her. Heath was going to have a field day with this one.

Shipman was out of chances, she knew that. The thought caused anger and disappointment to war in her stomach. Andy stabbed at the send button on her phone, having to hit it twice in her haste to get it sent before they hit the dead zone back to camp. Kate looked at her silently, her concerned expression coming into sharp focus as they passed a street light then falling into darkness again as they drove up into the mountain. They both knew everything had just changed. Andy felt the spectre of failure rise up out of the darkness. She quashed it with an angry twitch of her body, shoving her phone back into the pocket of her coat. Andy knew Troop 18 could very possibly go down in flames, and she intended to be there every step of the way.

Chapter Twelve

Andy shouldered her way out of her wet storm coat, taking a moment to hang it on the rack in the front hallway of the main house. She was soaked from her long walk up the driveway where Zeb had dropped her off before taking the silent and anxious troop up to camp. She was also irritable and on edge.

"Could you bring a little more water in with you, Andy?" Kurtz said, walking into the front hallway with her hands on her hips, a damp dishcloth slung over one shoulder. She still looked like a cop. It didn't matter if she was wearing jeans and a comfortable looking grey sweater and she was clearly in the middle of doing dishes. Kurtz was a cop and always would be. And right now her cop instinct was obviously kicking in. "What is it?"

Andy stood in the front entrance, unlacing and pulling off her boots while she filled Kurtz in on their episode at the athletic complex.

"What do you need from me?" Kurtz said bluntly, not offering an opinion because Andy hadn't asked for one.

"The phone," Andy said. "I need to take this to Lincoln."

Kurtz indicated the main room with a nod of her head, and Andy actually paid attention to the low rumble of quiet voices she'd heard since she walked in.

"Guests," she said. "Take the phone to the summer kitchen, if you want. Let me know if you need anything else."

It made sense, Andy decided as she grabbed the phone off its base and stepped across the soft, patterned carpeting. Kurtz opening a B&B in her retirement made perfect sense. She had always been accommodating, always more than willing to go to whatever lengths someone needed her to go. Always ready with a joke, advice, or an offer of shelter.

Andy stepped into the unheated room off the back porch, which served as a store room for the B&B, but was also a place for Kurtz to escape to if her guests were driving her crazy. Andy settled in on an old, overstuffed chair beside a lamp on a small coffee table, took a breath, and dialled Lincoln's number.

Shipman was finished. The directive Lincoln handed down to Andy in the first thirty seconds of their conversation was not a surprise. They'd been more than fair, and they'd been perfectly clear with the cadet. Andy knew it made sense. She agreed fully with the decision. If Shipman was unable to handle himself during the six month training, he had no future with the RCMP. Still, Andy was angry.

She sat stiffly in the armchair, staring grimly and unseeing at the boxes and bits of furniture around her as she listened to Lincoln and answered his questions. The decision had been made, and the committee would finalize the paperwork in the morning. But Lincoln wanted to come up himself to deliver the news. He asked a lot of questions about the incident, particularly about the rest of the troop. He asked for Andy's best guess as to what the troop was attempting to hide.

Andy could only offer her opinion that the troop had once again used camouflage and diversion to cover up something involving Foster and Frances and Shipman. But they hadn't all agreed on it. Lincoln jumped onto the fight between Shipman and Foster. It was the only crack they had ever seen in the troop. Lincoln wanted Andy to exploit it. When Andy argued, her instinct telling her it was the wrong move, Lincoln quickly changed his language. Pressure, he said. Apply some pressure. And prepare for the fallout.

They were just in the middle of arguing over the best action to take to accomplish this when Andy heard the creak of the summer kitchen door. Kurtz came in, and her blue eyes were intense, serious. She was holding the radio in one hand.

"What is it?" Andy pulled the phone away from her mouth, reading the urgency in Kurtz's stance.

"We need to get up to camp," Kurtz said. "Meyers just radioed down. Something's wrong with Trokof. Kate wants to get him to the hospital."

Andy launched herself out of the chair, quickly relaying the message to Lincoln. Lincoln swore reflexively, worry heavy in his voice, then said he was leaving tonight and would be up in the morning. Andy disconnected the call and followed Kurtz back down the hallway, listening to the rain hammering against the roof.

"It gets worse," Kurtz said, handing Andy the radio as she swung a large rain jacket over her shoulders, shoving her arms in and zipping it up in one fluid motion. "The road's beginning to wash out. A small slide opened up as the troop was making their way back into camp about twenty minutes ago. Meyers says the road could have stabilized or another four slides could have materialized by now. Hard to tell. He's getting the troop together. I said we'd radio when we got to the top of the highway."

Andy zipped up her cold, soaked jacket, shoving her hat on her head before pulling open the heavy door. Kurtz reached into the bed of the truck, grabbed a beat-up plastic container and handed it to Andy before they pulled themselves into the cab. "There should be flashlights and flares, take whatever you need."

Andy tested each baton, throwing the dead ones on the floor. She shoved five flashlights and seven flares into various pockets before closing up the container. She tried to visualize their next steps. "If the road's washed out, we're going to have to get Trokof to the Yukon—" Andy started to say, but Kurtz interrupted.

"Plan A is to get Trokof to the Yukon. Even that part of the road is a mess according to Meyers, so we'll have to see if we can back the Yukon down to the highway. Plan B is to get the sergeant all the way to my truck."

Andy's next question was cut off by the radio in her hand. "Camp Depot to Sgt. Wyles. Kurtz, you there?" It was Les, her voice stressed.

"It's Wyles. Go ahead, Sgt. Manitou."

"Andy, Kate says Trokof is deteriorating faster than she's comfortable with. She wants an ambulance waiting at the highway. Can you put a call into Emergency Services before you're out of cell range?"

Andy cursed in her head, trying to scare away the worry in her chest. Kurtz pulled over, stabbing at the button for her four-way flashers, the yellow lights blinking on and off as Andy pulled out her notebook awkwardly, made notes about Trokof's age, symptoms, and stats. Kate was in the background, calling out information to Les, her voice tinny and sounding very far away.

"Did you copy all that?" Les said, her voice cutting out a little at the end.

"Copy," Andy said loudly into the receiver, not entirely sure Les had heard. Andy pulled out her phone, tilting it towards the light to see if they were in range. "Take us back half a click," Andy said to Kurtz. Kurtz reversed down the side of the highway. Andy wasn't sure exactly how she could see anything.

"Try now," Kurtz said, slamming the truck back into park.

One bar. Andy hoped it would be enough. She called Kamloops emergency services, identifying herself, their location, and the vitals of the patient. The dispatcher was efficient and calm, almost bored, but police, ambulance, and fire would be dispatched to the scene. The dispatcher wanted Andy to stay on the line, but Andy explained that they needed to help the patient down from camp. When the dispatcher argued, Andy pointed at Kurtz to keep driving up to camp. Andy gave her own and Kurtz's cell numbers then let the cell tower disconnect the call for her.

Kurtz pulled into the entrance of the road to camp, killed the engine, and started to get out. Andy put an arm out to stop her.

"We need someone to stay at the highway, Kurtz."

Kurtz looked supremely annoyed. Andy was not supposed to be giving her orders, but Andy didn't have time to worry about Kurtz's feelings. Trokof didn't have time. "Take the radio. We'll need a link to the outside world and someone to direct emergency services in when they arrive."

To Kurtz's credit, she immediately slammed the door shut again and snatched up the radio. "Keep me updated, Wyles," she said, her blue eyes hard.

Andy nodded and opened her door, pulling out one of the flashlights. Andy started at a run, her footfalls landing wetly but solidly in the hard-packed gravel at first, but she soon bogged down in the softness of the loose rocks, the structural weakness just holding the road together. Her flashlight picked up the first wash-out between the highway and the Yukon. She jumped it, her brain working overtime thinking about getting Trokof back down this path.

Andy slowed, gravel and mud now sucking at her boots. The second wash-out was larger, the edges crumbling before her in the bright beam of the flashlight. She was pretty sure both these wash-outs were new since the troop had come down, and alarm rose in her chest as she calculated how quickly they were losing the road. Andy kept slogging through, wiping rain impatiently out of her eyes.

When she saw the third wash-out, Andy's heart sank. She stopped at its edge and aimed the beam of light up to see its origin. The torrent of water rushed down off the hill, diverted on one side by a boulder and on the other by a tree with massive, smooth roots that looked almost like a water sluice. Andy swore, her voice lost in the rain. The culverts never had a chance. She looked back to the wash-out in front of her, stamped her feet in the gravel a few times, and then backed up a couple steps and took a running start.

She launched off her right foot, but as the muscles in her thighs propelled her body up and forward, the ground softened and started to give way. The shifting weight of the flashlights and flares also unbalanced her, and she barely managed to clear the stream of water. Andy landed awkwardly and painfully on the other side, but she didn't stop or look back. She was too busy coming up with Plan C. Getting Trokof back down the road was impossible.

Andy arrived in camp moments later, briefly confused to see cadets ripping apart picnic tables in the quad, tossing two by fours into a haphazard pile. The cadets looked up as Andy approached but didn't stop what they were doing. Andy could make out Zeb, Mancini, and Awad through the blur of rain and dark.

"Where's Sgt. Trokof?" Andy said to Zeb.

Zeb pointed with the hammer he was using to pull nails free. "With the doc, medical cabin," he shouted over the rain.

Andy pointed to the pile of wood. "Traction?"

"Yep, and to bridge the wash-out."

Andy shook her head. "We can't go that way. New plan. We're going to have to take him down the mountain to the main house. Keep going though, we'll embed those boards in the mud for the upper part of the path. Hey, pass me your radio."

Zeb gave her his radio and went back to his task. Andy radioed Kurtz as she walked and told her about the road. She instructed her to drive back down to the house, call emergency services, and update their location to the main house. Kurtz swore, copied, and signed off. Andy shoved the radio into her pocket beside a few of the flares and took the steps into the cabin two at a time before pulling the door open.

Trokof had his eyes closed, in a half-sitting position on the bed, his skin an unhealthy grey colour. Kate instructed him to breathe in and out as she listened with her stethoscope pressed against his back. Trokof opened his eyes briefly when he heard the door, then closed them again, but not before Andy could see pain and a sad humiliation in his eyes. Trokof's jacket lay across his knees. His rumpled shirt was unbuttoned, and Andy could see the man's thin chest covered with light grey hair rising and falling as he strained to breathe.

Andy stood dripping on the mat, taking in Trokof's sad appearance, feeling awkward seeing him half-dressed, diminished, and ill. When Kate finished, she looked up at Andy and gently pushed Trokof back to a lying position, moved aside his shirt, and listened to his heart. Andy read the signs of Kate's stress. Kate wasn't panicked but definitely worried. Andy felt her own body calm slightly, felt the adrenaline in her body kick back down to a normal, functioning level.

Before Andy could say anything, Les came out of the back room with Kate's medical kit gripped in one hand.

"Andy, thank God you're here. Kate's got everything prepped, Trokof says he's ready to move, and Zeb and Meyers are mobilizing the troop, coming up with a plan to get him down the road to the ambulance—"

Andy cut her off. "The road is no longer an option. We're going to have to get Sgt. Trokof down the mountain to the main house."

Les's shoulders dropped with this news, her face stricken.

"Les, it's okay. We've got some time," Kate said calmly from Trokof's bedside. She turned to Andy. "Will there be an ambulance waiting?"

"Yes, and police and fire are on the way. I'm hoping they'll get up here in time to meet us part way. But I think we should assume we're on our own."

Kate nodded and Trokof groaned.

"Is the pain getting worse, Sgt. Trokof?" Kate said.

"No, the pain is the same, but you can add extreme humiliation to my list of symptoms." Andy appreciated Trokof making the effort to speak, but the thin, slightly slurred sound of his voice made Andy even more nervous.

Kate smiled and lay a hand on his shoulder but didn't comment. Trokof closed his eyes again.

"How quickly do we need to move?" Andy said.

"He's stable for now but his symptoms—heart arrhythmia, difficulty breathing, and dizziness—are becoming more pronounced. More than anything, we need to get him on a monitor to find out what's going on." She took a breath. "He's not emergent, Andy, but we need to get him to a hospital so we can keep him that way."

Les stood to the side, chewing on her fingers, a scared and seemingly unconscious motion. Andy was surprised. She had assumed that being a mother of four and a cop, Les would have better reserves than this. Andy checked her judgement. It was irrelevant right now. Les seemed incapable of independent thought or action, so Andy needed to give her something to do.

"Les, go make sure Meyers and Zeb know of the change in plans. Tell them they've got five minutes, then we'll meet in here and run through a step by step of what we're going to do to get to the main house. Got it?"

"Yes. New plan, five minutes, meet back here."

Les opened the door, looked at Kate's medical bag in her hand and seemed momentarily confused. Andy held her hand out and took it from her gently. Once she was gone, Andy looked up at Kate whose face mirrored Andy's look of disbelief.

"She's been a mess since I came to check on Trokof just after we got back," Kate whispered.

"You don't have to whisper on my account," Trokof mumbled without opening his eyes.

Kate looked down at him again and walked over to where Andy stood, still dripping wet, by the door. Kate slipped her warm hand into Andy's cold wet one and gave a reassuring squeeze. Andy returned it.

"Any idea what happened?" Andy said in a low voice.

"According to him, symptoms began about three days after arriving at camp. They were very mild at first but have progressed significantly over the last several days, peaking at around noon today when he realized he couldn't get out of bed without the pain in his chest becoming unbearable."

"And he didn't radio down to Kurtz," Andy said, the worry making her voice sound annoyed. This could have been avoided if only she'd gone with her instinct.

"He left the radio in the kitchen cabin after he had something to eat this morning," Kate said quietly. "There's nothing we could have done differently, Andy."

Andy didn't say anything. She didn't necessarily agree with Kate, but she knew it wasn't the most pressing issue right now. "Stress?" Andy spoke aloud a half-formed thought. "Did stress bring this on?"

Kate shook her head. "He has no known risk factors for heart disease or vascular conditions. Stress could make symptoms worse, but not cause the severity of what we're seeing."

They were both silent, watching Trokof's thin chest as it rose and fell. He was clutching his jacket in both hands like his uniform had become a lifeline. Andy's heart ached for the man.

"So you're saying it's just coincidence he became sick after he arrived at camp? Meaning it could have happened even if he'd never left Regina?"

"I really don't know, Andy," Kate said "It doesn't make sense that it's environmental, and the only meds he takes are vitamins of a dose low enough to be innocuous. He says his diet hasn't changed all that much since he came up here, possibly less red meat than he's used to but generally he's been eating and drinking the same…"

Kate trailed off and Andy, alert to the sudden tightness in Kate's shoulders, watched her carefully, waiting for her to finish the sentence. Instead, she turned away from Andy and walked quickly back over to the bed. She lay a gentle but insistent hand on Trokof's arm. He awoke immediately, his eyes growing wide and taking a moment to adjust.

"What is it?" he mumbled. "Time to go?"

"No, not yet. I just had a question. What did you eat this morning after we left camp?"

Trokof tried to wet his lips with a dry tongue, and Kate reached for a plastic glass of water on a table behind his head and handed it to him silently. Andy waited impatiently while he took a sip, wiped his chin, and handed it back.

"Tea and toast, like I always do. I had some orange juice while I was waiting for the kettle to boil. Not much of anything, really…" His voice petered out, like he'd forgotten the question. His eyes drooped again, blinked, and then he was out. Kate frowned, touched two fingers expertly to his neck and held them there without moving for a minute before walking back to Andy.

"I need to see the troop. All the cadets. Now."

Andy didn't quite understand what had happened, what facts had just emerged or what leap in logic Kate had just made. But it wasn't Andy's mystery to solve.

"I'll have them assembled in two minutes."

"Thanks," Kate said curtly, her thoughts obviously somewhere else. She started to move back toward the bed then stopped as Andy opened the door. "Wait, I need your phone." Andy reached into her inner pocket and handed her the useless cell phone silently. Kate took it without a word and Andy left the cabin, a suspicion forming in her mind.

Two minutes later, the medical cabin was filled to capacity. Those who had been outside were soaked and filthy, and the smell of wet mud permeated the room. The energy in the room was palpable as adrenaline and purpose flowed from one body to the next. The cadets sought each other out with their eyes, updated their component of the plan, disagreed, improvised, and revised. It was chaos.

"Troop 18, I need your attention and your silence," Andy called out. The troop quieted, and Trokof stirred on the bed.

"What is it…where's the troop…" Trokof mumbled, struggling to sit up, then going very pale and putting a hand to his chest, eyes wide. Kate pushed him back gently, spoke very quietly and he drifted again, his breathing laboured.

The cadets looked on in absolute silence. Andy saw fear, disbelief, and an echo of her own earlier awkwardness reflected in their expressions. Some of them had clearly forgotten that in just a few moments they were going to attempt to take a real, sick human being down a treacherous mountain path in the dark and rain. Reality settled heavily on the room. And then Kate started to speak.

"I know why you were all brought up here to Camp Depot. We all do. Sgt. Wyles, myself, Sgt. Trokof, your instructors—we all know why you are here at camp and not at Depot. We've known for weeks that you are hiding something, and that it has to do with drugs." Kate said it all in a quiet, firm voice. She had everyone's attention. The cadets were silent and still, all eyes on Kate.

"And right now I don't care about any of that. I don't care what you're hiding or how you've been hiding it. I don't care how hard you've worked to protect each other. Troop 18 has crossed a line, and I'm going to give you the benefit of the doubt and say you don't even know it. So I'm going to ask you one very important question and I hope like hell you give me the answer."

Dead silence except for the sound of twenty people breathing in the stuffy cabin air.

"Is there something in the kitchen cabin Sgt. Trokof could have unknowingly ingested in the last two weeks that could possibly explain his current condition?"

Cursing, exclamations of disbelief, pale faces and wide eyes, Petit putting his head in his hands, Frances taking two shaky steps back until he hit the cabin wall. Prewitt-Hayes gasped, covered her mouth with a shaking hand and stepped forward.

"Yes...oh, God, how did he..."

"Stop!"

Shipman pushed his way from the back of the room. He must have been one of the cadets working outside in the rain. His track suit was a ruined mess, completely covered from head to toe in mud. *Not a cadet*, Andy reminded herself of her earlier conversation with Lincoln. *Not a cadet anymore.*

"Tracey, stop. It's mine. I'll tell them," Shipman said but he wasn't looking at her, he was looking at Kate, his eyes intense. The rest of the troop were shaking their heads, Hawke Foster looked furious, and the rest of the troop looked like they were in pain. But no one stopped him from speaking. "It's methadone. He must have been drinking the orange juice. It's liquid methadone."

Andy heard the word, let the fact settle and the pieces fall into place. Then she saw Les leaning against the door, her face pale, her arms wrapped around her body. Andy turned her attention back to Kate, who was showing Shipman Andy's phone with the image of the chart.

"Are these numbers the individual dosages that were administered or the total amount that would have been mixed in the orange juice?"

Shipman obviously didn't know. He looked helplessly at Kate.

"Projected individual dosage," Prewitt-Hayes said miserably. "I tried to calculate a ratio based on volume of liquid and current weight."

"Tracey, no," Shipman said sharply, turning toward his troop leader.

"What?" Prewitt-Hayes nearly exploded. "Do you think it matters anymore, Greg? We've almost killed him—"

"Enough." Kate's tone was final. She raised her voice, and Trokof stirred on the bed but did not wake. "All of you listen to me. You need to pull together. That's the only way we're going to get Sgt. Trokof out of camp." Kate glanced quickly at Andy, telling her to take over. Then she opened a plastic drawer and started rummaging through her medical kit, pulling out an alcohol swab and a small, capped needle.

"Troop 18," Andy called out, her voice commanding. She needed to pull their attention away from what Kate was doing. "I need one person to tell me the plan. I want every step from this cabin until we load Sgt. Trokof in the back of the ambulance."

Prewitt-Hayes stepped forward and mobilized her troop. "Hellman, bring in the stretcher, and I want the two stretcher bearer teams to step forward."

As the cadets manoeuvred themselves in the small space, Andy checked out the makeshift stretcher. They'd converted one of the folding bathroom doors from the sleeping cabins. The door was lightweight but solid, and the cadets had fed leather and nylon-weave belts through the slats at four points to make sure Trokof was secure during his treacherous journey off the mountain.

"We've got two teams of stretcher bearers," Prewitt-Hayes said, nodding to the cadets who had come forward. "They'll spell each other off as needed. Advance team raise your hand." Two hands shot up. "Advance teams will check out the path and report back to the traction team. Traction team?" Another four hands. "They will be responsible for laying out the two-by-fours in the mud when the advance team calls for them. I'll be a light bearer, along with Awad."

There were adjustments, Andy putting herself on the advance team, Zeb asserting himself as one of the stretcher bearers, Meyers saying he'd lead the traction team.

"We're running out of time," Kate said from Trokof's side. "Let's get him on the stretcher."

Andy and three cadets stepped forward and followed Kate's careful instructions to transfer Trokof from the bed to the stretcher. Kate belted him in, tucking in a wool blanket around the silent and still sergeant. When she was done, Andy handed Kate her jacket from the back of the door while Les shouldered the medical kit like her life depended on it. The troop seemed to hold their collective breath, all eyes on Kate.

"Let's move, Troop 18," Kate said calmly.

"You heard the doctor," Prewitt-Hayes called out. "First stretcher team, you're up. Everyone else, you have thirty seconds to prepare your equipment."

Energy was high and progress was slow as they manoeuvred Sgt. Trokof's stretcher out of the medical cabin and onto the mountain path. The cadets were keyed up, their attention in too many places. Even Andy felt disoriented with shouts lobbed through the dark and rain. Andy pulled in a breath of air, ready to demand everyone's focus, but Prewitt-Hayes beat her to it.

"Pull yourself together, Troop 18! Advance team should be the only one speaking. Second team stretcher bearers fall back unless you're called. Keep formation, keep your focus. We've got this, troop. We will not let Sgt. Trokof down."

From her position at the front of the group, Andy felt a shift as the cadets regrouped and refocused, as if they remembered they didn't need light to communicate. They could seek each other out and anticipate each other's needs. This had been their strength all along.

The group began moving again, boots digging into wet gravel, rain pelting against trees and coats and soaking into the grey blanket that covered Trokof. Andy watched for obstructions and obstacles in the wide arc of her flashlight as she judged the strength of traction underneath her boots. As they left the safety of Camp Depot's only hydro pole and entered the forest, mud and darkness became their enemy. Something about the added layer of dark made Andy nervous. It was potentially the most hazardous part of this trip.

"Foster," Andy called out. "Take these flares and light up a path for us."

Foster ran ahead and soon the crack of the flares and their bright orange glare lit the underside of the trees.

"Traction team, we need you."

Andy quelled her impatience as a halt was called, and the traction team brought forward more wood and kicked it down into the mud until it stuck. Two stretcher bearers called in their sub, then they were moving again.

They had just about passed the last of the flares at the edge of the forest when a shout behind her made Andy tense.

"Shit! I'm losing my grip."

Andy heard the sound of stumbling, a cry of pain, and she dug her boots into the ground, and braced herself for the impact as the stretcher team hit her from behind. Meyers struck her painfully in the back as he tried to stop the downward momentum of the stretcher. Andy turned her shoulder against him, braced one boot down the hill and pushed back. Her boots scraped and slid half a foot, her flashlight hitting the ground and rolling crazily before the momentum stopped abruptly.

"Put him down, put him down," Meyers said, out of breath. He kept hold of the head of the stretcher so Trokof still lay flat. Trokof moaned. Andy could see his eyes, wide open and terrified. No wonder. It must be hell to be strapped down, unable to put out a protective hand to stop a fall.

Stretcher bearers spelled off at Prewitt-Hayes's instruction. Andy bent to pick up her flashlight and when she stood she saw Zeb leaning on Foster, holding his left foot off the ground.

"Kate," Andy called out, getting her attention and pointing at Zeb.

Kate picked her way around the stretcher. "Is it your ankle?"

"Slipped on a rock and twisted it."

"Can you bear weight?"

Zeb put his foot down, then stumbled and swore. Foster steadied him without a word.

"Nothing we can do here," she said bluntly. "Leave your boot on to minimize the swelling. Hawke, can you get him down off the mountain?"

Foster nodded, his face set in grim determination.

"Foster, Zeb, walk right behind the stretcher," Andy instructed. "Let's get moving," she said to the rest of the troop.

Though the rock was slippery, it proved easier for the team to navigate than the mud. The advance team occasionally called out the location of boulders or tree roots, but they were soon off the rock and back on gravel and loose stone again. When Hellman called out in an excited voice, Andy looked up from her constant sweep of the ground to see the main house lit up with the blues, reds, and yellows of an emergency response team. Four firefighters opened the gate to the meadow, their flashlights lighting up the field and flashing off the reflective strips in their uniforms.

A sigh of relief and a ripple of excitement went through the troop. They were close but not there yet.

"Keep it together, Troop 18," Andy warned. "We get Sgt. Trokof into the ambulance, just like we planned."

Andy walked ahead to meet the firefighters as they advanced. "Sgt. Wyles?" Andy couldn't see which body spoke.

"Yes."

"Captain Wilfred and crew. We just arrived on scene." Andy isolated the voice to the man slightly in front of the rest. "It looks like you might not need our services after all."

"I think we're going to make it," Andy said. "Is the ambulance here yet?"

"Yep, they're just playing emergency vehicle Tetris in the driveway at the moment. The ambulance is going to back up to the gate there. How is the patient?"

"Stable for now, according to the doctor," Andy said, intentionally mentioning Kate. Firefighters and paramedics hated cops offering their own medical opinion on anything.

The troop carried Sgt. Trokof through the meadow and the four firefighters guided them on the last leg of their journey. The ambulance backed up to the gate in a swirl of lights and a hail of drawn-out beeps. Efficient and slightly bored-looking paramedics opened the back doors, unlatched the stretcher, and let the frame and wheels fall open and lock. Kate left her position beside Trokof and gave them an update in a low, clipped tone.

Watching them transfer Trokof into the back of the ambulance, Andy realized it had stopped raining. Trokof's face was a sick, dull grey, and he looked like a stranger as the paramedics manhandled him into the rig. Without a backward glance, Kate climbed inside, and the ambulance doors slammed shut with a complete lack of ceremony. A few of the cadets took a step back, like they'd just been slapped. The ambulance driver shouted something over at the fire captain, who replied with a rude gesture, laughing. Then the rig eased its way back down the driveway. Andy could just see Kate through the small, high windows in the back, swaying with the movement of the van. At the last moment Kate looked up just before she and Trokof were carried away.

CHAPTER THIRTEEN

With the ambulance gone, the scene around Kurtz' B&B had been leached of all its energy. Kurtz and Meyers talked with the two local cops while Zeb leaned against a fence post, feigning like he wasn't in pain while talking to the fire guys. Doors to vehicles were open, overhead lights on, uniformed bodies half-wedged into cars as paperwork was balanced on a knee. It was the post-scene, something Andy was familiar with. It was the cleaning up, the following through, the documenting of times and people and places, statements to be transcribed and filed, awaiting the future possibility of a court case. Andy checked in with Captain Wilfred and thanked him and his crew for their time. She said nothing about methadone, nothing about the troop. That would be up to Lincoln.

Cadets stood in clusters, looking bewildered and lost and scared. Andy had to scan twice before finding Shipman, standing in the middle of his troop, looking exactly like every other cadet standing beside him. What he didn't look like was an addict. Though the story Shipman had given had made sense, confirmed by Kate who said intermittent doses of oral methadone could exactly explain Trokof's symptoms, Andy still couldn't make this detail fit with what she knew or thought she understood of Greg Shipman.

Finally, questions and paperwork were completed, gear stashed, crews reloaded, and the fire truck and cruisers left the Clearwater B&B.

"Come on, Troop 18, everyone into the house," Kurtz called out. "We'll find some way to feed you all and find you dry clothes." Without waiting for a reply, she marched the cadets around to the front of the house. The deep, cold wet of her uniform seemed to press against Andy's bones. Every inch of her was soaked and cold, mud up to her knees and streaked across her face. As she watched the cadets follow Kurtz, Andy felt the tug of control and responsibility. She hadn't figured out what they were going to do with the troop or the instructors tonight. *Let Kurtz help, let some control go,* Andy lectured herself. She heard boots behind her and turned to see Les with spent tears streaking her face.

"Christ, what a fuck up," Les said, her voice quivering.

Andy wasn't sure what she was referring to: the accidental overdose, Shipman admitting he was an addict, or her own behaviour. But as Les walked up to her, Andy put an arm around the woman's shoulder. Les gave a choked sound, furiously wiping tears from her eyes.

"I am living proof of the adage, 'those who can't do, teach.' I'm not proud of it, but there it is."

Andy said nothing, just squeezed Les's shoulders as they slowly followed the cadets down the gravel driveway to the front door. Andy didn't seem to be the only one supporting someone else. Up ahead, she saw Foster and Petit helping Zeb navigate the steps up to the porch.

"I'm really sorry, Andy. I'm sorry I wasn't more help…"

"Crisis is over, Les, let it go," Andy said firmly. "We got Trokof down from camp, he's in good hands, and Kate will call with an update. Right now I need you to help me take care of the troop."

Les used the heel of her hand to wipe away fresh tears. Then she shook her head like she was clearing away difficult thoughts or disturbing images. Andy wondered if something had happened in Les's past that made her react this way. She certainly wouldn't be the first officer to suffer from post-traumatic stress. But Les wasn't offering any details, and Andy wasn't going to ask.

"They need you right now," Andy said, her voice gentle.

"I'm in," Les said, forcing a cheerfulness she obviously didn't feel. But she was trying.

Wet gear and cadets dominated the inside of Clearwater B&B. The front door was a sea of neatly lined up, muddy black combat boots with coats piled nearby. Tara directed traffic, handing out towels, assigning cadets to rooms, saying they would bring up dry clothes shortly. Les and Andy pulled off their own boots and waded into the chaos. Kurtz and Tara's guests were in the middle of the living room, Penny handing out dry clothes with wide eyes, while her husband Al reiterated Tara's directions to various rooms in the house. They looked like they were having the time of their lives instead of being in the midst of a crisis.

"Use our room," Tara said to Andy, handing her a towel. "Find something to wear in the dresser then come help me feed the troop."

Andy gave her a swift kiss on the cheek. "I owe you," she said, wondering how many times she'd uttered those words in the last few weeks.

Tara gave a shake of her head, her long braid swishing against her back. "Don't worry. Rosie's already told me you intend to pay us back by staying for a visit," she warned, smiling her beatific smile.

Andy climbed the stairs, soaked cadets looking like half-drowned puppies were huddled outside rooms, waiting their turn to dry off and change. As Andy entered the upstairs hallway, they hushed and fidgeted. Shipman leaned miserably against the wall, his eyes downcast like he wasn't even really aware of where he was. And his former troop no longer knew what to do or how to protect him.

"We'll talk," Andy said to them, her sergeant's tone softened by the circumstance. "When everyone is dry and fed, then we'll all sit down and talk."

"But I'm done," Shipman said from his place on the wall. "We don't need to talk about that."

Andy waited for him to look up. He did, eventually. "Chief Training Officer Lincoln is on his way here right now. I expect him in the morning. He's the only one who can give those directives," Andy told the cadet. She wasn't fooling anyone, but the information could not come from her.

She left the cadets to silently contemplate Lincoln's arrival, seeking each other out as Shipman closed his eyes and shut everyone out. *Good luck*, Andy thought to herself. She was sure Troop 18 was not going to let him go that easily.

Twenty minutes later, Andy was standing at the stove in too-short track pants and a soft sweat shirt, stirring a hunk of frozen split pea soup in one pot, beef barley in another. Shandly and Tara were up to their elbows in flour and butter, mixing the ingredients for enough biscuits to feed an army. Kurtz and Tara's guests happily carried coffee and tea from the kitchen to the growing number of dried off cadets in the living room. Andy half-listened to Les's voice as she ensured everyone was accounted for, dry, and uninjured.

She pictured Kate at the Kamloops hospital, probably impatient and slightly bored, not allowed to treat Trokof, just sit with him and read his chart. Andy felt a pang of worry as she realized Kate must still be soaking wet and freezing. And probably hungry, Andy thought with a smile. Kate was always hungry.

Andy stirred soup and worried. Without Sgt. Trokof's steadying presence, without his innate ability to know exactly what the troop needed, Andy couldn't help but think the troop should be treated like suspects and witnesses with separate rooms, questions asked, and statements taken. Her cop instinct was telling her there was a case to be built. But Andy didn't have the energy for it. And if she was being honest with herself, she didn't have the stomach for it, either.

"What's on your mind, Sgt. Wyles?"

Andy hadn't heard Kurtz enter the kitchen and when she looked up from her simple, mindless task, she realized they were alone.

"I don't know if the troop should be supported or punished right now," Andy finally said, breaking up the last frozen chunk of soup with the wooden spoon. She put the lids on both massive stainless steel pots and adjusted the temperature. Then she leaned back against the counter, looking for advice from her former senior officer.

"Punish them for what?" Kurtz said.

"Shipman admitted he's been using, I have to assume the rest of the troop knows and, at the very least, they've been helping cover it up. It could be worse than that. More than one cadet may have actively engaged in illegal activity, possibly the procurement of drugs."

"Who do you work for?"

Andy looked at her, confused. "E-division," Andy said, slowly.

"Does your jurisdiction extend to investigating potentially unlawful activity at Depot Division?"

"No, of course not."

"And were you at any time requested by Staff Sergeant Finns or Chief Training Officer Lincoln to begin gathering evidence and building a case against a cadet or group of cadets?"

Andy considered this question, remembering every detail of her original conversation with Finns and Lincoln. "No," Andy said finally.

"Then keep the status quo, sergeant. I'd say that's what Lincoln expects from you right now," Kurtz said, picking up the baking bowls off the butcher block island and running them under hot water. "Sometimes you don't need to *do,* you just need to maintain."

"I hate not doing," Andy said, though she felt a little better having clarified her role.

"I know!" Kurtz said and thumped Andy energetically on the back. "That's one of the reasons I agreed to write the recommendation for your three chevies," Kurtz added, using the slang term for the sergeant's three chevron insignia.

Andy listened to the buzz of voices from beyond the swinging kitchen doors. Maintain, keep them together, wait for Lincoln to get here. Andy could do that.

Serving twenty-five people soup and biscuits was basically an obstacle course. Tara finally made everyone find a place to sit, and she appointed three people to help her serve. Andy wasn't the least bit surprised the cadets chose to all squeeze into the living room, squished onto couches, perched on chairs, and spread across the floor. Andy leaned against a wall and surveyed the scene, feeling true warmth for the first time in hours as hot soup heated her from the inside out.

The cadets seemed calmer, their senses lulled into warmth and comfort and camaraderie. Shipman had wedged himself against a wall underneath the window that looked over the back meadow. He was silent but colour had returned to his cheeks as he attacked his bowl of soup. Frances and Petit sat nearby, saying nothing but watching their friend with careful, worried expressions. Cadet Jacob Frances hadn't even touched his bowl of soup, and Andy was just wondering about this when the phone rang. The cadets instantly went quiet. A minute later, Kurtz signalled for Andy to join her in the kitchen, handing her the phone silently as the door swung shut behind them. Kate's voice was low and professional.

"Trokof is doing fine," she said immediately. "He's been triaged and seen by a resident and they've got him on a monitor. If his arrhythmia doesn't even out in the next few hours, they'll admit him for observation. But he's stable, and there's no reason to think he won't fully recover from this."

Relief flooded Andy's body. "Thank God," Andy said out loud, giving Kurtz a thumbs up. Kurtz returned it and headed back out of the kitchen. Andy assumed she was going to give the cadets the good news. "How are you?" Andy said.

"Damp. And cranky. That could be low blood sugar, though," Kate added thoughtfully. "How are you? How's the troop?"

"I'm fine, the troop's fine. Are you going to stay the night?"

"Probably. At least until I know if he's going to be admitted or released," Kate said. Andy wasn't surprised. "I hate to leave him here by himself."

"You're a good person, Kate."

"No cop left behind or something, right? Is that what I'm supposed to say now that I'm employed by the RCMP?"

Andy laughed. "Something like that. Call when you know what's happening, I'll come pick you up."

"Okay," Kate yawned. "Before I go, how's Shipman?"

Andy chose her answer carefully. "Resigned to his fate."

"Hmmm…" Kate said, clearly unsatisfied by Andy's response. "He would have had help beating the drug screens. We should have seen something behaviourally, if not medically."

"Are you saying you don't believe him?"

"I'm just saying it's not adding up for me yet," Kate said cautiously.

"You and me both," Andy said. "I'm going to talk to the troop, see what comes up."

"Okay," Kate said distractedly. "Trokof's waking up, I've got to go. Love you."

Andy returned it, the words warming her just a little more.

When she walked back into the living room, the cadets were talking in low, excited tones. Andy found Les in the far corner near the hallway with Zeb, who was sitting with his leg up on an ottoman, a bandage bulging with ice wrapped around his foot. The crisis had passed, and Les looked calmer.

"You've heard Sgt. Trokof is going to be okay." Andy raised her voice to address the whole room. "Dr. Morrison said they might admit him for observation, but he's expected to make a full recovery."

The words eased some of the tension in the room, but it wasn't entirely gone. Troop 18 still gestured and communicated their silent language. Andy waited, standing at the front of the room like their conversation was not yet over.

"Does he know it was us?" Cadet Shandly asked from the couch. She was wedged between Hellman and Awad, an empty soup bowl on her lap, her dark hair framing her pale face. "Does Sgt. Trokof know that we are the ones…"

Greg Shipman didn't let her finish the question. He stood up abruptly. "That I am the one who…" Shipman struggled with the words, like he couldn't force himself to finish the sentence. Andy watched him struggle but didn't help him out. "Who poisoned him. Accidentally. Who…who almost killed him. Does he know that?"

"I don't know," Andy answered. She hadn't thought to ask Kate and she couldn't be sure what Trokof had understood of the conversation in the medical cabin.

Shipman glared at Andy like she was keeping something back. She returned his look impassively. He then turned to his troop and gave them the same, warning look. If Andy was reading it right, he was telling them all to shut the hell up. Across the room, Les was clearly picking up the same signals.

"We know you had help covering this up, Shipman," Les said, her tone even and gentle. "We know the whole troop was involved." It wasn't quite an accusation but a reminder of the basic facts.

But Shipman was shaking his head. "It was me. It was only me. I did this on my own." Shipman's voice was robotic, repetitive, desperate. He was lying, and every single person in the room knew it. Prewitt-Hayes had her head in her hands, and Andy was pretty sure she was crying. Foster's gaze was fixed on Shipman across the room. Andy was shocked to see the intense anger in his eyes, his hands clenched into fists at his side. Frances sat dejectedly behind Shipman, his head hung low. He was still holding a full bowl of soup. A tremor shook through the cadet. The soup spoon rattled against the ceramic dish, and Frances clenched it tighter. Another tremor caused his knee to jump involuntarily, splashing soup onto the leg of his pants.

Facts raced, information surfaced and retreated, details refocused and strengthened, leaving a firm trail of suspicion in Andy's mind. Andy addressed the troop, choosing her words very carefully. "We don't need to do this now," Andy said to the room. "Chief Training Officer Lincoln will be here in the morning. He will have a lot of questions. And my advice might not mean a damn thing to any one of you, but I suggest you spend some time tonight thinking about why you're here." Andy paused, every eye riveted to her.

She thought briefly about Kate saying the troop would trust her. That she offered them a way out. "I think you should all spend some time thinking about what motivated you to apply to Depot, and what you've accomplished as individuals and as a troop since you arrived. And you should think about where you want to go from here. Because your answers to the TO tomorrow will shape a lot of lives."

Andy left it there, reminding herself she could only lead them to the right decision; she couldn't force them to make it. Shipman had angled his body against the wall so Frances was now almost completely hidden, but she saw Frances was shaking almost uncontrollably now, the sound of the spoon against the bowl a very soft but distinct sound in the room.

"Assign teams, Cadet Prewitt-Hayes," Andy said. "Dishes, laundry, and bedding. Let's treat Kurtz and Tara's place with some respect, okay?"

But Prewitt-Hayes seemed incapable of pulling herself together. She sat on the couch shaking her head, tears streaming down her face. Shandly took a long look at her troop leader and stood up.

"Take a break, Tracey, we've got this. I'll be on dishes with three volunteers. Petit, talk to Tara about the laundry, and Mancini start figuring out with Kurtz where everyone is going to sleep. Everyone else just stay out of the way."

The cadets broke up, the relief of a goal and action evident in the way they moved. Each of them glanced at least once at Frances before looking at Shipman who gave an imperceptible nod or a glare, like he was reassuring them that he had it under control.

Andy wound her way through the living room to where Les and Zeb were still sitting. Meyers materialized out of nowhere, wearing an extra-large green t-shirt with the name of a hunting camp splayed across the front. Andy assumed Kurtz's guests had donated some clothing to their cause.

"Let's let them off the hook tonight," Andy said in a low tone. "They're coming undone, and Lincoln might as well be here for the fall-out."

Zeb bounced his good knee up and down, clearly jittery. "Fucking hell…methadone. Fuck. Heroin?"

"Shhh," Les admonished Zeb. "Not now, not here."

Meyers looked pointedly at the corner where Shipman was bent over, talking to Frances, blocking the cadet from view.

"I know," Andy said, almost under her breath. "We need to keep an eye on them. Both of them."

Meyers nodded. "I'll go find Kurtz," he said quietly. "I'll tell her she's assigning sleeping quarters, and Shipman and Frances are to be out here where they can be watched." Meyers faded into the background, a skill Andy now recognized and admired in the man.

"You going to make it, Constable Zeb?" Andy said, trying to pull him out of his low mood.

"Fucking ankle," he said bitterly, not taking the bait. "Fucking troop. Jesus."

"Good to see you're taking this all in stride," Les said sardonically. Zeb shot another foul-mouthed answer right back at her. Les winked at Andy and dropped into a nearby chair, fully engaging Zeb in a verbal match. Andy backed away, thinking it was exactly what they both needed to balance out their moods. The rain started again as Clearwater B&B buzzed with the night-time preparations. It sheeted against the windows, closing them in even more tightly, marking the boundaries of the closed, warm space against the wet, cold dark outside. Penny and Al cheerfully took the offered upgrade of the honeymoon cabin and not long later four cadets squeezed into the room meant to house only two. Night settled more completely outside the windows as conversations drifted and flowed, blankets and pillows tossed across the room, t-shirts traded for socks.

Andy watched it all silently, a mug of hot coffee in her hand, feeling much like Prewitt-Hayes as she counted, re-counted, and tracked the movements and moods of the cadets. Lights were dimmed near midnight and a thoughtful, introspective quiet stole across the house. Andy hoped they were hearing her warning. They could talk and analyze and plan and whisper all they wanted with each other. But these were the moments where they were in their own heads, where worries and truths and decisions played out in dramatic, imagined detail that no one else could witness. Andy looked at Zeb across the room and she nodded once, releasing the cadets to his care for now.

Les was rinsing out her mug in the sink, talking in low tones to Kurtz who was sitting on a tall stool at the island. Tara had gone to bed once the task of arranging for the care of their overflow of guests had been completed. Les announced she was turning in, making a joke about pulling rank and claiming a bed for herself. She hugged Kurtz and Andy quickly and Andy wished her a good sleep, knowing they needed it more than anything.

Once Les was gone, Andy took the seat beside Kurtz, feeling an ache in the centre of her back where Meyers and the stretcher team had struck her earlier. It seemed like so long ago, and Andy felt the energy drain very suddenly out of her body.

Kurtz took a long look at Andy before going to the liquor cabinet tucked into a corner of their walk-in pantry. Andy looked with idle appreciation around the kitchen, admiring the space. She would love to have a kitchen like this with a pantry and enough counter space to cook a full-course meal. As Kurtz came back with her bottle of whiskey and poured some into Andy's coffee without asking, Andy let the image of cooking for Kate and their friends drift out of her head with a sad, lost pang. She wondered where she and Kate would go next. She couldn't imagine going back to separate apartments, couldn't imagine one more day of Kate not having met her friends, of not sharing every piece of their lives.

"How you holding up, kid?" Kurtz said.

"I'm beat."

"No wonder. You carry too much. You always have."

Andy said nothing to this, taking a sip of her spiked coffee, feeling the double-heat hit her bloodstream almost instantly. She was going to have to be careful. This was not a night to get fall-down drunk, though a small part of her urged her to do just that.

"Who is it?" Kurtz said quietly. Kurtz wasn't stupid. She'd made her own assessment of the cadets.

"Frances is my bet," Andy said, just as quietly. She wished suddenly Kate was here, so they could talk this out or at least confirm or deny the others' suspicions. But her instinct held her steady. Walking back through every detail she'd read or discovered about Cadet Jacob Frances and Troop 18 over the last few weeks, everything added up to Frances being the addict. "Shipman is covering for Frances. He figures he's gone anyway, might as well take the fall for the whole thing."

Andy took Kurtz's silence as support, but she had nothing to add. They sat quietly, the tick of the clock above the pantry providing an easy, subdued metronome. Andy took another sip of her coffee, the caffeine and alcohol hitting all the right neurons in her brain. Or all the wrong ones. Andy wasn't exactly sure anymore.

Her phone vibrated insistently on the counter and the screen blinked on, a text message from Kate rolling down the screen.

"Trokof being admitted to cardio. Precautionary only, he's fine. May have ride back. Will text."

Andy quickly thumbed out a text back. "Good. Did you eat?"

Kate returned the text. "Bad coffee and oatmeal cookie count?"

Andy laughed quietly to herself, texted back that no, that didn't count as a meal and who was the ride from?

"Const. Reilly. Feel free to call local station to verify I'm not being kidnapped."

Andy laughed out loud this time and turned the screen to Kurtz so she could see what Kate had written.

Kurtz snorted. "She's a funny one. And she knows you well, apparently. Reilly's a good guy, he's one of the uniforms who responded to the 9-1-1."

Andy texted back saying Kurtz had verified that Constable Reilly was legit and to keep her updated. The phone went silent again, and Andy felt the fatigue and worry weigh down her whole body, the smell of the spiked coffee suddenly making her sick. She wanted to crawl into bed with Kate and sleep and sleep and sleep.

"You don't have to wait up with me, Kurtz. Go on up to bed."

Kurtz just sipped her coffee. They ended up talking for hours, their conversation moving from past to present with the ease of people who had been friends a long time. They were both fiercely proud and protective of the agency they had committed their lives to, but Andy could recognize a note of bitterness in Kurtz's tone. Kurtz talked to Andy like she thought her former junior officer was still a wide-eyed rookie, unwilling to recognize the cover-ups and corruption. They argued quietly, Andy trying to defend her position, not believing Kurtz's argument of cognitive dissonance. Kurtz ended the argument by punching Andy in the shoulder, laughing delightedly at a heated comment she'd made.

"I've missed you, kid. There's a lot I don't miss about being a cop, but I've missed talking with people like this. I've missed talking like a cop."

Andy grinned back, appreciating Kurtz's view on the world, wondering again what it must be like to retire. By one thirty in the morning, Kurtz had switched to scotch and Andy had stopped drinking altogether.

Kate texted again. "En route. Twenty minutes."

Andy got up from the stool. Her body felt cold from sitting still for so long, her bruised muscles tight and unwilling to move easily. She opened the fridge and pulled out the leftovers Tara had put aside earlier, heating up the last of the beef and barley soup in a small saucepan. She buttered a thick wedge of Tara's homemade bread, then went back to the fridge and moved aside veggies and roasts until she found a hunk of extra-old cheddar, Kate's favourite. Next she filled the kettle, plugged it in, and found some herbal tea. Then she waited for Kate, listening for the sound of a car to announce her arrival.

Kurtz had been watching Andy quietly as she moved around her kitchen. "You've found her, haven't you?" Kurtz said with a gentleness Andy didn't think she'd ever heard before. She'd seen it, though. It was evident every time Kurtz looked at Tara.

"Yes," Andy said, and a deep sense of rightness filled her entire body.

"It's amazing, isn't it?"

Andy smiled. "Yes, it is."

Kate arrived just before two in the morning and came straight back to the kitchen, dropping her medical kit by the pantry. Kurtz handed her some clean clothes, bid them goodnight, then left the two of them alone. Kate looked exhausted, her face pale and her hair frizzy from having been wet and dried. Andy pulled her in and enfolded Kate in a tight embrace, rocking her gently. Eventually Kate disengaged, running her hand down Andy's back and giving her a reassuring smile, telling Andy she was okay.

"Go get changed. I'll serve you some food," Andy said.

Kate looked at the clothes on the butcher-block island: worn jeans, wool socks, and an old RCMP sweatshirt from Kurtz. With a tired but distinctly mischievous look, Kate started pulling off her clothes where she stood. Andy had to laugh.

"What?" Kate said, her words muffled by the shirt coming off over her head. "No one's awake."

"You'd better hope not," Andy said, pouring hot soup from the saucepan into the bowl and sliding it on to the counter.

"They're not. I checked on my way in." Kate zipped up the too big jeans and hiked herself up onto a stool. She sighed as she dipped her spoon into the soup, blew on it gently, and took her first bite.

Andy wondered if she should wait, decided she couldn't. She needed to hear it from Kate. "Even Frances?"

Kate looked at Andy sharply, confirming they were on the exact same page.

"Poor guy," Kate said quietly, tearing off a piece of bread and dunking it in her soup. "What's going to happen?"

"That's up to Lincoln. And it's up to the cadets to figure out if they're going to break down and tell the truth or try to keep up a hopeless lie," Andy said, realizing she really had no way of knowing which way the cadets were going to land on this one. She hoped for the truth with every tired and frayed nerve-ending still firing at this early hour of the morning.

They talked quietly while Kate worked her way through her only hot meal in the last twenty-four hours. Andy poured them both some tea while Kate updated Andy on Trokof. He'd slept most of the time she was there but had been awake and lucid long enough to figure out where he was and ask about the cadets.

Kate had told him they were all fine and offered to share what they had learned, but he'd asked her to wait until the morning when he could process it properly. Andy was just about to add something to this when they heard a light tread on the floor. The kitchen door swung silently open and Cadet Frances walked in, his skin grey, eyes bloodshot, hair sticking up at the side, and his borrowed clothes baggy. He looked like shit and he shook as he ran a nervous hand through his hair.

"Are you all right, Jacob?" Kate said, the compassion clear in her tone.

He looked at her blankly, switched his gaze to Andy then back to Kate.

"What do you need?" Kate said again, turning all the way around on the stool to face him.

"I need some paper," Frances said. "And a pen."

"What for, Cadet Frances?" Andy said, using his title, possibly for the last time. But she was trying to snap him out of his stupor, hoping for a straight answer.

Frances swayed slightly and trembled. "I want to write it all down. All of it. So they don't have a choice. I won't let them lie for me anymore."

Andy went to the wood hutch on the far wall and found a pen and a pad of lined paper. She handed it silently to Frances, who sat heavily on a chair and began to write, seeming to forget Kate and Andy were even there. Andy had to wonder how long he'd lain awake, tortured by guilt and indecision as he listened to his troop fall asleep.

He wrote line after line but couldn't stop shaking, the tremors getting harder and harder to watch. Finally Kate hopped off the stool and rummaged through her medical bag until she found sample size packages of Tylenol and anti-nausea meds. Kate ripped open the packages and signalled with a jerk of her head for Andy to get a glass of water. She placed both the water and the pills on the table.

"That will put me to sleep," Frances said, pointing almost accusingly at the small, orange tablets. "I need to finish this."

"You'll be done by the time it kicks in," Kate said, pushing them closer.

"I shouldn't. I want to be awake when the TO arrives. I... have things I want to tell him," he mumbled.

Kate looked back at Andy, seeking support. Andy shrugged. They couldn't make him take the meds. Kate picked up one of the orange pills, broke it in half with her fingernail then picked up the two Tylenols and held them out.

"This won't put you to sleep, but it will take the edge off." She kept her hand out and pushed the water closer. Frances hesitated. "Don't punish yourself, Jacob," Kate said quietly. "If you want to be lucid tomorrow when you talk to Lincoln and when you face your troop, you need to deal with the symptoms of withdrawal now."

Frances took the pills and drank the water, and then he picked up the pen and began writing again like his life depended on it. Kate and Andy withdrew to the other side of the kitchen where they whispered quietly. After ten minutes, they stopped bothering, Frances didn't seem to notice they were there, leaning against the island. Andy checked the clock: three thirty in the morning. Her body's exhaustion and extreme alertness warred with each other, her muscles screaming fatigue while her brain just couldn't stop. Kate leaned her head up against her hand, looking tired and thoughtful.

"You should go to bed," Andy said quietly.

Kate yawned and smiled. "Oh yeah? Where?"

Shit. There really wasn't a chair, a spare blanket, or even a cushion left from the chairs in the dining room. Andy had forgotten to find them a place to sleep. A bubble of laughter rose in Andy's throat, and she bit her lip to choke it back. Kate's brown eyes widened with her own suppressed laughter and for a moment they silently dared each other not to laugh out loud. Frances's intense scribbling pulled them back down to reality. Andy looked around Tara's incredible kitchen where they were basically pinned down for the next few hours.

"Want to make some pie?" she said to Kate quietly and the absurdity of the question, of their situation, almost had them laughing again. What else to do with their time? They had no case to build, no suspects to follow. They had to monitor Jacob

Frances as he wrote the history of why they were all here, so they had nowhere else to go.

"Apple?" Kate said.

Kate and Andy made pie. They cut flour and chilled butter together, the sharp tines of the pastry cutter working against the sides of a ceramic bowl. Kate found a bag of apples in the cold cupboard off the back porch and began peeling, coring, and slicing enough for four pies, occasionally stopping to squeeze lemon juice over them so they didn't brown.

They talked quietly together about small things, things that didn't matter really but took on a different significance at four in the morning. Frances kept up his scribbling, stopping for moments and putting his head in his hands. Andy and Kate continued what they were doing, and Frances would occasionally look up and watch. If he found what they were doing odd, he gave no indication of it. In fact, he seemed to find their quiet presence reassuring.

Kate pushed Andy aside as they began fluting the edges of the pastry, her deft, physician's hands being more suited for the task, Kate said. Frances put down his pen with finality. His chair scraped back against the floor as he stood, the sound harsh in the silence. For a moment, no one moved in the kitchen. Frances ran his hands through his hair again, and then he looked around the kitchen. He headed for the back door exit just off the pantry with a single-minded attention that made Andy nervous. She stepped into his line of vision.

"I don't want you to be out there alone," Andy said, wondering at her choice of words. She'd meant to say 'you can't.' It was supposed to have been an order, but it hadn't come out that way. Andy felt sorry for Jacob Frances.

"I just need some fresh air," Frances mumbled. "I'll sit on the steps."

Andy stepped back, letting the cadet open the door and close it very quietly behind him. Andy went to the sink where she could see him easily out the window in the overhead porch light.

Frances had pulled out a pack of cigarettes, lit one with cupped, shaking hands and stood staring off into the night, looking more lost than any one person had a right to.

Kate wasn't quite tall enough to see through the kitchen window. "He's okay?"

"Well, he's not going anywhere," Andy said. "Not now at any rate."

Without a word, they both turned and looked at the kitchen table where Frances's missive sat, folded thickly. Apparently, the cadet had a lot to say. Andy's curiosity burned. She'd been asking herself so many questions over the last few weeks, and she suspected the answers were in those sheets. But she wouldn't touch them. Those words weren't meant for her.

Kate stood at the island and finished rolling out dough and covering the last of the pies. Andy made coffee, bypassing her favourite whole beans and opting for the much quieter fine grind. She checked on Frances periodically, now sitting on the top step, staring into the darkened back field. They didn't talk now, the long day and night catching up to them in a stretched-out weariness. Kate put the first two pies in the oven, the hiss of the gas stove a comforting back drop to their exhaustion.

Andy slid her hand around the back of Kate's neck and massaged her lightly. Kate leaned back into her. They stood quietly together, listening to the house sleep, having arrived at the part of the night-morning where it seemed you were the only people awake in the whole world.

Andy registered a new noise, the arc of light on the windowpane indicating a car was coming up the driveway. Andy disengaged herself from Kate's embrace and checked the clock in the kitchen. Just after five in the morning. As she opened the back door, Frances was pulling himself up from his spot on the step, leaning awkwardly against the railing and looking to Andy for direction. Andy told him to wait and she descended the few steps down to the driveway where the car had come to a stop not too far from the garage.

It was Lincoln, and Andy could not deny how happy she was to see him. Their mission had seemed to careen and shift so quickly out of control in the last twelve hours, coming to a sudden, jarring halt. As she stepped off the porch, Andy was both relieved and nervous that everything was coming to a close. Troop 18, who had already suffered losses, was about to suffer more.

Lincoln straightened out his rumpled uniform, looking exactly like he'd been travelling all night. He put out a hand, almost formal, and Andy shook it.

"Thanks for taking care of my troop and my instructors," Lincoln said. "I knew you were the right person for the job."

Andy gave only a quick nod of acknowledgement, not entirely sure she deserved his thanks. Frances was a mess, Shipman was about to be released, and Trokof was in hospital. They stood by the car, looking back at the main house while Andy updated Lincoln. She was sure Lincoln had seen Frances standing by the back door, nervously smoking another cigarette, but he waited for Andy to fill in the details. Once she was done talking, Andy waited quietly while Lincoln seemed to absorb everything she'd just said.

"Methadone," Lincoln said on an expelled breath, shaking his head. "Christ on a crutch." Andy couldn't imagine the implications, the investigation, and the paperwork this was going to mean for the TO.

"He wants to talk to you." .

"Then let's go talk," Lincoln said. Andy couldn't be sure, but a note of regret seemed to be mixed in with his anger and his resolve.

They approached the cadet together and Frances immediately came down the steps and stamped out his cigarette in the wet gravel. He picked the butt off the ground and threw it into a metal can half-hidden under the stairs. Frances had spent so much energy being flat and uninteresting so as not to attract any attention, Andy never really had the chance to get to know him as a person.

Lincoln released Andy with a quick, appreciative nod of his head, and Andy climbed the back stairs again. The smell of apple pie and coffee hung heavy in the warm air of the kitchen and Andy's stomach gave a small growl, as if her body just remembered it was morning. Kate sat at the island, a mug of coffee steaming in front of her. Andy was pretty sure she'd had her eyes closed just before she'd walked in.

"Lincoln," Andy said, answering Kate's silent question. "He's talking to Frances right now."

More waiting. Andy felt almost impatient now that her body had switched over to a new day. She fidgeted, toyed with her mug, checked on the pie, and wished more than anything she could go for a run. Kate watched her silently from her perch, her body still for once. Andy didn't mind showing impatience and nerves in front of Kate. It was acceptable.

"It's going to be all right, Andy," Kate said finally. "You've done everything you can."

Andy didn't confirm or deny but she did finally sit again.

By five thirty, the second set of pies were in the oven and they heard a heavy tread on the back stairs. Lincoln entered the kitchen alone, looking tired and worn. Andy introduced him to Kate, Lincoln giving his thanks and saying he wished they were meeting under better circumstances. They sat at the kitchen table, Kate only joining them when Lincoln asked her to. She first poured him a coffee, which he accepted gratefully.

Lincoln ran his hand up and down his jaw, fingers rubbing at the grey bristles from his overnight beard as he lined up what he wanted to say.

"Jacob Frances knows his contract with the RCMP has been revoked. Or will be as soon as I reach the committee members at a more reasonable hour," Lincoln said, to no one's surprise. "He's already found a drug rehabilitation facility in Kelowna," he continued, and Andy's eyes went wide. This was news. Kate breathed out sharply, indicating her own shock. Andy wondered where Frances had found the time to do that. She wondered how long he'd been thinking about it and researching it, waiting to find the courage to go. "He wants to go now."

"Before he talks to the troop?" Kate said.

"He doesn't want to see them. He led me to believe he'd written a letter—that one I assume," he said, indicating the folded pieces of paper. "He said it would explain everything."

The clock ticked loudly in the silence of the kitchen, the gas stove flame puffing quietly as it came to temperature again. Andy thought about Jacob Frances sitting on the back step, imagined the courage it would have taken to explain to the Chief Training Officer of Depot Division that you needed help. *He'll be in rehab for the holidays*, Andy thought suddenly. Christmas was less than two weeks away.

"Are you going to take him?" Andy said.

"Yes."

"They worked so hard," Kate said, her face troubled. "I know they shouldn't have. I know they shouldn't have lied for him," Kate amended, looking up at Lincoln, "but they worked so hard to protect him. It seems wrong that he's just going to disappear." Kate struggled, still shaking her head. "There's no closure this way."

"He's making a decision for himself," Andy said to her quietly. "That should be honoured."

"And it's time to cut the strings. Frances has accepted that he's on his own in this battle."

Kate stared blankly at her coffee mug on the table and Andy wondered whether or not Kate was thinking about her own battles, both recent and in the past.

"Which facility?" Kate said to the TO.

Lincoln named it and Kate nodded. "Let me call them," Kate said, looking to Lincoln for permission. "It will help to have a physician make a referral."

Lincoln nodded gratefully and Kate carried the phone into the corner of the kitchen. As she waited for someone to pick up,

Kate stretched herself up on her toes so she could look through the window, checking on Frances.

"How'd you get here so fast?" Andy said.

"Choppered into Medicine Hat then drove through the night."

"Want me to take Frances?"

"No, I think it should be me. I'll be back in a few hours, and I'll want to talk to the troop. There's still that mess to clean up."

Yes, Andy said to herself, thinking of the rest of Troop 18 sleeping, totally unaware of what was happening. *That mess.*

It seemed like minutes, and Kate was off the phone, Lincoln was gulping the last of his coffee, and then collecting Frances who sat rigidly on the back step. Kate and Andy stood on the back steps as Lincoln drove him away, the only two to witness Cadet Jacob Frances' sudden exodus from Depot.

CHAPTER FOURTEEN

The night sky over Clearwater B&B faded into the deep richness of blues and blacks with the first idea of stars as Kate and Andy walked hand in hand up the driveway toward the meadow. They moved with the fatigue of a day and a night and another day passed without sleep. They moved with the heaviness of those still trying to make sense of what had happened, of those who had been witness to other people's pain and misfortune. Though Troop 18 had left hours ago, following orders to pack up and ship out with red-rimmed eyes and trudging feet, the weight of their presence could still be felt. Andy felt it in the tightening of the muscles in her back and the way her thoughts flashed to moments and words and images from the day, her mind unsettled.

Kate squeezed her hand as they got to the metal gate. Andy wondered if she was thinking about Trokof being loaded into the back of the ambulance right here, just under twenty-four hours earlier. Trokof had been released earlier that day and had insisted, with all the bluster of a drill sergeant who would not be taking orders anymore, he would take the bus back with the fourteen remaining cadets of Troop 18, Greg Shipman, and the instructors. Andy pushed the cold, metal gate behind them with a soft clang and felt a little better knowing Trokof was on the bus, trying to remind herself that what happened to the troop no longer mattered to her.

But it did. It mattered to her more than she could really reason with. Andy couldn't stop thinking about the expressions on the faces of the cadets when they realized Jacob Frances was gone. Shipman, Prewitt-Hayes, and Foster had stumbled, bleary-eyed into the kitchen just before six in the morning, demanding in panicked tones to know where Frances was. Andy had told them to wake up their troop and assemble in the living room. Kate had put on more coffee. Shipman followed orders, Prewitt-Hayes started to cry, and Foster looked like he wanted to punch something. But they'd roused their troop mates and sat together to hear the news.

"I wonder how they're doing," Kate murmured quietly, breaking their shared silence. Andy knew she was also struggling to let them go. But Andy just squeezed Kate's hand reassuringly. Clouds were moving in, marring the perfect night sky, and the cold, damp air reminded Andy that Kurtz had mentioned they might see some snow. Andy caught herself wondering what camp would be like in the snow, then she reminded herself that camp was empty. The cadets and instructors had spent the day stripping it bare of linens and food and gear and equipment. No trace left that Troop 18 had been there at all. The next time it opened, once Kurtz and Tara figured out the washed-out road, it would be for corporate retreats, men and women in expensive adventure jackets and brand new hiking boots. No roll call at six a.m. in the quad. No more push ups. No more drills.

Gravel turned to ice-crunched grass as Kate and Andy followed the path up to the honeymoon cabin. The guests were back in the main house, and Tara had made up the room for Kate and Andy while Kurtz had, without permission, called Staff Sgt. Finns to request a couple days off for his sergeant. Finns had agreed to two, and Andy decided she didn't have the energy or the right to be pissed off. Only grateful that Kurtz had once again provided her with exactly what she needed.

Andy thought of a line from Frances's letter. *What I needed most in that moment...* Prewitt-Hayes had read the letter out loud after hearing that Frances had left to check himself into a drug rehabilitation facility. Shock didn't quite describe how the cadets took the news. Loss, Andy decided. Troop 18 continued to exude such a deep sense of loss.

Some of this you already know. Some you don't. Bear with me, Troop 18.

I put off applying to Depot for three years. I knew it meant a lot to my dad. He'd get all jumpy around me, biting his tongue, not wanting to be that dad who pushed his kid. But I'd been talking about Depot since I was eight. I just knew it was something I wanted to do. Fourth generation RCMP had a nice ring to it. I guess I didn't expect to go so off course. I can't even tell you why or how I started using. Just the closer I got to finishing my criminology diploma, the more anxious I got. I started having trouble concentrating, was picking fights with my girlfriend. I even blamed her for losing one of my applications. I'd been telling everyone for so long this was what I was going to do, but the closer it got, the more worried I got that I would fuck it up. They wouldn't let me in or I'd hate it or I'd fail out. Christ, could anything be more embarrassing than that?

When I finished my diploma, I immediately got a job as a security guard. Said I wanted some time to work, get used to a uniform, make a little money before I ran out to Saskatchewan. More excuses. I started using about a year after graduation, when everyone kept looking at me, waiting for me to announce my application. When I began to lose weight, I blamed it on my new exercise program, my training schedule for Depot. My dad thumped me on the back, still biting his tongue but not able to rein in how excited he was. I thought I was going to be sick. I wasn't something to be proud of. I was a functioning junkie. I was nothing the RCMP was looking for.

I got clean on my own. That made me feel strong, like the last 3 years of my life had been a blip. I broke up with my girlfriend, started training, kept the Depot application on my fridge and a photocopied picture of my great grandfather in uniform in with my money. So if I felt the urge to pay for some more, I'd have a good reason not to.

The pressure came back the day I saw the envelope with the RCMP logo sticking out of my mailbox. The urge to use came crashing back, like I hadn't spent the last 18 months clean. But I fought it every step of the way to Regina. Showed up with my bag of shit and the urge to use. Picked up my cadet kit and still had the urge to use. Stood in formation with the rest of Troop 18, fighting the urge to use.

Troop 18. You were my saving grace. I was completely undeserving of your friendship. I hadn't realized until I showed up that I'd spent the last few years basically on my own. Depot was different, hanging out with you guys was different. Maybe it's just being forced to spend most of your waking days and hours in cramped quarters, everyone going through the exact same shit. Well, almost everyone. As far as I could tell, none of you were battling my demons.

When we lost J.T., I lost the will to keep fighting. I know a lot of you did, too. Shipman, I'm talking to you. But remembering J.T. dropping to the ground in front of us shorted out my brain. There was nothing left but that picture in my head, and I knew what I needed to do. I remember very clearly leaving the bar where the rest of you were drinking heavily, walking through the dark streets of Regina. I asked a few questions, followed a few shady people, exchanged some money and walked away again. I stood alone for a very long time with the rock in my hand. A very long time. By the time it was in my bloodstream, the euphoria completely masked my self-loathing.

My half life was back again. So much fucking harder now. Some days I was up, so up and everything was on. My target, my assignments, my fitness were dead on. Some days I shook like I really had the flu I kept telling you all I was getting. Petit, I know you figured it out first. I didn't know it at the time but you must have gone to Shipman, then to Prewitt-Hayes. And you all arranged my fucking intervention. Instead of going to a bar like we usually did on a Saturday night, when I'd sneak off to buy some more, use, then come back, we went to that high school football field. I balked at first, swore up and down that I wasn't using, that you were all assholes, that if you really thought that then they should just turn me in. You were all so quiet, so calm, waiting for me to finish my ranting until I cried like a little baby. Totally broke down. RCMP material, that's me.

Tracey, you had a plan. Of course you did. Asked me if I'd gotten clean before, and I explained about the methadone clinic. I was shaking then, from talking about it with you guys and from the need to use. Hawke, you saw me. You were more of a loner than me, not outside the circle, but on the edge, always walking the perimeter. When you walked away from the group, I thought I was sunk. Figured you thought I was the most pathetic thing you'd ever seen. I thought it was disgust on your face. It wasn't. Five minutes later and you came back with the names of three local methadone clinics. Told me to get started, brother. You guys walked me there, waited. It was the strangest feeling, having these people watch me swallow what I needed most in that moment. The two things I needed most—the drugs in my system and a troop of people believing I'd make it through this. I still can't believe what you guys did for me...

Tracey had trailed off, flipping it over to the next page. Then she surveyed the room, checking in with each of the other cadets. By that time, the audience included Lincoln who had let himself in quietly and stood at the back of the room. The cadets had seen him, had shared his presence with each other with a jerk of their heads, but they'd remained quiet, absorbed in Frances's words.

"I think we should say this part in our own words."

Lincoln walked to the front of the room, pulled up a chair, and sat in front of Troop 18. "I'd like to hear it in your own words."

Troop 18 had talked—haltingly at first, like it went against instinct, like they were fighting off the last two months of their camouflage. But then they tripped over each other to talk, adding details, correcting, excising their abundance of sins. They had lied. Foster, Shipman, and Mancini all copped to helping Frances cheat the drug screen. They explained how sick Frances would be when they couldn't get the methadone and how Jessup and Mercier had snuck in alcohol and marijuana to help him deal with his withdrawal. Frances had been furious with them. Foster said he was sure Frances had been suicidal when Jessup and Mercier had left. They had watched him carefully, working incredibly hard to keep him under the radar, to keep them all flat and uninteresting so they wouldn't show the turmoil and chaos they felt they could only share with each other.

Andy had watched their confession with a sick, sour feeling in her stomach. Every detail of it was awful. She couldn't quite believe how these cadets had managed to lie and cover and support and protect through one of the toughest six month training academies in the nation. If she hadn't just spent the last two weeks with Troop 18, she would have assumed it was an impossibility.

They couldn't explain the hypodermic needles found in their classroom. It hadn't come from Frances. Their best guess was that some of the other cadets or troops had figured out what was going on and planted it there. This answer jibed for Andy. The cadets had no reason to lie anymore, and Depot certainly had its fair share of assholes.

Shipman took over when they talked about Camp Depot and how prepared they had been to keep Frances hooked up to methadone, even remotely. Before they'd left Depot, they had researched clinics and looked into storing liquid methadone. Prewitt-Hayes discovered they recommended taking it with orange juice, so they did, adding a half bottle of lemon juice and a cup of salt so no one else would even consider drinking it.

They talked about how sick Frances was, how the dose was different or messed up or something. It wasn't working. Twice Shipman left Depot, walked all night, impersonated Frances and stole extra methadone from the clinic. Shipman wasn't boasting. He wasn't proud, but he said it with a kind of defiance that made Andy think he would make the same decisions again if he had to. Damn the consequences.

Andy felt a brush of cold wind as they followed the old wood fence along the path leading up to the honeymoon cabin. The porch light shone through the winter-bare trees in the distance. But she slowed, not yet ready to enter the cabin and take her thoughts about Troop 18 through the door. Kate seemed to understand, and she stopped on the path.

"You haven't said anything about Lincoln's final decision," Kate said quietly, aiming her comment up into the sky where dark grey clouds had begun to muscle their way over the night.

Andy didn't respond. She wasn't sure what to say because she really had no idea how she felt. Her sense of justice and her strong belief in consequences for actions warred with the mitigating circumstances. She knew the cadets in Troop 18 were good people and would make good cops. So Andy really had no idea what she felt when Lincoln had thanked the troop for their honesty and closed himself in Kurtz's hideaway office with his phone for an hour while he discussed with the Human Resources Officer and the Cadet Training Officer what the official Depot response was to their transgressions.

Andy looked blankly up at the sky, remembering how grim Lincoln's face had been when he asked the troop to reassemble. The troop had stood at near attention in the living room, the bright, warm sun shining brilliantly in painful contrast to the nervous fear gripping the room as Lincoln gave his final decision.

Shipman and Frances were released from their Cadet Training Agreements. Everyone else had another chance. Their six month probation was extended to a year, and they would be closely monitored and held to the most rigid of standards, but they all had another chance. As the cadets dared to show relief, stealing guilty looks at Shipman who sat very still at the back of the room, Lincoln held up a warning hand.

"This is not a gift I'm giving you," Lincoln said. "If you make it through the next two months at Depot, I am in effect sending you out into your rookie year with a handicap. Everyone will be watching you. Rumours will precede you wherever you go. Some cops won't like you before you even arrive. Many won't trust you. Get used to it. Get through it. Figure out how to stand on your own two feet, cadets. It's the only way you're going to have a career as a Mountie."

Andy toyed absently with Kate's cold fingers. She pressed them between the heat of her palms. Kate smiled and waited.

"I want to fast forward five years…one year even, to see where the cadets end up. Then I'll know if it was the right decision," Andy said, knowing she was avoiding the question. "I think half of them won't make it through their rookie year," Andy said finally. "But I think they deserved their second chance."

Kate nodded, and then she touched her fingers very lightly to Andy's face, as if telling her to re-listen to her own words. So she did. And she heard it this time with finality, with a kind of inevitability. The ache and the uncertainty about the troop left her body and her mind in a rapid, draining exodus. The last grip of her responsibility and control over the cadets slipped away in the cold air. It was gone. They were gone. Andy smiled at Kate, the first time she'd smiled today.

"Thanks," Andy said, kissing Kate lightly then slipping her arm around Kate's waist as they continued walking.

Andy was just about to ask Kate a question when her cell phone beeped from her back pocket.

"It's my parents," Andy said, anticipation building in her chest. She fumbled with the keys, finally opening the message as Kate held her breath. "It's a girl!" she said. "Born 4:43 p.m. after fourteen hours of labour, nine pounds, three ounces, lots of hair. They've named her McKayla Andy…" Shock froze the words in her throat. Kate grinned, tears sparkling in her eyes. "McKayla Andy Wyles," she read out loud, this time with the most incredible sense of wonder.

"You have a namesake," Kate said as Andy answered the text then shoved the phone back into her pocket.

"Yeah," Andy said, her throat tight. "Guess we should go to Calgary to meet the little creature."

Just as they reached the porch of the cabin, snow began to drift down from the sky in slow, soft spirals of white that melted the second they touched the ground. Kate gave a small cry of excitement and turned her face toward the sky. Andy did too, the flakes brushing against her face, tumbling down until they caught on her hair and jacket.

"Can we sit outside for a minute?" Kate said, her voice hushed, like speaking too loudly could break the spell of snow.

"Sure. Give me a minute."

Andy entered the cold cabin, lit the already built woodpile in the fireplace, and pulled a well-worn wool blanket from a drawer. She joined Kate on the porch step, spreading the blanket over their legs, arranging themselves so they were comfortable and close. They watched the snow and processed the long day. Andy's thoughts followed no logical order. She felt no weight, no immediacy, no pressure to do or remember or think. Kate curled against her side.

"Two days off together," Kate said into the silence, still entranced with the snow falling onto the meadow.

"Two days," Andy repeated. They'd rarely had time to themselves, even before their months apart.

"Two days, then back to Vancouver. Back to my two jobs," she said, as if she was testing out the thought, still getting used to how it sounded.

"Back to our two apartments," Andy added, not exactly sure what made her say it.

Kate looked up at Andy, and she knew they were both thinking about that moment in Hidden Valley when Kate had asked Andy to move in with her. Andy always felt guilty about that moment and Kate's expression when she assumed Andy was rejecting her. It wasn't rejection. Andy had just been trying so very hard to be careful, to make no wrong moves with Kate. It had backfired badly.

Kate gave Andy a knowing, sympathetic smile then tucked her head into Andy's shoulder, hiding her eyes. Andy wanted to say the right thing this time. She stroked Kate's hair gently.

"When you're ready, ask me again," she said quietly.

Kate only nodded slightly, a small movement against Andy's neck. Andy calmed a little, relaxed, reminded herself that there was no hurry. They had time.

The snow picked up as more clouds moved in, a heavier blanket now blocking their view of the meadow. It closed them in together in the most wonderful way, helping them retreat from the world.

"Andy?" Kate's voice was soft.

"Yes?"

"When we get back to Vancouver, will you move in with me?"

Andy lit up with joy, struggling to hold herself as still as Kate. She reined herself in and calmed herself down.

"Yes," she said, not able to keep the intense happiness out of her voice. She felt Kate's smile, though she didn't move. Andy wondered why, an unwelcome thread of worry unwinding in her stomach. Kate took a breath, as if she was steeling herself for something.

"Maybe I should have qualified the question before I let you answer," Kate said, sitting up. Andy could see the resolve in the set of her mouth. Andy readied her brain, her body, and her heart. She would take whatever qualifiers Kate wanted to place on this. If Kate wanted to take this slow, Andy would take it slow.

"When I ask you to move in with me, I don't mean you start spending more time at my place than yours, or that you store more clothes in my house and have a drawer for your stuff. I mean three days from now, you are giving your landlord your two months notice, and you and I are arguing about whose couch is more comfortable and how many lamps we need in one apartment and which brand of shampoo we're going to buy.

"And I mean that we finally meet each other's friends, we have them over to our place, *our place,*" Kate repeated, as if she could tell Andy was having trouble accepting this, "and you cook for them and I…do whatever it is that I do. And I tell the phone company as many times as I need to that you are my girlfriend, that you are my partner. And we never see each other at Christmas because we both always take the shitty holiday shifts so people with families can be home with their kids."

Andy just stared, her heart pounding. They'd arrived at the conversation, the only topic they had ever avoided with each other. Kate picked up Andy's hand and linked their cold fingers together. When she spoke again, her voice was soft but very sure. "And we finally admit to each other that neither of us wants to have kids." Kate let this sink in for a moment before carrying on. "But we're there to see our nieces and nephews and your godson grow up. We're there for all of it. So…that's what I mean."

Andy sat very still, her shock at Kate's words slowly turning to amazement. She'd never met anyone like Kate. There had never been anyone like Kate.

"So ask me again," Andy said, her voice hushed. "Ask me what you really want to ask me."

The sweetest smile touched Kate's face and she leaned in, brushed her lips over Andy's cheek, and whispered in her ear.

"Will you marry me?"

Andy closed her eyes, felt the heat of Kate's breath against her cheek, the incredible warmth of belonging in her chest.

"Yes."

About the Author

Jessica Webb spends her professional days working with educators to find the *why* behind the challenging behaviors of the students they support. Limitless curiosity about the motivations and intentions of human behavior is also a huge part of what drives her to write stories and understand the complexities of her characters and their actions.

When she's not working or writing, Jessica is spending time with her wife and daughter, usually planning where they will travel next. Jessica can be found most often in her favourite spot on the couch with a book and a cup of tea.

Jessica can be contacted at: jessicalwebb.author@gmail.com

Books Available from Bold Strokes Books

Divided Nation, United Hearts by Yolanda Wallace. In a nation torn in two by a most uncivil war, can love conquer the divide? (978-1-62639-847-4)

Fury's Bridge by Brey Willows. What if your life depended on someone who didn't believe in your existence? (978-1-62639-841-2)

Lightning Strikes by Cass Sellars. When Parker Duncan and Sydney Hyatt's one-night stand turns to more, both women must fight demons past and present to cling to the relationship neither of them thought she wanted. (978-1-62639-956-3)

Love in Disaster by Charlotte Greene. A professor and a celebrity chef are drawn together by chance, but can their attraction survive a natural disaster? (978-1-62639-885-6)

Secret Hearts by Radclyffe. Can two women from different worlds find common ground while fighting their secret desires? (978-1-62639-932-7)

Sins of Our Fathers by A. Rose Mathieu. Solving gruesome murder cases is only one of Elizabeth Campbell's challenges; another is her growing attraction to the female detective who is hell-bent on keeping her client in prison. (978-1-62639-873-3)

The Sniper's Kiss by Justine Saracen. The power of a kiss: it can swell your heart with splendor, declare abject submission, and sometimes blow your brains out. (978-1-62639-839-9)

Troop 18 by Jessica L. Webb. Charged with uncovering the destructive secret that a troop of RCMP cadets has been hiding,

Andy must put aside her worries about Kate and uncover the conspiracy before it's too late. (978-1-62639-934-1)

Worthy of Trust and Confidence by Kara A. McLeod. FBI Special Agent Ryan O'Connor is about to discover the hard way that when you can only handle one type of answer to a question, it really is better not to ask. (978-1-62639-889-4)

Amounting to Nothing by Karis Walsh. When mounted police officer Billie Mitchell steps in to save beautiful murder witness Merissa Karr, worlds collide on the rough city streets of Tacoma, Washington. (978-1-62639-728-6)

Becoming You by Michelle Grubb. Airlie Porter has a secret. A deep, dark, destructive secret that threatens to engulf her if she can't find the courage to face who she really is and who she really wants to be with. (978-1-62639-811-5)

Birthright by Missouri Vaun. When spies bring news that a swordswoman imprisoned in a neighboring kingdom bears the Royal mark, Princess Kathryn sets out to rescue Aiden, true heir to the Belstaff throne. (978-1-62639-485-8)

Crescent City Confidential by Aurora Rey. When romance and danger are in the air, writer Sam Torres learns the Big Easy is anything but. (978-1-62639-764-4)

Love Down Under by MJ Williamz. Wylie loves Amarina, but if Amarina isn't out, can their relationship last? (978-1-62639-726-2)

Privacy Glass by Missouri Vaun. Things heat up when Nash Wiley commandeers a limo and her best friend for a late drive out to the beach: Champagne on ice, seat belts optional, and privacy glass a must. (978-1-62639-705-7)

The Impasse by Franci McMahon. A horse packing excursion into the Montana Wilderness becomes an adventure of terrifying proportions for Miles and ten women on an outfitter led trip. (978-1-62639-781-1)

The Right Kind of Wrong by PJ Trebelhorn. Bartender Quinn Burke is happy with her life as a playgirl until she realizes she can't fight her feelings any longer for her best friend, bookstore owner Grace Everett. (978-1-62639-771-2)

Wishing on a Dream by Julie Cannon. Can two women change everything for the chance at love? (978-1-62639-762-0)

A Quiet Death by Cari Hunter. When the body of a young Pakistani girl is found out on the moors, the investigation leaves Detective Sanne Jensen facing an ordeal she may not survive. (978-1-62639-815-3)

Buried Heart by Laydin Michaels. When Drew Chambliss meets Cicely Jones, her buried past finds its way to the surface—will they survive its discovery or will their chance at love turn to dust? (978-1-62639-801-6)

Escape: Exodus Book Three by Gun Brooke. Aboard the Exodus ship *Pathfinder*, President Thea Tylio still holds Caya Lindemay, a clairvoyant changer, in protective custody, which has devastating consequences endangering their relationship and the entire Exodus mission. (978-1-62639-635-7)

Genuine Gold by Ann Aptaker. New York, 1952. Outlaw Cantor Gold is thrown back into her honky-tonk Coney Island past, where crime and passion simmer in a neon glare. (978-1-62639-730-9)

Into Thin Air by Jeannie Levig. When her girlfriend disappears, Hannah Lewis discovers her world isn't as orderly as she thought it was. (978-1-62639-722-4)

Night Voice by CF Frizzell. When talk show host Sable finally acknowledges her risqué radio relationship with a mysterious caller, she welcomes a *real* relationship with local tradeswoman Riley Burke. (978-1-62639-813-9)

Raging at the Stars by Lesley Davis. When the unbelievable theories start revealing themselves as truths, can you trust in the ones who have conspired against you from the start? (978-1-62639-720-0)

She Wolf by Sheri Lewis Wohl. When the hunter becomes the hunted, more than love might be lost. (978-1-62639-741-5)

Smothered and Covered by Missouri Vaun. The last person Nash Wiley expects to bump into over a two a.m. breakfast at Waffle House is her college crush, decked out in a curve-hugging law enforcement uniform. (978-1-62639-704-0)

The Butterfly Whisperer by Lisa Moreau. Reunited after ten years, can Jordan and Sophie heal the past and rediscover love or will differing desires keep them apart? (978-1-62639-791-0)

The Devil's Due by Ali Vali. Cain and Emma Casey are awaiting the birth of their third child, but as always in Cain's world, there are new and old enemies to face in post Katrina-ravaged New Orleans. (978-1-62639-591-6)

Widows of the Sun-Moon by Barbara Ann Wright. With immortality now out of their grasp, the gods of Calamity fight amongst themselves, egged on by the mad goddess they thought they'd left behind. (978-1-62639-777-4)

18 Months by Samantha Boyette. Alissa Reeves has only had two girlfriends and they've both gone missing. Now it's up to her to find out why. (978-1-62639-804-7)

Arrested Hearts by Holly Stratimore. A reckless cop with a secret death wish and a health nut who is afraid to die might be a perfect combination for love. (978-1-62639-809-2)

Capturing Jessica by Jane Hardee. Hyperrealist sculptor Michael tries desperately to conceal the love she holds for best friend, Jess, unaware Jess's feelings for her are changing. (978-1-62639-836-8)

Counting to Zero by AJ Quinn. NSA agent Emma Thorpe and computer hacker Paxton James must learn to trust each other as they work to stop a threat clock that's rapidly counting down to zero. (978-1-62639-783-5)

Courageous Love by KC Richardson. Two women fight a devastating disease, and their own demons, while trying to fall in love. (978-1-62639-797-2)

Pathogen by Jessica L. Webb. Can Dr. Kate Morrison navigate a deadly virus and the threat of bioterrorism, as well as her new relationship with Sergeant Andy Wyles and her own troubled past? (978-1-62639-833-7)

Rainbow Gap by Lee Lynch. Jaudon Vickers and Berry Garland, polar opposites, dream and love in this tale of lesbian lives set in Central Florida against the tapestry of societal change and the Vietnam War. (978-1-62639-799-6)

Steel and Promise by Alexa Black. Lady Nivrai's cruel desires and modified body make most of the galaxy fear her, but courtesan Cailyn Derys soon discovers the real monsters are the ones without the claws. (978-1-62639-805-4)

Swelter by D. Jackson Leigh. Teal Giovanni's mistake shines an unwanted spotlight on a small Texas ranch where August Reese is secluded until she can testify against a powerful drug kingpin. (978-1-62639-795-8)

Without Justice by Carsen Taite. Cade Kelly and Emily Sinclair must battle each other in the pursuit of justice, but can they fight their undeniable attraction outside the walls of the courtroom? (978-1-62639-560-2)